"GIRL, I MEAN TO RIDE ALONE," SAID LONGARM . . .

"Pooh, I can ride as good as you," Flora replied. "Do you want me to show you how I shoot?"

"Honey, you're a Canadian. They'll be sore as hell if you aid and abet me any more than you have."

"To hell with the law. Those sons of bitches killed my family."

"I know," said Longarm patiently. "You still can't tag along."

"How are you going to stop me?"

He smiled. "You're too pretty to shoot. Maybe I'll just spank you."

"I dare you to try," she cried and there was something in her wide amber eyes that made Longarm's heart skip a beat . . .

*Also in the LONGARM series
from Jove*

LONGARM
AND THE MOUNTIES

TABOR EVANS

A JOVE BOOK

First Jove edition published January 1980

10 9 8 7 6 5 4 3 2 1

Printed in the United States of America

Jove books are published by Jove Publications, Inc.,
200 Madison Avenue, New York, NY 10016

Chapter 1

Longarm luxuriated in the steam room of The Turkish Delight. He was a little awed by what kept coming out of his hide. It wasn't as if he hadn't bathed recently, and he'd scraped himself down a couple of times since coming in here to soak in the scented steam. He'd felt sure his pores were empty as well as open, but as he ran the spatula along his thigh again, he was astounded at the crud he'd absorbed in his travels. The hardwood spatula kept plowing more of what he figured to be an equal mixture of coal smoke, trail dust, old sweat, and powdered horse turd out of his glowing, steam-wet skin. But this time there was less of it, and Longarm figured he was getting to the bottom.

He was running out of time, too. The office would be open any minute. So he got up from the wet wooden bench and stepped into the shower room next to the steam chamber. He soaped his reddened flesh, took a deep breath, and turned on the cold-water tap, hard. Ice-cold mountain water crashed down to close his pores and wake him up for a while.

That had been his main purpose in stopping at the steam bath after saying goodbye to a certain lady from Leadville at the Drover's Rest an hour ago. He'd told himself it was a work night when she started smiling at him in the restaurant, but the next thing he'd known, it was Wednesday, and he hadn't slept enough to mention.

Longarm turned off the shower and, still shivering, staggered into the dressing room to dry off and get ready for work. He'd picked up a fresh shirt and new underwear to go with his newly cleaned hide. There was little he could do about the smell of Denver still clinging to his tobacco-brown suit, felt Stetson, and leather goods.

He strapped on his cross-draw rig and adjusted the hang of his holstered .44 before putting on his frock coat. The shoestring tie the Justice Department made him wear hung a mite crooked, but then, so did everything else, this morning. With luck, he'd be able to sneak forty winks during his lunch break.

Outside, the sun was shining and the air was crisp. But Denver was dirty and brown as usual. A sparrow pecking at a road apple in the gutter chirped a cheery good morning up at him as he crossed Larimer Street, and Longarm muttered, "Aw, shut up."

It was no better at the Federal Building. The clerk playing the typewriter out front shot him a pleasant howdy, despite the fact that the world was going to end any minute. His boss, Marshal Vail, was disgustingly happy to see Longarm.

The pudgy man with the bushy eyebrows, sitting behind the desk, waved Longarm to a seat and said, "You haven't gotten to work on time in recent memory. What happened, were you up all night?"

Longarm fished out a cheroot, crossed his legs and struck a sulfur match on his bootsole, and said, "The taxpayers don't rate explanations as to how I spend my own time, Billy. But I'll tell you, man to man, I just tangled with a perfumed man-eater. I hope you have a nice tedious chore for me this morning, like escorting a prisoner to court or serving somebody with a summons. If you ask me to fill out any papers, I'll just have to shoot us both. I can't seem to get my eyes adjusted to the cold gray light."

Vail said, "You can sleep your hangover off on the train. I'm sending you to Montana. You remember that case you handled up on the Blackfoot reservation a while back?"

Longarm frowned and said, "Yep. I remember civilizing hell out of those jaspers pestering the Indians, too. Don't tell me somebody else has started killing Blackfoot."

Vail said, "I won't. Nothing happened to the Indians, this time. It was Durler, the Indian agent. You remember him, don't you?"

"Sure. Last time I saw Calvin Durler, he'd busted up with his wife and was drinking pretty good. What other sort of trouble is he in?"

"He's dead. He was gunned in the town of Switchback during an unfriendly game of cards. Durler was a federal employee, so killing him makes it a matter for us to handle."

Longarm swore softly under his breath and said, "I remember the local law up there was a man named Murphy with a yellow streak that showed. I can see you've handed me another bitch case, Billy. It's sort of tough to solve a killing after half-baked amateurs have messed with the clues and handed you a cold trail."

Vail said, "There's nothing to solve. We know who shot the Indian agent. It was done in a crowded saloon in front of a dozen witnesses. Yellow or not, Sheriff Murphy took a mess of statements down. All you have to do is pick the killers up."

"Killers? More than one?"

"The man who gunned Cal Durler was a drifter called Canada Jack. Durler chided him about the way he was dealing stud, and Canada Jack pumped three rounds into him, under the table. He then stood up, smiling, tipped his hat to a barmaid, and sauntered out. Since he rides with a gang of about a dozen men, just about as mean as he is, nobody saw fit to discuss the matter with Canada Jack at the time. Sheriff Murphy showed up in his own good time, took everybody's statements, and was kind enough to pass them on to the Justice Department as a federal matter he

7

didn't reckon he had any further business poking his nose into."

Longarm nodded and said, "That figures. So my job is to mosey back up there, discuss the matter with this big, bad Canada Jack and see if I can persuade him to come quietly."

Vail said, "That don't seem too likely. You'd best take a couple of other deputies along to back your play. Canada Jack has killed before, and the young owlhoots he rides with are pretty ugly. They're a mixed bag of Canucks and Yanks, and they've raised pure Ned on both sides of the border. I know you're pretty good, Longarm, but no one lawman would stand a chance against the gang, so—"

"Let's eat this here apple a bite at a time, Billy. Is this Canada Jack an out-and-out border bandit, or just surly?"

"He's not wanted for anything but killing folks, if that's what you mean. He hasn't robbed any banks or stolen any cows. You might call him an unpleasant tourist. I wired the Mounties, and they say they have no wants or warrants out on him."

"Hell, in that case, he's sure to have made for the border by now. You're sending me on a fool's errand, Billy. He'll have jumped the line by the time I can possibly get to Montana Territory. Why don't we ask the Mounties to pick him up for us?"

Vail sighed and said, "I already did. Fort MacLeod sent back an awfully wishy-washy reply, so I checked higher up in diplomatic channels. Canada Jack has friends in high places. We can't touch him, north of the border."

Longarm blew a thoughtful smoke ring before he mused aloud, "I don't understand you, Billy. The Northwest Mounted Police are sort of stuffy and formal, next to us, but they're pretty good lawmen, and a cut above some I've met when it comes to honesty. How the hell can a murderous saddle tramp have the Indian sign on the Mounties?"

8

Vail said, "He doesn't. His family does. Canada is a British Dominion, and Canada Jack's elder brother is a belted earl with a seat in the House of Lords."

"Canada Jack is an *Englishman?*"

"Yep. Black sheep of a fine old family with a heap of influence. His real name is John Chumley, and he went to Eton, so he talks funny. He was kicked out of Eton for beating up a teacher or something. They bought him a commission in the British army and sent him to India to make a man out of him. But he cheated at cards and started shooting at Hindoos for the hell of it, so the army sent him home. His family owns a cattle outfit on the Peace River, so they sent him to Canada to run it, hoping the outdoor life would improve his disposition. He didn't seem to think herding cows was all that interesting, so he started riding around with a gang of other young no-goods, and when the Mounties started to get proddy about the noise they were making, they came down across the border to give *us* their business.

"Just why Chumley cheats at cards is a mystery. He gets an allowance from his family in England. The general opinion is that he's simply crazy-mean. So, like I said, you'd best take a backup team with you, this time."

Longarm shook his head and said, "I work better alone, Billy. I'm not trying to prove I'm a hero. I just don't like to have to worry about where other folks might be when the situation gets complicated. Do you remember the time when James Butler Hickock gunned his own deputy in that free-for-all shootout?"

Vail looked disgusted and said, "I remember Wild Bill drank a mite, too. You ain't fooling me, Longarm. I know why you like to work alone, and this time, I warn you in advance, don't do it."

Longarm stared at his boss in wide-eyed innocence as Vail nodded and continued, "You just stick to the rules and regulations of the Justice Department, this time. I don't want to hear about any rough justice and, since you brought it up, I don't want you messing with the Mounties anymore."

Longarm frowned and said, "I didn't say that much about the Mounties, Billy."

Vail said, "I know. That's how I know you're still pleased with yourself about the time you made a blithering idiot of their Sergeant Foster. It might interest you to know that Crown Sergeant William DeVerrier Foster is now in command of the troop at Fort MacLeod."

Longarm grinned and said, "Old Foster got promoted? That's good to hear. We had our differences, that time he and I were after Cotton Younger, but he's a good old boy."

Vail tried not to smile as he said, "You tricked him into riding all the way to Canada with an overripe corpse he thought was his man. He never found out you'd fooled him with the wrong body until he got home, smelling like a rose. If Foster ever catches you on his side of the border, he means to have a word with you, and I doubt it will be the least bit friendly. So don't ride north across the line, Longarm—that's an order."

"What if this Canada Jack cuss has lit out for Alberta?"

"He won't be gunning folks you have to worry about. I don't care if we bring him to trial or run him out of the country, just so the shooting stops in our jurisdiction." Vail paused, then knitted his black eyebrows and leaned forward on his desk. "Are you getting any of this, Longarm? Sometimes I think you don't hear too good when I'm giving you a direct order. I want you to take some boys and go up to Montana. If Canada Jack and his gang are still on U.S. soil, I want them arrested or whatever. If you don't catch up with them on this side of the border, I want you to turn right around and come home. Is that understood?"

Longarm said, "No. I already told you, they figure to be gone when I get there."

"Maybe you'll meet a nice-looking gal on the train. You often do. I know I may just be sending you on a sightseeing trip. The point is that we have to go through the motions after a federal employee has been murdered. You're right about the Mounties being good, and a good lawman knows when it's time to bend the rules to bring a killer to justice. So let *them* worry about the family influence and such. Stay out of Canada. There's more to it than this vinegarroon, Canada Jack. You could get us into a diplomatic flap if you tangled with the Mounties."

Longarm frowned and asked, "Are we fixing to have a war with Canada, Billy? The last one was a draw, and it was a while back."

Vail said, "They're fixing to have a revolution, north of the border. It's touchy as hell. Washington isn't clear as to the rights and wrongs, and our orders are to stay the hell clear of the mess."

"I can see why. Who's rebelling against who, this time? Last rebellion I remember up there was the Métis Rising, under Louis Riel, a Red River breed."

Vail nodded and said, "The half-breeds in Western Canada are fixing to rise again, and their leader, Riel, is plotting against the government in Ottawa, from up in Montana."

Longarm whistled softly and asked, "Do you want Riel picked up too?"

Vail said, "No. Canada has a death warrant out on Louis Riel, but they ain't serious, as long as he stays out of the country. They don't want to make a martyr out of him, and Riel has been granted political asylum by the U.S. Government. So stay the hell away from him. I only brought the matter up so you could see how important it is to behave yourself, this once. The Mounties are on the prod and watching the border. Crown Sergeant Foster hates your guts. Do I have to draw you a picture?"

Longarm said he understood, clamped his teeth down on his cheroot, and got up. He said he'd go back to his furnished room and pack while Vail's clerk typed up his travel orders, vouchers, and so forth.

After Longarm had left, the pimply-faced clerk with heavily macassared hair came in with the already-prepared papers and put them on Vail's desk. He said, "You look sort of pleased with yourself, Chief."

Vail grinned and said, "I am. I just told Deputy Long to behave himself, and you're my witness if he gets in Dutch."

"Do you really think he'll disobey you, Marshal Vail?"

"Don't he always? There's not another man I have who'd be worth sending up there after a killer two hoots and a holler from the border. Canada Jack has jumped the border before, after killing folks down here. Nobody up there seems to give a damn."

The clerk nodded and said, "In other words, you're sending a man, this time, who doesn't stop for technicalities once he's on an outlaw's trail."

Vail smiled and said, "Longarm don't stop for brick walls, and they don't even have the border posted with keep-off-the-grass signs. He'll trail that crazy English killer to the North Pole if he has to."

"But what about the Mounties and the trouble up there, sir?"

"Hell, I told Longarm about it while I was telling him not to cross the line!"

The clerk sniffed and said, "Well, I know he's good, sir. But the Mounties are pretty good too. What if he can't avoid them?"

Vail chuckled and said, "If they know what's good for them, they'd better avoid Longarm. The murdered Indian agent was a man he knew, and I've seen that look in his eyes before."

It didn't rain as much on this side of the Rockies, so the old burial ground at Switchback, Montana, was starting to summer-brown. The fresh grave of the murdered Indian agent was banked with flowers. Some were already faded, but there was a nice nosegay of forget-me-nots near the wooden marker. Longarm bent and plucked them from the grave. Then he walked over to another marker in the lonely plot, and removed his hat before he knelt to place the flowers gently in the grass as he murmured, "I never forgot you, Sally. It's just that I've been busy in other places."

A shadow fell across the grave of the girl he'd once known, and he looked up, feeling foolish. A sober-faced Blackfoot stood there with a tin star pinned to his white man's vest, and Longarm said, "Howdy, Rain Crow. I was just visiting with Roping Sally here. You know, she was the only gal I ever met who could rope better than me?"

The Indian said, "She was beautiful too. Does it help you to know you got the man who killed her?"

"Nope. It still hurts like hell when I think of finding her dead out there on the prairie."

Rain Crow said, "It hurts me too. I was with you. But you did not return here to investigate old crimes. The Indian police have not been invited to hunt for the killers of our agent, Durler. I was wondering if you could tell me why. You have always spoken straight. For a white man," he added with a chilly trace of a smile.

Longarm got to his feet, dusting off his trouser leg with his Stetson. He said, "You Blackfoot lawmen are feds, the same as me. We've ridden together in the past, and I know you and your boys are better lawmen than the shiftless skunk the local voters saw fit to elect in these parts."

"But we are Indians," Rain Crow reminded him sardonically.

"There you go. Since you asked for it straight, I'll tell you true. Canada Jack's gang is white as well as dangerous. If someone who didn't know what was going on was to see a posse of redskins chasing white men across the prairie, they could jump to all sorts of hasty conclusions."

13

The Indian police officer said, "We can take care of ourselves in a fight."

Longarm smiled and said, "Colonel Custer would probably agree, even though you Blackfoot deny being there. But you and me are peace officers, Rain Crow; we're not paid to smoke up the territory. The government assigned me to round up the gang because I'm white, not because they aimed to insult your ability."

They headed for their two mounts tethered near the cemetery gate, and Longarm said, "I've got a bottle of Maryland rye in my saddlebag. I was coming out to the reservation to jaw with you in any case, but meeting you close to town has saved me a trip. I wanted the views of a lawman I respected before I lit out after Canada Jack."

Rain Crow said, "It's against regulations to give an Indian a drink."

Longarm smiled and answered, "Hell, there's nobody looking, and if I get caught, I'll say you held a gun on me, you ornery savage."

Rain Crow smiled warmly for the first time and said, "It was good to ride at your side, Longarm. I see you are still color-blind. Sometimes people smile at us until they get what they want from us. You are not like that. My grandfather would hate to hear me say this, but I think you must be a good person."

Longarm opened the saddlebag, glanced around to make sure they were unobserved, then pulled the cork with his teeth before handing the flask to the Indian, saying, "Have a slug and stop blubbering about my sweet disposition. Let's hunker down here by the fence, and study on the killing. Were any of you Blackfoot in town at the time?"

Rain Crow took a swallow, handed the bottle back, and dropped to his haunches as he said, "No, but I have spoken to friendly whites who saw the shooting. They say Durler had been drinking again, but he was not wearing a gun and he was never mean when he drank, anyway. He just cried when he got drunk enough. He was a decent enough Indian agent, but we thought he was a sissy."

Longarm hunkered down by the Indian and returned the flask, saying, "I know. I was here in town when he busted up with his wife. Before I left Denver, I checked the lady out. Mrs. Durler's living in Dallas with a saloonkeeper who beats her regular and makes her entertain his customers."

Rain Crow nodded and said, "Heya! The old women out at the reservation predicted such an end for her. How do you suppose the old ones read the future, Longarm?"

"By getting old and having seen it all before, I reckon. Nan Durler made a play for me one time, which don't make her a whore, exactly, but leaves me unsurprised that she seems to be headed there pronto. The point is that Canada Jack wasn't doing a favor for a lady when he gunned your agent. I read the witnesses' statements at the sheriff's office before I rode out here. I was too polite to ask where Murphy was while the shooting was going on, but it seems to be an open-and-shut case—the cold-blooded murder of a harmless drunk."

"They say Durler caught the Canadian cheating him at cards."

"I know. I read that part. Some people don't seem to understand this, but it's against the law to shoot a man, even when he makes a mild suggestion about a fresh deck. Your agent was alone and unarmed. The killer gunned him, laughed, and raked in all the money on the table before he just got up and moseyed out of the saloon like he owned the town."

Rain Crow scowled and said, "The white men there were cowards."

But Longarm said, " 'Stunned' would be a politer way to put it. Canada Jack's having about a dozen men with him at the time might have had a mite to do with it. I'd say the killing made Canada Jack at least a tiny bit thoughtful, since he was last seen riding out of Switchback. He and his gang rode slow and easy, but the point is, they ain't in town now."

Rain Crow took another swallow, coughed, and said, "I know. I think they rode back to Canada. When Murphy got around to telling us our agent had been murdered, I asked around the territory. They have not been seen anywhere on this side of the border. I know you think we use a tom-tom, but—"

"Now, you just pull in your horns," snapped Longarm, adding, "I'm finding these here remarks sort of tedious, Rain Crow. I read the telegram you sent us. What in hell's eating you, this morning? *I* never rode against the Blackfoot, and even if I had, the Indian Wars are supposed to be over."

Rain Crow smiled sheepishly and said, "I'm sorry. It gets to be a habit, and I keep forgetting how you saved my red ass that time. I think I must be angry because I liked Agent Durler, and now it looks like the men who killed him have gotten away."

"They're still on this continent, ain't they? Where in Canada do you reckon they might be headed?"

Rain Crow blinked. "You're not serious?"

"Do I look like I'm laughing? Canada Jack left a cattle spread on the Peace River. I misdoubt he'd go there to cool off. Too many folks on the Peace know him, and he ain't popular. I hear they're building a railroad over near Regina. You Indians called it Pile of Bones when it was still a gathering place in the Shining Times."

The Blackfoot nodded and said, "I, too, hear the Canadians have started a railroad to the West Coast. But why would Canada Jack want to go there? He is not a railroader."

"No, he's a troublemaker craving action, though. There's usually whores and tinhorns following the railroaders. I figure they might have beelined north to Alberta, and about now they'd be just drifting east, taking their time as they sniff about for more fun and games."

16

The Blackfoot looked uncomfortable as Longarm had figured he might. It was a good sign.

Longarm said, "I have to slip up there quiet, without the Mounties pestering me for papers and such. I understand there's trouble brewing up that way."

"I have heard this too," said Rain Crow, looking away.

Longarm said, "The last time the half-breed Métis rose against the Canadian government, they got stomped. This time, I understand Louis Riel plans to enlist at least two full-blood chiefs to join his army. They have a red-and-white flag sewn up, and they aim to form a red-and-white independent nation in western Canada."

Rain Crow shrugged and didn't answer.

Longarm said, "The Cree of Canada are related to the Blackfoot, ain't they?"

"We speak the same language, almost. But there are no Blackfoot involved in Riel's rebellion. Not U.S. Blackfoot, anyway."

"I know. I can see you'd hate like hell to see breeds and Indians *win* up there. You're going to have to help me, Rain Crow. Like our drinking habits, it'll be unofficial."

"You want me to ride across the line with you? I am ready to go now."

Longarm shook his head and said, "We'd both wind up blundering into a Mountie patrol. I need someone who can help me move about without attracting attention. I can't hunt that gang much, if I'm being hunted myself. I figured if I had friends among Riel's rebels up there, it would make my task a mite easier."

Rain Crow said, "I don't know any Cree that well. *I* trust you, but Cree who didn't know you might be tempted by the horse and guns of a lone white."

Longarm took a deep breath, let it halfway out so his voice would sound calm, and asked, "Rain Crow, where can I meet up with Louis Riel?"

The Indian didn't answer.

Longarm said, "Come on, I know he's in Montana. He's not wanted by the law, this side of the border. I could track him down in a week, maybe less, if the State Department in Washington has his last address. I'm just trying to save us all some time."

Rain Crow asked, "What makes you think I know where the leader of the Red River breeds might be?"

"Shit, don't play cigar-store Indian on me, old son. Asking a western tribesman where to find Riel is like asking an Irishman if he's ever heard of the Fenian Society. Neither one may *tell* you, but they both know what you're talking about."

"What would you do to Riel if you found him?"

"Not a thing. I only want to talk to him; I'm not interested in his revolution. The men I'm after are white. At least one is a high-born Englishman whose brother helps run the empire that Riel is sore at. I figure there's a fifty-fifty chance I can get Riel and his Métis rebels to help me. If he says no, that's the end of it. I can promise you, man to man, I won't lift a finger to harm Louis Riel or his cause. So how about it? While we're sitting here playing games, those killers are getting away."

Rain Crow stared at the ground for a long time before he said, "Hear me. This is how you find the place where our half-red brother is waiting for the raising of the flag that is red and white."

Chapter 2

The flag above the little schoolhouse wasn't simply red and white; it was the red, white, and blue of the United States. It was four in the afternoon, and the kids had gone home, as Longarm slowly walked his bay gelding across the schoolyard and reined in by a water pump. He dismounted and tethered his horse to the pump before he walked over to the doorway, mounted the two steps, and knocked. A deep but pleasant voice called out, "Come in, it's open."

Longarm did as he was told. Inside, he found a man seated at the teacher's desk in a shiny black suit and a soft linen collar. The teacher looked up with a puzzled smile. Longarm saw that Louis Riel was about thirty-five, with black hair and a Louis Napoleon beard and mustache. Only his rather high cheekbones and swarthy complexion hinted at possible Indian blood. He saw that the man at the desk expected him to say something, so he took out his wallet as he walked down the aisle between the desks and said, "I'm a deputy U.S. marshal, Mister Riel."

The Métis leader nodded and said, "You have orders to investigate my teaching American youngsters?"

Longarm noticed that Riel had a slight French Canadian accent, but otherwise, his English was more cultivated than that which most folks spoke on either side of the line. Longarm said, "I took the liberty of asking about that already, sir. You've been teaching the kids just fine."

"Considering I'm a dangerous rebel? Would it surprise you, *m'sieu,* to know I am an admirer of your Washington and Lincoln?"

"No, sir, I've always thought they were fine gents too. I'm not here to tell you how to teach the three R's, Mister Riel. Officially, I ain't here at all."

"Oh? What's this all about, Deputy Long?"

Longarm hooked his rump over one of the kids' desks and took out two cheroots. He offered one to the Canadian, who declined it. Longarm put the spare away and lit up, saying, "First, I have to tell you the story of Cal Durler, an Indian agent who was just murdered not far from here. Old Cal wasn't much, but he tried, and the Indians liked him."

"You don't have to butter me up, *m'sieu.* I am as much a white man as I am an Indian. As a matter of fact, we Métis used to think we *were* white, until the Canadian government explained our position to us."

"Yeah, I heard the Red River breeds were descended from French Canadian fur traders and their Indian wives."

"I thank you for saying *wives* instead of *squaws.* You are almost correct in your thumbnail description, but our white ancestors were not all French. Many were Scottish or English, most worked for the Hudson Bay Company. They settled western Canada long before the capital at Ottawa was anything but a trapper's cabin in a swamp."

Longarm knew the man had made this speech before, and he figured they'd get it over with if he kept quiet, so he tried, as Riel continued, "The Hudson Bay Company dealt fairly with the Indians as well as its white employees. When Queen Victoria got around to noticing western Canada at all, we'd tamed it for her. There was no reason to change the ways we'd always done things, but what politician can leave well enough alone?"

"Yeah, I heard Canada was reorganized about the time of our own war between the North and South."

"Changed completely, and not for the better,

20

m'sieu. They took all political powers away from the old Hudson Bay Company and resurveyed the western provinces. Those of our people who'd taken to farming had settled in the old French manner—small villages surrounded by long, narrow strips of farmland. The Anglo-Saxons now in power seem to find this uncivilized. They drew new maps, divided the country into sections, acres, and so forth. They began to lay out town sites and roads across the prairies. Never mind if a Métis settlement was already there. We were treated as if our towns and farms were temporary Indian camps. We were told to move aside and not block progress."

"Progress can be a pain. Couldn't you fight them in court?"

Riel laughed bitterly and said, "How? We are Indians. Savages. Mere wards of the state."

Longarm frowned and said, "This ain't none of my business, but you don't look all that Indian to me."

Riel shrugged and said, "I am about three-quarters white, biologically. Your Chief Ross, of the Cherokee Nation, was *seven-eighths* white. Canada is not alone in its legal niceties. An Indian is an Indian. I attended a university for whites. I hold several degrees and, as you were just kind enough to mention, I am not wearing feathers and paint."

Longarm nodded. "In other words, you ain't allowed to vote." He knew where they were, now. He'd heard the same complaint from a Cherokee M.D. who'd written a book on forensic medicine.

Riel's face stayed calm, but his brown eyes smoldered as he said, "Exactly. They told us Métis we were to be administered by a kindly white Indian agent who'd know what was best for us. When a white bully named Thomas Scott tried to evict some of my people from land their grandparents had carved from the wilderness, I killed him. The rest you know."

"Yep. Canada sent in the militia to restore order, and formed the Northwest Mounties to make sure it

21

never happened again. That leaves you sitting here, plotting the second round, and that's what I want to talk to you about."

"The fighting around the Red River is over," Riel said. "Concessions were made by both sides, and if the whites won't respect us, at least they've learned to leave us alone."

Longarm shook his head and said, "Let's not pussyfoot. The survey lines have reached Saskatchewan, and both you Métis and the full-bloods are sore as hell. Canada's in a hurry to build her railroad to the Pacific and settle her west with cattle and wheat spreads. You've been down here behaving yourself for a few years, and the new MacDonald government they just elected up north is anti-United States, anti-Indian, and anti-anything that's in their way. I give it between next Tuesday and five years before you have another all-out fight up yonder."

Riel smiled thinly and asked, "Really? Who do you think will win, this time?"

Longarm met his gaze as he answered, "Them. I had this same conversation with a Sioux I liked, one time. He was right as rain about the justice of his nation's claim to the *Paha Sapa*. But Uncle Sam said the *Paha Sapa* was the Black Hills, and it was *his*."

"We Métis are not as unprepared as our Dakota cousins were, *m'sieu*."

"You must be some hell of a fighting force, then. Red Cloud had the finest light cavalry that ever rode this earth. He won the first few battles, too. You're an educated man, Mister Riel. How come, if I can see it, you can't?"

"We shall fight because we have no other choice. I agree that our forces seem modest compared to those of the British Empire, but what else can we do?"

Longarm said, "Beats me. I never came here to talk you out of a war with Queen Victoria. I need your help for a more modest invasion of Canada."

Riel sat still long enough for Longarm to fill him in

about the murder of the Indian agent and Canada Jack's flight from justice. Longarm saw he'd scored a point when he mentioned that the wanted killer's big brother had a seat in the House of Lords. But when he got near the finish, the Métis leader said, "What you ask of me is impossible, *m'sieu*. If I were to put you in contact with rebels in Canada, I would be putting their lives in your hands!"

Longarm asked, "Why? I don't have a warrant on any Métis. I told you, the current Canadian government is anti-U.S., and Washington ain't all that fond of Prime Minister MacDonald, either."

"Nevertheless, you would know too much. What if you were to fall into the hands of the Mounties?"

"I'd say howdy, and they'd be delighted to boot me out of their country. One of them's a personal enemy, so if I got picked up by *his* troop, I'd probably wind up in jail until the American consulate bailed me out."

"Oh? You say you have had trouble with a member of the Northwest Mounted Police?"

"Nosir, *he* had trouble with *me*. It was a similar situation. Old Sergeant Foster was down here looking for a gent who'd killed someone in Canada. I figured I had the better claim, so—"

"Just a moment," Riel cut in. "Are we speaking of William DeVerrier Foster, Crown Sergeant at Fort MacLeod?"

"That's him. I hope he ain't a pal of yours."

Riel scowled blackly and growled, "The pig is part French. He denies his Indian blood, of course!"

"Jesus, you mean old stuffy Foster is a *Métis*?"

"I mean he is a *pig*. I spit in his grandmother's milk, red *or* white!"

"Well, it's nice to see we agree on something. Anyway, I sort of made a fool of Foster, and they say he's never forgiven me."

Riel sounded interested, so Longarm told him the whole story about how he had switched dead bodies and let the Mountie pack the wrong stinking corpse all the way back to Canada that time. When he'd finished, the Métis leader was laughing. Most folks did when he told the tale.

Longarm waited politely for the man to regain his composure, but quickly saw that he'd never lost it. The Métis leader said, "I can see how you would have your problems with the Mounties. Just where in Canada did you want to look for your gang of killers?"

Longarm thought and answered, "North of the border, but south of the Peace River. I don't figure they'd be west of Fort MacLeod, at the foot of the Rockies, or east of Regina, at the end of the rails moving west."

Riel frowned and said, "You've given yourself a lot of territory to search, *M'sieu* Long. Two provinces with two governments and two Mountie commands."

"Well, it's mostly open prairie, ain't it?"

"Forgive me, but it is not. Alberta may be mostly high plains country, but as you work east into Saskatchewan, you will encounter lakes, pot holes, uncharted streams, and tamarack swamps. And by the way, the Canadian Pacific crews have built past Regina. By now they should have reached Moose Jaw, to the west."

Longarm nodded and said, "That's why I need help from folks who know the country up there, sir."

Riel stared hard at him for a long, unwinking moment. Then he asked, "Where are you staying in town, *m'sieu*?"

"I hired a room at the boardinghouse next to the Wells Fargo. Why?"

"Go back and stay there for no more than twenty-four hours. If nobody contacts you, you will know you are on your own. Do not look me up again, no matter what. We live in interesting times, and my people are—how you say—'on the prod'?"

"I follow your drift, sir. How will I know if you decide to help me?"

"You won't. My name is not to form part of any

conversation you may have with any person who may offer to act as your guide."

"Right. If we're caught jumping the border, you know nothing about it."

Riel smiled thinly and said, "They told me you were a man of uncommon common sense, *M'sieu* Long. I give you another high mark for understanding the delicacy of my position as a political refugee."

Longarm frowned and asked, "You say somebody *told* you about me, sir? Does that mean you were expecting this visit?"

"But of course. How do you think a stranger such as yourself *reached* me? When I learned that a lawman was looking for me, I naturally made certain inquiries of my own. You have a reputation for being a man of honor, with the sort of madness my Indian blood finds amusing."

Longarm saw that the teacher was looking past him, and saying something with his eyes. So he turned casually and nodded to the two young half-breeds covering him from the back of the room. They neither smiled nor nodded back, but he saw that they were pointing their shotguns politely at the ceiling.

Turning back to Riel, Longarm chuckled and said, "I've been accused of some funny things. But this is the first time anyone ever suspected me of being a British spy."

Riel shrugged and said, "Return to your room and wait until we make certain you are not. I would like to hear more of your refreshing views on the Northwest Mounted Police, but I have papers to mark and a lesson to prepare for my students. So, if you will excuse me . . ."

Longarm nodded and put out a hand. Louis Riel ignored it as he stared down at the papers on his desk. Longarm knew the interview was over, and that it wasn't likely they'd ever see one another again. He nodded and turned away. As he headed for the door, he saw that the Métis pair who'd been covering him had slipped away like Indian smoke. That had been what Riel was signaling with his eyes. Had the tall American not turned when he had, he'd never have known they were there.

As he walked outside and mounted up, he wondered where they were covering him from, now. He didn't look around for them. He knew he was still being tested by the teacher.

Longarm had been told to wait in his hired room, but the wallpaper wasn't all that interesting, and there was a taproom downstairs. So he was seated in a corner with a smoke, a beer, and the latest issue of *Captain Billy's Whiz-Bang* when the waiter came to him and told him there was a Red River cart out front. Longarm put a dime on the table and strolled out to have a look.

Like the Green River axe or the Pennsylvania rocking chair, the Red River cart was a frontier folk invention. Nobody knew who'd made the first one; they simply filled a need. The one out front was typical of its kind: a one-horse, two-wheeled vehicle with a canvas top like that of the larger prairie schooner. The wood was unpainted and put together without metal nails or hardware. Like Indian snowshoes or an Eskimo sled, the Red River cart was held together with rawhide lashings. Even the rims of the spidery-looking wheels were tallow-cured leather. At rest, the Red River cart looked like it was on the verge of total collapse, but Longarm knew the light, springy construction could tote a season's worth of furs or hides just about as far as the driver aimed to travel with them.

Longarm stepped off the plank walk and moved forward for a view of the driver sitting under the sunbonnet canopy of patched and faded canvas. He saw that it was a woman of about twenty-five. She wore moccasins, and a wraparound skirt of dark blue calico. Above her red-sashed and trim waist, she wore a short-fringed buckskin jacket. She wore no hat, and her straight black hair hung down in a raven's-wing on either side of her high cheekbones. Her pretty face was a shade darker than Longarm's own tanned features, but her wide-set eyes were cornflower blue, and they regarded him the way a dubious cat's might size up any stranger. Longarm seldom tried to pet a cat he didn't know, so he nodded and said, "They call me Longarm."

The Métis girl said, "I am Claudette, me. My English she is not good, so we will do better not to ask too many questions. I am traveling to the Oldman River Country, perhaps as far as the Saskatchewan. If you wish to keep me company, put your possessions in the back and tether your pony, him, to the rear of the cart."

"Your English is better than my French, and I'll be proud to come along and maybe protect you, ma'am. Just wait here and I'll be back in a jiffy."

Longarm trotted into the rooming house and fetched his things. He loaded them in the cart bed, noticing that the interior had been fixed up with a double bed of hides and blankets. He told Claudette he'd be right back with his mount from the livery across the street.

He'd paid in advance, so it only took him a few seconds to get his army-issue bay gelding, but the short interval had been enough time for a couple of town loafers to notice the pretty half-breed. As Longarm led the bay toward the cart, he saw that they were pestering her.

Usually, such nonsense ended as soon as such fellows saw that a woman had an escort. So Longarm walked quietly up and began to tether the horse to the rear of the cart, hoping they'd get his meaning.

They must have been drunker or dumber than they looked. As Longarm finished and started around to the front, one of the grinning yokels asked Claudette, "Hey, is it true you breed gals rub noses instead of kissing?"

His partner slapped his back and chimed in, "I rub noses good as hell. I got something else I'd like to rub you with, honey!"

Longarm cleared his throat and said quietly, "This lady is with me, gents."

The first loafer eyed him owlishly and answered, "Lady? Hell, she's just a squaw."

Longarm said, "I'm going to forget you said that, mister. Then I'm going to commence counting. If you're still here when I get to five, I'm going to start by tearing your face off."

"What are you, a squaw man?"

At this point, Longarm decided to dispense with further formalities.

Claudette sat quietly, holding her cart horse steady, as Longarm picked the first one up by the scruff of his neck and the seat of his pants, to toss him headfirst into a watering trough. By this time, the other was running in the general direction of North Dakota. Longarm waited until the one he'd tried to drown came up sputtering to the surface and rolled over the far side of the trough to chase his partner down the street.

Then he climbed up beside Claudette and said, "Sorry about the ruckus. They must have been drinking."

The Métis girl clucked to her cart horse, and as they started moving, she said, "That was a foolish thing to do, you. Now you have attracted attention. People will be speaking tonight in the saloon of the big white man and the blue-eyed squaw."

"Well, I couldn't just stand there and let them talk to you like that, could I?"

"Why not? I am used to it. I am used to taking care of myself, me, too."

"I noticed you don't seem worried about traveling across the prairie alone. You're probably right, but they had no call to be so free with words like 'squaw.'"

"Pooh, I *am* a squaw, me. It simply means 'woman,' in the language of my mother's people."

"I know, but they gave it another meaning, the way they used it."

28

"I know. Tell me, were you angry with them for insulting you as well as me?"

He shook his head and said, " 'Squaw man' ain't an insult, as far as I can see. I've never been ashamed of having Indians for friends."

She shrugged and said, "Before you tell me how beautiful you think I am, I must tell you that I am only doing a job for a friend. I will get you across the border if I can. Please don't expect me to *like* you, white man."

Just getting to the borderlands from Riel's headquarters near the Great Falls of the Missouri chewed up the better part of a week, and Longarm found the trip tedious as hell.

The early pioneers had named the high plains the "Sea of Grass," and the name fit. The prairie rolled in long, smooth swells, as if some long-forgotten ocean had frozen in place under a tawny carpet of buffalo grass, and the Red River cart creaked and groaned over the stationary waves like a ship at sea. They'd sail slowly up for a look-see at the distant horizon all around, then sink down into the draws between the crests, where the air hung dry and furnace-hot. Big gray prairie locusts played at being flying fish as they bounded ahead of the cart horse's plodding hooves, and spotting a cow or an antelope in the distance broke the monotony much like spotting a whale from the deck of a clipper offered diversion for bored seamen. From time to time, they'd pass a bleaching buffalo skull or a lonesome clump of cottonwood in a draw, but if Longarm commented on the way the overgrazed country was getting stripped down to grass and cows, he got no answer.

Like the stern captain of a more imposing vessel, Claudette maintained silence on the bridge. The Métis girl seemed more oblivious of her passenger than sullen. When she didn't ignore him outright, she tended to answer in monosyllables. It didn't take the big lawman long to lapse into a silence of his own as he sat there, chewing an unlit cheroot and wishing he was anywhere else, with perhaps an uglier lady who spoke English.

After a bit of awkwardness the first night, he got used to the sort of inhospitable camping routine. Claudette slept in the cart, ground-anchored and tilted on its lodgepole shafts, with the horses hobbled to graze. Claudette cooked one hot meal a day, at sundown, and didn't thank him when he gathered cow chips for their little fires. Morning and noon meals consisted of pemmican, dry sourdough, and cold coffee. Longarm was used to rough fare, but sleeping alone on the grass in his bedroll made him sort of wistful.

A less truthful man would have managed to convince himself he didn't want the sulky little breed. Longarm, like most old trail hands, was used to the celibacy away from town or his home spread. But, while doing without on a long hunt or trail drive was one thing, doing without in the company of a beautiful gal you had all to yourself was another.

Privacy was impossible as they traveled alone together, and Claudette didn't bother trying all that much. When nature called, she'd stop the cart, walk around to the far side, and simply squat. Longarm didn't peek, but he had sharp ears and a vivid imagination. When it was his turn, he'd mumble something about scouting ahead, then mount his bay, and put a rise between them before he unbuttoned his pants.

Claudette slept nude. He didn't learn this by peeking, either. She had a little hurricane lantern hanging from the middle bow of her canvas top, and the shadow show she put on at night as she prepared for bed was rough on Longarm's glands.

By the afternoon when she said they were almost to the border, he wasn't sure whether he hated her or was falling in love with her. She'd been nice-looking when he'd first seen her perched on the cart seat. Day by day, she seemed to get prettier. He knew himself well enough to understand what was happening. It reminded him of the old army joke at Fort Apache. The story went that you could tell when a trooper was overdue for a transfer, because he started to see blondes instead of brunettes doing their laundry along the White River. By now he'd have settled the matter, had Claudette been like most gals. He didn't get every pretty gal he met, but it seldom took him this long to find out whether it was win, lose, or draw. Claudette didn't even bother to let him know she hated him; she just sat there, hour after hour, pretty as a picture and quiet as a tomb.

Longarm was an experienced plainsman in his own right, so he spotted the distant dot on the horizon as they topped a rise near sundown on the day Claudette had said they were nearing the line. He didn't say anything. They were headed for whatever it was he'd spotted, and when the Métis girl felt like commenting on it, she would.

They dipped down into a draw, and he lost sight of the dot. The next time they rode over a rise, he was watching for it and got a better look. He decided it looked more like a house than anything else. They went down through another draw, and the next time it appeared, Claudette said, "That abandoned Hudson Bay post, ahead, is just this side of the border."

He nodded and asked, "Who's meeting us there?"

"Nobody. The soddy, she was built on a trader's cutoff in the Shining Times, before the border she was carefully surveyed. It has not been used for years. Sometimes someone camps there. The well has caved in and the firewood is all gone. Some buffalo hunters, they burned the last roof timbers many years ago. There's no reason for anyone to be there now."

He nodded, but asked, "Why are we headed for it, then?"

She said, "*Merde alors*, one must be headed *someplace*, yes?"

He stared at the northern sky and said, "Right. It's still daylight and anyone watching the border can see for miles from any rise. But don't you reckon the

Mounties know the old trading post has been abandoned?"

"Of course, but they are most proper and never cross the line. We could be looking for wood. We might be homesteaders, meaning to file on the land, with our soddy half-started." She looked away as she added softly, "We could be a white man who wishes to be alone with the squaw he picked up."

Longarm said, "That was your notion, not mine. As I see your plan, we're to pull in at the ruins on this side of the border, wait until it's good and dark, and make a run for it."

She shrugged and said, "I can see why they told me you needed help. One does not run, as you put it. One crosses quietly, when—how you say—the coast, she is clear?"

"That makes sense. The Mounties can't be everywhere along such a stretch of nothing much. There's going to be a hunter's moon tonight. We'll hunker down for a spell, and later on I'll scout ahead before we try to sneak this cart across."

Claudette swore in what might have been French or Cree, and said, "*Sacre* Goddamn, you are not in charge here. You are my passenger, and you talk too much."

He felt like doing some cussing of his own by now, but he tried to keep his voice polite as he said, "Look, honey. I ain't trying to run this expedition, but I'd sort of like to savvy it better. Aside from the Mounties we might trip over, there's a dozen half-cracked killers somewhere up ahead with guns. If I find myself having to make sudden moves in the next few hours, it might be best for us both if I knew what the hell I was doing."

She relented slightly and explained, "We shall stop at the ruins ahead, as if we are camping for the night. We shall do nothing while the moon hangs high. When it is dark, well after midnight, we will move on, if we get the signal."

He relaxed a bit and said, "You're right. I hadn't thought it out all the way. I might have known you'd

32

have friends up ahead. Some Métis or Cree has been staked out quiet all afternoon, keeping an eye out for prissy riders in red coats. If they've passed by, he'll signal us. If they're dug in and waiting up ahead, he won't. That way, they can't catch him, either."

"You are learning. Why do they call you Longarm? It sounds like an Indian name. But you are not an Indian, and your arms are not too long for your body."

He laughed and said, "I've been asked that before. It's sort of dumb, but my last name's Long, and Uncle Sam uses me as what you might call the long arm of the law."

"I see. You are right, it is dumb. I am not too clear, me, why they want me to help you. But I know you are not enforcing any law at the moment. You are trying to *break* the law, yes?"

He shrugged and said, "Well, there's laws and there's laws. I reckon Queen Victoria might take a dim view of my illegal entry, but the men I'm after didn't cable London or even Ottawa for a tourist visa, and they sure busted some laws all to hell. On either side of the border, it's considered ornery to murder folks. My job, as I see it, is to reach out and grab those jaspers for Uncle Sam, no matter where they've run to."

"Won't this make trouble between your government and Canada?"

"It might, if Canada ever hears of it. Your Prime Minister MacDonald is a muley cuss when it comes to cooperating with the States."

She grimaced and said, "Please, *m'sieu*, MacDonald is not *my* prime minister, him!"

"Sorry. I forgot you Métis consider Louis Riel your prime minister, president, or whatever."

Claudette's face went cigar-store Indian as she murmured, "Louis Riel? I have never heard the name before, *m'sieu*."

"Oops, forgot *that*, too! I can see why you're so unconversational, ma'am."

For the first time since they'd met, the Métis girl

allowed a trace of warmth to creep into her voice as she said, "I already observed *m'sieu* was learning, him."

Once more, the cart rode them up for a look around and Longarm said, "There's a painted pony grazing about a quarter-mile west of the ruins."

Claudette said, "I saw it, me. She looks like a stray, him or she."

Longarm frowned and objected, "Strays or wild mustangs don't like being on their own. That pinto should be exploring for company unless it's crippled or there's other critters nearby. You'd better pull up here, while we're below the skyline in this draw."

Claudette pulled her cart horse to a halt, but said, "Few people know of this trace north. Even if it was an ambush, why would they allow that pony to roam free, him?"

Longarm said, "That's what I aim to find out. You stay here while I ride in on my bay and have a look-see."

She started to object, but he added, "Look, Claudette, you're in charge, as far as getting me across the line goes. I'm in charge when things come up that you can't savvy. Is it a deal?"

"Pooh, nobody ever comes this way but those of us who remember when this part of the high plains was part of Canada. I think you waste your time, me. But the sun, she will not set for an hour or more. You go ahead and play *les* cowboys and Indians while I rest my horse."

Longarm swung down from the cart's seat and went around to untie his mount. He swung himself into the saddle and rode out, but not in the direction they'd been going. Anyone watching from the ruins would be expecting to see more of him as he topped the next rise. So Longarm rode east along the draw. As he'd expected, the rise on either side grew less steep as it wandered away from the Rockies.

He used the low-hanging sun and the set of the shadow he cast to keep track of just where everything

34

was. A mile away from where anyone might be watching for him, he spurred his bay up and over, saw that there was no further low ground between himself and the ruins, and headed in at a jogging trot. He didn't like trotting very much. It was the least comfortable gait for both mount and rider, but a man bobbing awkwardly made a tougher target, too.

The painted pony spied Longarm's bay and nickered as it headed to join them, or tried to. Longarm saw the way its hind off-leg was drawn up as it limped their way, and he muttered, "Busted, sure as hell. Somebody left you out here for the wolves and buzzards, Old Paint."

The pinto reached them as Longarm reined in just out of pistol range of the ruins. As the two critters nuzzled one another like long-lost kin, he drew the Winchester from its scabbard and dismounted on the wrong side. This was a trick he'd learned the hard way, from a Shoeshone he'd been set to gun as the Indian dismounted. Since then, he'd known most Indians got on and off the right side. It could still surprise most hidden marksmen, waiting for an easy shot at a cuss hung with a foot in the stirrup.

Longarm walked around the horses as he levered a round into the chamber, and when he stepped from behind cover, the odds were more reasonable.

He knew there was no sense in looking for things to hide behind, as he strode in across the short-grass, so he just kept a sharp eye on the ruins and hoped for the best.

He heard the buzzing of flies as he approached the open gap in the sod wall where the door had once been. He sniffed, considered, and moved on in. It hardly seemed likely that anyone alive was hiding behind that wall. The smell of death was strong enough to turn the stomach of a coyote.

The bloated body lay spread-eagled on its back inside the roofless shell of the old trading post. The buckskin pants had split, and the buttons of the red checkered shirt had all popped off, exposing a watermelon of purple, swollen paunch. Night critters and ants had been working on the horror that had once been a human face, but Longarm could see that the man, for that was what the corpse had been in life, had worn his hair in Indian braids. Over on the grass in a corner lay a battered black felt hat with a feather in its snakeskin band. The dead man had been an assimilated Indian or a breed.

There was a black circle of burned-out grass where a cow-chip fire had been. There was an overturned coffee-pot and a fresh can of beans amid the older, rusted-out cans and sun-faded coffee grounds of earlier campers. The slanting rays of the sun shone on something in the grass, and Longarm bent to pick it up. It was a spent cartridge. There were three just like it nearby. Longarm held it up and read *Webley .38* on its brass base. He put it in his pocket, muttering, "Someone put four rounds from a British revolver in this poor cuss, and reloaded before he rode on."

He picked up the hat and walked outside to look around before going back to his bay. It was easy enough to read the sign of other horses. A party of about a dozen riders had ridden in to find the lone camper brewing coffee. There were no signs pointing to much of a fight. They'd simply gunned him by his fire, for some reason.

As he walked over to the horses, thinking it over, he spotted the old Indian agency brand on the pinto's shoulder, and nodded. "Yep, that's it. Old Paint was stolen over near the Blackfoot reservation where Cal Durler was murdered. He hung up a leg in a dog hole, and they needed a fresh mount. The dead man never came out here on foot. They gunned him for his pony before they ran north across the border!"

Longarm led his own mount clear of the crippled pinto, and held the bay's reins firmly as he raised the Winchester in his free hand. As the hurt and lonely Indian pony struggled to rejoin them, Longarm raised the muzzle and fired at point-blank range. As his army mount shied and tried to break free, the pinto collapsed with the .44 slug in its now pain-free brain, and Longarm soothed, "Easy, pard. I know he was a friend of yours, but it's better this way."

The spooked bay settled down as Longarm explained about his rough surgery, and after they'd waltzed a bit more, he was able to mount up and slip the Winchester back in its boot. As he rode toward the draw he'd told Claudette to stay in, he spotted her Red River cart topping the rise and coming his way, fast.

He rode to meet her, waving the dead man's hat as he called out, "Rein in, ma'am. There's a mess of dead meat around here, and you're fixing to spook your cart horse!"

Claudette did as he suggested, and as he joined her, Longarm held the hat out to her and said, "I sure hope you don't aim to tell me this belonged to the Métis watching this border crossing for you."

Claudette gasped, "*Mais non!* But I recognize that *chapeau*, me! It belongs to one of our couriers, a Cree named Red Knife. We have been expecting him for some time, with dispatches from the north. Where did you find his *chapeau*, you?"

"About ten feet from his body. They gunned him for his horse."

"Aha! It was our enemies, *les* Mounties, *non?*"

"Not hardly. They get their mounts from Queen Victoria. Red Knife was murdered by the gang I'm after. But you were right about them being enemies. Men like that are enemies of the whole human race. From the mess they left, I'd say they have at least a ten-day lead on me. You wouldn't know what Red Knife's pony looked like, would you?"

"But of course. It was a dappled gray mare with the black mane and tail."

"That'll help. I thank you for carrying me this far, ma'am. But from here on, the trail looks sort of spooky.

37

You just tell me who my next contact is, north of the line, and I'll be on my way alone."

She looked startled and said, "Don't be crazy, you! In the first place, those were not my orders. In the second, it is broad daylight and—"

"I know how you folks have been crossing," he cut in, "but as I read the sign, there's no Mountie troop patrolling this stretch, and those killers are already too far out in front of me for comfort. I'd like to shilly-shally around, playing games with shadows in red coats. But I'm on serious business."

"*Merde alors!* Do you think our revolution is not serious?"

"Oh, revolutions are serious enough, ma'am. They're time-consuming, too. I don't know too much about you Métis and your cause, but I've jawed with Fenians fighting to free Ireland, and I've talked to Mexicans trying to get rid of Diaz, and the last time I heard, old Sitting Bull was over on the Pine Ridge, plotting another rising of the Sioux. I reckon, sooner or later, all your revolutions will get going, but I ain't after Canada Jack as a way of life. I just want to *catch* the rascal and get it over with. I haven't time for secret meetings in cellars, or singing patriotic songs in the back room of some saloon. Hunkering down over there in them ruins is a waste of time. I aim to ride on as soon as I bury the dead man."

"You wish to bury Red Knife, *m'sieu*?" She cut in.

He nodded and said, "Somebody sure ought to. I noticed you have a tool kit over your left wheel. Why don't you hang on to the horses here, while I do the job?"

She said, "Red Knife's people live far from here, but if we got word to them—"

But Longarm shook his head and said, "I'll mark his grave and they can do as they like, in time. You can't just leave a man laying there like a cow pat. He's got to be buried decent before I ride on."

As he dismounted to take a shovel from the side of

the cart, the Métis girl said, "*Bien*, I will help you, me. You are most right, of course, but your concern surprises me. I told you he was an Indian."

"What's that supposed to mean? I thought he was a friend of yours."

"He was, but you are white, and you never knew Red Knife. Few of your kind go to so much trouble for one of my mother's people."

Longarm hefted the shovel and said, "You stay here and hold the horses. You can come closer and maybe join me in a few words, after I tidy up."

"It is that ugly?"

"He's been in the sun for a spell. I ain't saying you ain't tough enough to handle the sight, but he wouldn't want to be remembered by a pretty gal in the condition he's in right now. I'll wave you in when I've made him fit to receive visitors."

He left her there with the horses as he walked back to the ruins. The smell hadn't gotten any better, and the dead pinto would be adding to the aroma in a few hours. As he walked around the horse he'd shot, he muttered, "I'm sorry, fellow. Digging a hole for *you* would be ridiculous."

He stepped through the opening, took off his coat and hat, and tossed them on the grass. Then he went to work, upwind and as close as he could manage to the corpse. By the time he'd cut through the sod and gotten down four feet, he was sweating, the bluebottle flies had found him, and the smell was getting to him. He straightened up, braced a palm against the small of his back, and told the dead Indian, "That's going to have to do you, old son. This clay soil is hard digging."

He got the shovel blade under the dead man's center of gravity and heaved. Red Knife rolled over wetly and fell face down in the shallow grave. His exposed back was a crawling mass of maggots, and Longarm quickly blotted out the horror by scraping dirt in, fast.

It only took a few minutes to fill the grave and pat the mound firm with the back of the shovel.

He picked up his hat and coat, and stepped to the doorway to wave the Métis girl in. Claudette drove her cart to within rifle range and dropped her cast-iron ground anchor before leaping down. Leaving the cart and the uneasy horses beyond the sickly sweet scent of murder, she walked wide around the dead pinto to join Longarm. She stared soberly at the mound for a long, unblinking moment, then she walked over, dropped to one knee, and crossed herself to say an *Ave* over the dead Cree.

She took a rosary from under her buckskin jacket and Longarm stood respectfully, hat in hand, as he waited for her to pray some more. But Claudette simply put the rosary atop the mound, pressed it in with her fingers, and stood up, murmuring, "He was a Catholic."

Longarm said, "If we could rustle up some scrap lumber, I could make a marker with my jackknife, ma'am."

But Claudette said, "You have done enough. His people will be told. They will be surprised by your *beau geste*, but they will not be displeased."

He shrugged and said, "My mother wasn't much for praying, but she told us about the Golden Rule. Let's get out of here, ma'am. The sun will be down soon and this ain't a pleasant place even by daylight."

As he walked her back to the cart, he put on his frock coat and said something about her returning to the town they'd come from. Claudette said, "You can't go on alone. The Mounties are watching for strangers."

He said, "I know. But they just let a least a dozen riders cross the line not far from here. One more might not matter."

"I don't understand you. You risked your life approaching our leaders because you said you needed help. Now you say you wish to ride on without me."

He shrugged and said, "I never figured they'd give

me a young gal to guide me. The men I'm after play rough and mean. I'd rather risk a set-to with Crown Sergeant Foster than have you hurt by a gang of desperadoes who swat folks like flies."

"But I know the country ahead. I can guide you to safe hiding places and help you avoid the Mounties."

Longarm raised an eyebrow and asked, "What happened to your accent, ma'am? You're starting to talk like one of those British spies your friends are so worried about."

Claudette smiled and said, "I have to work at it when I'm with people I don't know. Sometimes it helps to be remembered as an unwashed primitive. The Mounties have several wanted posters out on me, each with a different description."

He nodded and said, "I figured you could pass for a white gal if you wanted to. Chasing you Métis must be a chore. Most of you can look red or white, as the occasion calls for."

Her mood darkened as they reached the cart. She said, "It was the Tories in Ottawa who decided we were savages. Now they must live with what they've made of us. If we can't be full citizens, perhaps we can beat them as wild Indians."

Longarm helped her up on the cart, but remained standing as he said, "That ain't my fight, ma'am. And I'm beginning to see that my fight ain't yours. It's almost sundown, so we'd best part friendly, and both of us will be free to work things out as best we can."

She hauled in her ground anchor, but held her cart horse steady as she asked, "If I were a Métis *man*, would you be so unwilling to ride on with me?"

He shook his head and said, "Nope. But you ain't a man, and there's another reason. I asked for help to avoid trouble with the Mounties. I never swore away my freedom. I'm a professional, and a fair hand at staying alive. I don't feel comfortable as a package to be delivered."

She nodded and said, "I know. I was not easy on you. Would it help if I explained?"

"You don't have to, ma'am. They sent you on a fool's errand with a man you weren't sure of. I told you I had Indian friends. I've met up with some of you undecided folks too, and I know you got a tough row to hoe. Some of my kind don't have much sense, and they can get silly as hell about the advantages of their complexion. I wasn't too surprised by your attitude, but it did get tedious."

She said, "Tie your bay to the back and get in. We are going on to Canada together."

He hesitated and she added, "With you in charge."

Longarm grinned and said, "I'll settle for a partnership. You tell me when I'm about to step in something dumb, and if I tell you to hit the dirt and stay put, you're to do it with no argument. Agreed?"

Claudette smiled back and said, "*Oui*. Together we advance against the common enemy, *non*?"

He wasn't sure how she meant that, but he didn't argue. Canada Jack and his gang were enemies enough, for now. If the Métis tried to mix him up in their revolution, he'd just have to come up with a graceful excuse. He only wanted to avoid the Mounties. It wasn't his job to tangle with them. If Crown Sergeant Foster met him riding with a wanted Canadian rebel gal . . . Well, he'd cross that creek when he came to it.

Chapter 3

Longarm was anxious to press on, while Claudette was still in favor of waiting until at least moonset. In the end, they both got their way. They crossed early, but the night was black as a dungeon.

The high plains only average ten or twenty inches of rain a year, but when it does rain, the prairie sky makes up for its long dry spells of cobalt blue. Longarm had noticed that the sunset was redder than usual, but the stars were coming out as Claudette clucked to the plodding horse ahead of them and said, "We are now in Canada."

The prairie looked just the same, but the evening sky looked like the Lord was drawing a big wool blanket over the world as He put it to bed for the night. Longarm said, "We're in for a cloudburst, sure as hell. We'd best pull up here. That's a deep draw out in front of us."

"I thought you were in a hurry."

"Not to drown. Any border patrols around here will be making for home or high ground about now. This rise we're on figures to become an island any minute, so we'd best stay put."

Before she could answer, the evening breeze reversed and a raindrop big enough to fill a shotglass came down to lick the dust from his booted toe on the running board. He said, "See what I mean? Drop the ground anchor. I've got to hobble my gelding before he's spooked by summer lightning. We ought to be safe enough here on midslope. Lightning hits the ridges, and the floodwaters won't rise half this high even if she rains all night."

As they went about their chores, the rain started coming down in earnest, and Longarm was soaked by the time he'd unsaddled his bay and hobbled it. He threw his McClellan and possibles under the cart and ran around to see if Claudette needed help.

She'd hobbled and unharnessed the cart horse, and the cart sat at a crazy angle with its grounded shafts aimed down the slope. Longarm said, "Duck inside. I aim to swing the shafts around to level her. The rain will come in the back if we leave her like she is."

Claudette said, "I will help, it's heavy." But he said, "Get up under the canopy, damn it. I ain't a sissy, and there's no sense in both of us catching pneumonia!"

She didn't argue, but she didn't do as he suggested, either. She grabbed one of the lodgepole shafts, and together they righted and turned the cart on its wheels until it sat level. By now they were both as wet as if they'd gone swimming in their clothes, so he simply shrugged when she bent at his side to help him chock the wheels.

She didn't invite him to join her as she climbed up into the cart at last, but he had no intention of standing there in the rain, and as he hauled himself up under the canopy, she put out a hand to steady him.

He shifted his weight gingerly as he made sure the cart was steady and tried to figure where to drip. Most of the floor space was taken up by her bed. The rest was covered with supplies. There was less space, all told, than in a Concord coach.

Claudette pointed out a barrel for him to perch on, and began to unfasten her buckskin jacket as she said, "We have to get out of these wet things before we get chilled, *non?*"

It was pretty dark, but not that dark, and Longarm said, "I've been wet before. I sure wish you'd face

44

the other way, though. You ain't wearing a shift under that jacket and, while I'm trying to remember my manners, I'm only human."

Claudette glanced down at her firm, moist breasts, as if surprised at the sight herself, and said, "Living in a Red River cart, one must be *practique.* False modesty makes for needless difficulty in such close quarters, *non?*"

"If you say so, ma'am. Maybe I'd best take off at least my coat and vest and such."

Fooling with his own buttons gave Longarm's numb fingers something to do and a place to keep his eyes. The Métis girl moved her hips from the buffalo robe of her bed and drew the wet calico skirt off over her head. He wasn't looking at her, and it was night-time with no lantern lit, but he couldn't miss the fact that she was sitting knee-to-knee with him, stark naked. She laughed as she took a wool blanket from the pile at the foot of the bed and wrapped herself in it, asking, "There, is that better, *m'sieu?*"

He peeled off his soaked-through undershirt and answered, "It helps a mite. Do you have another blanket to spare, ma'am?"

She nodded and handed him one. He was starting to shivver as he draped it over his chilled shoulders and said, "Thanks. This is right nice and fluffy."

She said, "Nobody makes blankets like the Hudson Bay Company. That's a four-beaver blanket and it's been in my family since the Shining Times. Why don't you take off your boots and britches? I can't see."

He saw no reason to argue, so he followed her suggestion. It was sort of awkard, peeling under the blanket with a lady sitting close enough for him to smell her moist hair and flesh, but he managed, and as he piled the wet things in a corner, he was sincerely grateful to the Hudson Bay Company. He had a monstrous erection. Probably because he was cold, he decided.

By now it was almost pitch black, and he could

45

feel her nearness more than he could see it. The rain was drumming harder and he said, "Listen to that gullywasher out there. It's coming down salt and fire. Sounds like it's settled in for the night, too. We'd have had some lightning by now if she was just a summer squall."

Claudette said, "I know. You forget, I was raised on the prairie in a Red River cart. I have been listening for the cry of a loon, but I think our friends on this side of the border are not expecting us tonight."

He started to ask what a water bird would be doing out on the prairie, even in a cloudburst. Then he nodded and said, "I've always wondered why Indians signal with out-of-place bird calls. I heard an Apache trying to sound like canyon jay one time, a day's ride from any canyon."

She laughed and said, "Few white men are as observant. One must, of course, make one's bird calls a little unusual. How else could a friend know he or she was not hearing a real bird?"

"Oh, I figured that out long ago. It's just a wonder anyone's ever fooled by it."

"Some men are easier to fool than others. Has m'sieu fought many Indians?"

"I've never traded shots with Cree, if that's your question."

"In other words, you've killed your redskin."

"The first man I killed was white, and I never gloated over it. Since then, I've traded shots with all sorts of folks, from blue-eyed blondes to Cimmarron blacks. I've never shot anyone who didn't need to be shot, and I've bought drinks or offered a smoke to more men than I've had to fight. The Lord in His wisdom made more decent folks, of every shade, than He made skunks. But when I meet up with someone looking for a fight, I fight the son of a bitch. I don't ask about his family tree."

Claudette chuckled and said, "I don't think I'd better fight with you, then. I don't know why I brought it

46

up. Sometimes I go a whole day without remembering I'm a breed."

She struck a match and lit the hanging lamp, and as the glow filled the tiny space they shared, Longarm caught a glimpse of one breast she'd exposed by raising her bare arm. He looked away and said, "I'd just as soon we left it dark, ma'am."

She said, "The lamp will burn some of the chill from the air in here. You'd be surprised how a soapstone oil lamp warms a bark wigwam in the winter. I remember playing naked as a child in my grandmother's wigwam up on the Quill Lakes, with the wolf-wind howling and the snow almost up to the smoke-hole."

He said, "I noticed modesty ain't your strong point, ma'am."

"Surely you've spent enough time in Indian camps not to be repelled by a glimpse of flesh?"

"Repelled ain't the word I was looking for, ma'am. As to what I may or may not have glimpsed while visiting with Indians, it ain't the same. It just seems *natural* for Indian ladies to wear fewer duds than most. I hope you won't feel insulted, but you don't seem Indian to me. By the time I've seen most white gals in the buff, I'm usually more sure of the cards I'm holding."

"Are you suggesting you'd feel less awkward cooped up with me if you made love to me?"

He frowned and answered, "That was your suggestion, not mine. But as long as you brought it up, I think we should act one way or the other. It's this sitting on the fence between formal and intimate that makes a man broody."

The Métis girl nodded and said, "*M'sieu* has a point. It would be more sensible to get the tension out of the way, *non*?"

Then Longarm's breath caught as she let the blanket fall away and lay back, nude and inviting, across the bed. Her knees were almost touching his, and as she spread them wide, she murmured, "Come. Let's get it over with."

47

His groin tingled and his cheeks began to burn as he gazed down at her flawless, tawny body in the warm lamplight. But he scowled and asked, "What do you take me for, a goddamned Jersey bull that needs to be serviced so he won't gore the hired help?"

"What's the matter, don't you want it?"

"I don't want *it*. I could use a woman, but I like the real thing too much to get any pleasure from an *it* that's just trying to be, uh, sensible."

She sat back up with a puzzled frown, still fully exposed, and, if anything, more desirable with her big blue eyes staring into his at closer range. She licked her lips uncertainly and asked, "Are you as angry as you look? I am trying to understand you, *m'sieu*, but you are so different from other men I've met."

"I reckon you've met lots of other men, huh?"

She smiled bitterly and murmured, "Ah, now we are on more familiar ground. You think I'm just a half-breed slut, yes?"

He said, "Nope. I think you're of the prettiest gals I've ever met, and I want you right now, so bad I can taste it."

"Then what makes you so hesitant? I told you I didn't mind."

He reached up and dimmed the light before he said, "Let's call it *respect*. You and me are grown-up human beings, not critters with no feelings, or kids who'll whimper if they don't get some candy. I don't want a woman who's only servicing my body. I want— Hell, I *need* a woman who considers me a fellow critter, not some sort of randy goat."

She looked down and blushed a dusky rose as she murmured, "You fool, don't you understand the defenses of a girl who's been rejected by your kind since childhood?"

He started to answer, then he saw that no words were needed as he leaned forward, took her cheeks in both his palms, and kissed her eyelids as she tried to blink away her tears. His own blanket fell away as he

48

raised her mouth to his, and Claudette was suddenly on her knees between his naked thighs, her breasts his chest as he enfolded her in his arms. She kissed him warmly and hungrily as she wrapped her own chilled arms around him, but the position was awkward for both of them, so he leaned off the barrel and half rose, aiming them both across the bed. As he worked them into a less awkward angle, her thighs were suddenly hugging his ribs, and the next thing he knew, he was in her to the hilt, the way old lovers found the way without having to grope for it. Her eyes opened wide in the dim light as they both gasped in surprised pleasure. He started moving silently, knowing anything he said at this moment would sound dumb, and to his relief, she responded with a passionate silence of her own.

They made love naturally on the firm pile of hides, the way men and women were designed to do it before folks started writing books and making up complicated rules. She didn't say anything coy, or lie to him about never having felt this way before. He could tell when she was coming, and he could tell she knew the way there. As they climaxed, she moaned like a cougar and gave herself completely. It wasn't until they'd done it again that she turned her head away and sighed, "*Sacre*, what must *m'sieu* think of his naughty squaw now?"

He stayed where he was and thrust roughly, saying, "Aw, bullshit! Don't try to kill the magic, Claudette. What do I have to do to show you I don't hate Indians, stand on my head?"

She laughed and asked, "*Merde alors*, in a Red River cart?"

And then they were both laughing, meeting one another's eyes.

She cupped a nipple up to him as she sighed, "I like the way your mustache teases. It is most strange, but I do not feel as ashamed as I expected."

"Hell, we've done nothing to feel ashamed about, Claudette."

"Perhaps, but I tried so hard to fight what was happening to us. I knew from the first that I wanted this. But I was so afraid."

"Jesus, you sure put me through a long initiation. But I'd say it was worth it. After wanting you so many nights, I don't feel like we've done it twice already. I feel like we're just starting."

"I know. I feel what you have inside me. It's even better, now that I feel surer in your arms. I—*Merde*, why talk about it? Let's just *do* it."

They did, and then, since they were still able, they did it again. When they paused to get their breaths, the rain had stopped.

He said, "Storm's over. I wonder what time it is."

But Claudette dug her nails into his buttocks and murmured, "The time, in here, is *now*. Who cares what time it is in the rest of the universe?"

They rode north across the prairies of Alberta as the buffalo grass greened back after the rains. Like so many parts of what the ignorant called "the great American desert," the life forms of the high plains took advantage, fast, of such few favors as the severe climate offered. They forded the shallow Milk River their first morning north of the border, and found the sand bars of the braided stream covered with waterfowl enjoying the change in the scenery. Claudette explained that a week before or a week in the future would find the Milk reduced to a string of stagnant puddles with dust devils blowing among the cottonwood and willow of its banks. Cheat grass would sprout, go to seed, and die along the riverbed before it filled again. That evening, they camped by a prairie lake ten miles across. Mallards and sandhill cranes dabbled in the grassy shallows for fairy shrimp, and Longarm was surprised to find the water salty when he started to fill the coffeepot for Claudette. The laughing Métis girl explained that the lake was only a brine pond, five hundred feet or less across, most of the time.

By the third day north of the line, they could see the green bases of the revived grass from the cart's seat, and he spied pronghorn in the distance, gorging themselves on the unexpected bonus-growth. He asked why there were no cows, and Claudette explained, "We are in dangerous country for cattlemen."

He nodded and said, "I should have seen that without asking. North Mexico and South Texas are the same. It hardly pays to graze cows near a border, with the price of beef high and employment for the uneducated low. Where do you Métis range your stock?"

"Mostly north of the South Saskatchewan and south of the North Saskatchewan."

"Two rivers with the same name, right?"

"Of course. They join near a new town the Anglo-Canadians want to call Prince Albert. We Métis still hold the triangle between the west branches of our Swift-Running Rivers, and we spit on Queen Victoria's new maps. The territory of Saskatchewan is ours. They have no right to name our villages after dead English princes."

"I think Prince Albert was German, but let's not worry about it. I thought we were in Alberta."

She nodded a bit grimly and said, "We are, at the moment. As we trend northeast, we will be in Saskatchewan. In the Shining Times, our ancestors, red and white, met at a place called Pile of Bones to trade and court one another. Now they call it Regina, another stupid English name."

Longarm nodded and said, "I've been going over the map they sold me, back where we met up. This country is sort of confusing, the way you Métis, the full-bloods, and the Canadian government give different names to the same places. It's none of my business, but you do need more names out here. All your Métis places seem to be named after saints, and the Indians didn't show much imagination. You've got two Saskatchewan rivers and a Saskatchewan Territory and a town called Saskatoon. Ain't that a mite confusing?"

"Not if you speak French or Cree!" she snapped, adding, "Those of us who *belong* here know our way around. We did not name things for the strangers trying to steal our land and change our ways."

He saw they were getting into murky waters, so he tried to steer them back to subjects they could agree on. He said, "The gent you say you never heard of told me the railroad was about to Moose Jaw by now, and I explained why I figured Canada Jack and his gang might be headed there. I maybe shouldn't mention this, but my map tells me Moose Jaw is directly east of here, and we seem to be headed north."

Claudette said, "I know. I told you we were going to the Oldman River. That's a tributary of the South Saskatchewan. We can follow the river valley east to La Coteau. There, the river elbows north and we can cut southeast for the railhead at Moose Jaw."

He closed his eyes and tried to picture his map. Then he nodded and said, "I see some good and some bad in your notion, Claudette. The good part is that we'll be approaching from a direction few Mounties would expect from a border jumper."

"But of course. What is the bad part?"

"It's the long way around. Canada Jack might have headed more directly for the bright lights and piano music. I've been watching for signs along the way, but I haven't cut trail since we left the deserted trading post. He's already got a good lead on me, as it is. If he just lit out direct, across country . . ."

"*Merde*, they told you that you needed a guide. What seems the short way, on your map, is not the best way, on the ground. There is—how you say—a *grain* to the way the hills and rivers run up here. Many years ago, there was a great glacier. The land is furrowed into finger lakes and treacherous swamps. The men who build the railroad are learning this.

That is why you Americans beat Canada by so many years with your own railroads."

"In other words, the shortest distance in these parts ain't always a straight line."

She nodded. "Exactly. That is why we find the survey of the central government so foolish as well as so unjust. We who know the country live with the way God made it. Our carts, as you know by now, are slow. But they get us there. No Indian or buffalo ever climbed over a steep ridge or ploughed through a tamarack swamp just to save going around the easy way."

"Hmm, Canada Jack's been up here a while, and he may have some Canucks riding with him. Now that I study on it, I can see where following the old Indian trails makes sense. But don't the Mounties patrol the known trails?"

"Of course, as well as they are able. The country is big and the Mounties can't be everywhere."

"I can see that. But I only worry about them patrolling a stretch I happen to be using. If *you* know the easy way to Moose Jaw . . ."

"Pooh, the Mounties travel alone; we do not."

Longarm stared around at the rolling prairie. He was damned if he could see any company. But he remembered that she was part Indian, so he said, "I noticed some smoke to the north just after dawn. I figured it was just a small grass fire."

She smiled without answering.

He asked, "Uh, just how close do those friends of yours move in at night?"

Claudette laughed and said, "Not that close. They know my cart, and they are not concerned about what may or may not be going on inside it after dark."

He grinned and said, "Your friends are good. I've been scouted by Comanche, Apache, and such. I generally notice."

She nodded and said, "The Mounties are good too. They are also quite direct about questioning people

53

they consider curious. Most of our counter-patrols are led by Métis, with at least one or two full-bloods out on point. Before the Cree got horses, they hunted on these plains afoot. It takes a good hunter to approach a buffalo or pronghorn within arrow range."

They drove on for a time before she asked slyly, "Have you been watching that coyote, about a mile out to our left?"

Longarm glanced at the distant gray dot and said, "Sure. Looks like an old dog-coyote sunning himself while he waits for a foolish jackrabbit to graze within sprinting range."

Again she didn't answer, but her hint had been enough. Longarm stared hard and muttered, "Come to study on it, that coyote's ears are sure droopy. I've heard the Sioux used to creep up on buffalo wearing old coyote skins."

Claudette said, "I know. So did the Cree. Look, M'sieu Coyote has seen we are not being followed and has disappeared from the skyline. Are you still afraid I'll lead you into a Mountie ambush, Longarm?"

He said, "Nope. But the Mounties ain't my main worry."

By the time they reached the Oldman River, Longarm had formed an odd double-image map of western Canada in his head. There was the official version, made up of grid coordinates, bench marks, and an imposing road network that appeared mostly on paper. The survey teams of the central government had divided vast areas into neat, square townships, and had provided name after name for towns nobody had built yet. Rail stops were neatly lettered in on open prairie the tracks would not approach for years, and the Royal Post was prepared to deliver mail if anyone ever addressed a letter to a nonexistent post office in an uninhabited peat bog or tamarack swamp.

Underlying the crisp, inked certainty of the cartographer's Canada lay the hazy reality of a sparsely settled, complex land known to the white and Métis settlers, the Indians, and other wild creatures who really lived there. Claudette showed him lakes and streams not on the map. She skirted wide of settlements and lonely cattle spreads she wasn't sure of, but more than once, they shared the wry amusement of noting that a sizable collection of buildings wasn't on the map, while, ten miles or more away, an empty stretch of open range pretended to be a county seat.

When he asked her about the inhabitants of the places she avoided, the Métis girl explained, "Some are Métis. Others are pure French, or maybe something else. Our cause has friends among pure Scots, and even English who understand and sympathize with our problems. On the other hand, there are Métis and even full-bloods who wish to be well-thought-of by the government. By the time one knows for certain, it may be too late."

He nodded and said, "It reminds me of the Fenians. Sometimes it seems the Irish rebels worry more about each other than they do about the English. Have you had any Fenian troubles this far west, Claudette?"

"Very little. The Irish Catholics are, of course, opposed to the Protestant domination of the central government. But when they are not fighting the Orangemen, the Irish tend to fight the French or Indians. It got so bad in Quebec, a few years ago, that French and English militia units fought side by side against some mad Irishmen invading Canada from your country."

"I heard about that. They were Irish veterans of the Union army. They kept their guns when they were mustered out, raised a green flag, and marched on Montreal for reasons best known to themselves. It was embarrassing as hell for Uncle Sam."

She said, "There have been many raids since, though not so *dramatique*. They have held up some banks. They have robbed some trains. But they do not seem as serious about their revolution as we are about ours."

Longarm shrugged and said, "Oh, the Irish rebels in Ireland are as serious, I'd say. But revolutions are funny things. We've got some gents, down Missouri way, still fighting a rebel cause they lost fifteen years ago. I'd have a higher opinion of Jesse James if he just held folks up 'cause he needed money, but some men need excuses, and revolution can be a fine excuse for larceny."

Claudette frowned and asked, "Are you accusing Louis Riel of being a common bandit?"

He smiled and answered, "I thought we said we'd never heard of *M'sieu* Riel. Don't cloud up and rain all over me, honey. I just said there was all kinds of rebels. Some are doubtless sincere, some are maybe a mite crazy. Others are just rascals."

"Oh? And what sort of rebel do you make of Louis Riel?"

"Hell, I never made him a rebel, it was his own idea. He struck me as a man who's at least three-quarters reasonable, but maybe a quarter over the edge into the dreamland of the desperate."

Then he saw he'd hurt her feelings, so he quickly added, "If you're right about him having decent white settlers backing his claims, he'll likely make out all right in the end. Canada's a democracy, even if Prime Minister MacDonald can't understand that at the moment. You Métis only need a few just men who can vote, voting the right way, and you'll get your justice without having to kill nobody."

"And if the new white settlers coming in won't help us?"

"You'll lose, right or wrong. I'm sorry as hell, but I don't make the rules. If I were Riel, I'd be leery as hell about recruiting full-bloods. Not because *I* consider your Cree relations savages, but because, like it or not, most white settlers will. Red Cloud had a deal on paper with our government, and a lot of white men in our Congress were starting to say the Sioux were getting flimflammed. Then Custer went and got himself killed, and all bets were off. It took our army less than two years to smash the Dakota Confederacy and lock up every spokesman they had as some sort of wild man. They tell me Sitting Bull still writes to friends back East, and subscribes to the *Washington Post*. But no matter what he says, since Little Big Horn, it's taken as the rantings and ravings of a wild Indian. You Métis are already tainted with feathers and paint, back east in Ottawa. You kill one white, Indian-style, and it's over for you. They'll hunt you down like Sioux."

This much talking all at one time tended to make Longarm a trifle light-headed, so he broke off and sat back to catch his breath as Claudette shuddered and said, "I know. Some of our leaders are opposed to joining with the full-bloods for the reasons you just gave. But Louis is safe in Montana at the moment, and there will be no rebellion of any kind this summer."

He saw that they were making for a clump of trees, and as they topped another rise, he spotted a soddy and a windmill as well. He said, "Up to now, you've been steering wide of windmills, Claudette. I hope our philosophical discussion hasn't upset your navigation."

She said, "The cattle spread ahead belongs to friends of our cause. I don't think you'd better discuss our cause at all with them as I pick up supplies and dispatches. I say this because the family you'll be meeting in a few moments is pure white. Like my father, Ian MacTavish used to work for the Hudson Bay Company. He and his wife and children are Scottish Protestants, and loyal to Queen Victoria on every subject but one."

"You mean Mister MacTavish don't hold with robbing folks who might have an Indian grandmother?"

"Exactly. Like yourself, old Ian is color-blind when it comes to simple justice. Don't tell him you're in Canada illegally, though. He would never knowingly break the law."

"Ain't helping wanted rebels sort of *bending* it?"

"Not according to MacTavish. He didn't vote for MacDonald in the last election, and he claims our prime minister is the outlaw. He's a rather crusty old dear, but I think you'll like him."

Longarm laughed and said, "He sounds like an uncle I had in West-by-God-Virginia. The old man backed the Union and paid his taxes regular, but he never did get used to the notion that he didn't have the God-given right to make his own corn likker. I don't reckon he'd have stolen a red cent, but he sure scared hell out of some revenuers from time to time."

They drove on in restored humor as Claudette prattled on about her father's friend and the Shining Times. It seemed odd that the new government saw fit to ignore the network of trails and trading posts already laid out over several generations by the old Hudson Bay men. MacTavish, like so many other old-timers, had settled in to homestead what had once been a way-station on the trail to the beaver grounds of the Rockies. He didn't bother to take out his map to check it. He knew nobody back east had put the cattle spread on paper. Since MacTavish had the vote, he'd probably manage to convince them of the error of their ways, when and if some fool surveyor showed up to plant a railroad station in his kitchen.

As they drew near, Claudette reined in and murmured "There is something odd here. The vane of the windmill tells me there have been no Mounties around here recently. But why is it so quiet?"

Longarm nodded and said, "I noticed. We're sitting plain as day on this rise, almost within rifle range. You say they have kids?"

"Oh, the MacTavish children are teenagers. But they have a yellow Indian dog and—

"Stay here. I'll have a look-see."

Longarm got down, walked around to the rear of the cart, and got his Winchester before he moved in the rest of the way on foot.

He called out a couple of times on the way. The folks who lived in this isolated soddy could be in the back, and the sudden sight of a stranger moving toward their door with a rifle could upset some folks.

He saw no sign of livestock. A dog might not bark at a cart he knew, but Longarm had never met the critter. He spotted the corner of a corral behind the soddy, and swung wider as he moved in. There were no horses there, and the rails of the gate were down.

Watching the curtains of the one small window facing his way, he got almost to the door before he spied a patch of reddish yellow in a clump of weeds near a corner. He moved closer and saw that it was a dead yellow Indian dog, missing half of its head.

He said, "Oh, come on, Lord, not *again!*"

But he knew, as he kicked in the door, that Death had visited before him. He tried not to breathe as his eyes adjusted to the gloom inside and enabled him to start counting. The bloated body of a teenaged boy was sprawled near an overturned table. The corpse of what could only be MacTavish, himself, lay behind the table with its head in the fireplace. The fire had gone out long ago, but not before the dead or dying Scotsman's head had been baked black on the coals.

He saw the spent shells on the floors, but he didn't bother to pick any up. He could tell from here that they matched the one in his pocket.

A door across the room stood ajar. He didn't want to, but he went over and into the bedroom anyway.

The bloated, naked body of a gray-haired woman lay on the blood-encrusted mattress in an obscene position. Her wrists and ankles had been tied to the bedposts with pigging string. Like her blood, the matted semen between her legs had dried, but he could see that she'd been gang-raped before one of her assailants had shoved a gun up her vagina and pulled the trigger. There wasn't much expression to be read on her fly-blown, bloated face, but she didn't have to tell him she'd died degraded and terrified.

Longarm took off his Stetson and said, "I'm sure sorry, ma'am. I mean to make somebody pay for what they done here."

Then he took out his knife and cut her free before tossing a torn blanket from the floor over her.

He thought for a moment that he was about to throw up, but he held it down with an effort, placed the hat firmly back on his head, and had a tight rein on his feelings by the time he'd walked out and back to Claudette and the cart. He put the rifle on the seat and went around to the side, without comment, to get the shovel.

Claudette gasped, "*Mais non!* Not another killing!"

He said, "More like three. You said there was a daughter. I didn't find her body. I hope that means she got away."

"And if she didn't get away?"

"They've got her. If they ain't killed her by now, she's likely wishing they would. The folks inside have been dead for some time."

Chapter 4

They followed the Oldman River east until they reached a little trail town that Claudette called Petit Arc. What the Canadian maps called it was anyone's guess. It squatted on low ground near the river, and was mostly made of logs floated downstream from the Rockies.

Claudette steered the cart into a fenced yard near the edge of town, and told Longarm not to show his face around the settlement if he could help it. The quiet Métis couple who came out to help with the horses were friends, she explained, but the others in town were a mixed lot of Métis and whites who might tend to blow with the prevailing breeze from Ottawa.

The Métis couple spoke no English and Longarm didn't have enough French to matter, and in any case, few Frenchmen from Paris could have carried on a comfortable conversation in the Métis dialect. They knew who Longarm was, however, and made him welcome to their humble cabin. As the wife served him hash and coffee with an uncertain smile, Longarm was able to follow Claudette well enough to see that they were here to spend the night, pick up a fresh cart horse, and reprovision her cart.

It was getting toward evening, and, after learning that no mounties had been through in the past few days, Longarm told Claudette he meant to have a look around the settlement.

She said, "But no! I thought I just explained that conditions were unsettled here in Petit Arc!"

He nodded and said, "You did, and I follow your drift. But I didn't come all this way to avoid everybody. If the men I'm after passed this way, somebody will have noticed. A dozen riders stand out in a town only twice as big, and one of them's riding a dapple gray. How many saloons and such do you have in Petit Arc, Claudette?"

"One, if you wish to call it that. The trading post, the general store, and the post office are one and the same. They sell liquor too."

He glanced at their shy-looking Métis hostess, decided she wouldn't know many bad words in English, and asked, "How about houses of ill repute?"

Claudette looked uncomfortable as she admitted, "There are a few squaws, down by the river. I have heard bad things about them. There is no formal establishment, as such."

"Independent businesswomen, huh?"

"Perhaps they are hungry. Since the fur trade died . . ."

"I get the picture. I wasn't asking as a prospective customer. I told you the young owlhoots I'm after seem to crave excitement."

"Do you think they could be here in Petit Arc?" she asked, obviously alarmed.

"I sure hope so. It's about time I got a break."

She murmured something in her Métis dialect, and their host nodded in agreement. She said, "Jacques will go with you. He knew the MacTavishes."

But Longarm said, "No. This ain't his fight, even if MacTavish was a friend. Your outfit needs this quiet hideout, and I might have to work noisy. Tell Jacques I thank him, but I want him to stay here and guard you ladies. No woman alone is safe with those wolverines running loose within a week's ride."

As Longarm had expected, the appeal to his manhood calmed the Métis down. Longarm finished his coffee, stood up, and said he'd be back in about an hour. Claudette asked what she should do if it took longer, and he said, "You go on to wherever without me. The whole town could just about hide in a Texas hat, so it can't take long to explore. If I'm not back in less than two hours, it'll mean I'm in a mess I don't want you in. If you hear gunshots, take off like a scalded cat. If I win or lose, it's sure to attract attention."

She asked, "Won't you need my help in getting away?"

He said, "Nope. Your cart rolls slower than I had in mind with a Mountie on my tail. It might help if I had some addresses between here and Moose Jaw where I could maybe hide out and wait for you."

Claudette stared down at her feet for a moment before she replied, "If you make it to La Coteau, you will go to confession at the little Church of Saint Denis. Father Marcel may help you."

"*May*, Claudette?"

"It is the best I can do. Do not allow yourself to become separated from me, and there will be no problem. It is your idea to go to the trading post. You know I am against it."

He said, "I'll be back directly, Lord willing." Then, since the others were staring at him, he decided not to kiss her. He just nodded at all three and stepped outside.

He got his own saddled bay from the barn, and led it behind him down the rutted road to the middle of town. If he had to light out, he didn't want to leave a trail leading to the door of Claudette's friends.

He had no trouble finding the only action in Petit Arc. It was a long log building with a veranda along its street front and a pair of swinging doors set in the middle. He looked the horses at the hitching rail over, didn't see a dapple gray, and went inside.

The barnlike interior was illuminated by hanging oil lamps, and looked like a mixture of general store, gin mill, and natural history museum. The long bar or counter ran the length of the rear wall, and the log walls were hung with everything from new hats to a moth-eaten moose head above a crate filled with bottles. The far ends were filled with shelves and barrels, but the four or five men inside were gathered under the moose head, so he figured that was the place you got drunk.

The proprieter and his Canadian customers eyed Longarm thoughtfully as he bellied up to the bar and asked for rye. The proprietor was a morose-looking man of about sixty, with red hair gone to gray. He filled a shotglass and withheld comment until Longarm placed a silver dollar on the counter and asked if he stocked three-for-a-nickel cheroots.

The man nodded and said, "Aye, but they're two for thruppence here. We don't see many Yankee dollars this far north, ye ken."

Longarm took a sip of rye and said, "Good stuff. To save you gents some backing and filling, I just rode up from Montana Territory."

"Did ye, noo? I thought ye might be a Yank. What brings ye to the bonny banks of the Oldman?"

"I've been hunting."

"Ooh, a hunter ye are? Well, I fear ye've come a wee bit late, if it's buff ye're after. Aye, the herds are fading fast. Though I hear there's still buff to be hided north of the Peace."

One of the others said, "Not hunting alone, there ain't. The goddamned Cree are starting to make smoke talk, north of here. It's that goddamned breed's doing. They should have hung Riel back in the seventies when he first showed his true colors!"

Longarm noticed that the Scot running the place looked uncomfortable, and he wondered what that meant. Since they'd accepted him as a fellow white man, he said, "I ain't studied things in Canada much, since the way you boys run your country ain't my business. I've been looking for a gent from the States who said he might be passing this way. We call him Tex. He rides a dapple gray mare with a black mane and tail."

The Canadians exchanged puzzled glances. Then one of them said, "Didn't one of them two just in here ride a dappled gray, MacAlpin?"

The proprietor nodded but said, "Aye, and it was a mare, but he's not a Yank named Tex. He's the short Canuck the others called Stubs."

Longarm shook his head and said, "Must be another fellow riding a gray. Old Tex is long and lean."

He took another sip before he added, grudgingly, " 'Course, he might have swapped with someone. You gents say there was a *bunch* of riders?"

MacAlpin nodded and said, "Aye, about a dozen. They said they were surveying for the C.P.R.R. The main party moved on, but Stubs and another called Ryan said they had to meet someone on the westbound stage. They should be back any minute. The stage is due just after sundown, ye ken."

One of the others snickered and said, "I know where they went. They went down to Indian Mary's, in Squaw Alley."

MacAlpin said, "Ooh, that's nain of ye're business, Slade. I'll fetch the smokes ye wanted, Yank."

As the rather prim MacAlpin fetched the cheroots, Slade told Longarm more than he really wanted to know about the morals and probable diseases of the unfortunate Indian Mary. He was offered directions to Squaw Alley too, but he pretended not to care. At least two of the gang had hived off to wait for the arriving stage. That part was interesting as hell.

He bought a fistful of smokes and tucked them away as he casually asked how often the stages ran and so forth. He struck pay dirt when he heard one of them say it only came through once a week, and MacAlpin said, "Aye, Ian MacTavish should be joining us any minute. His daughter Flora is coming back from Medicine Hat on yon stage. If it ever gets here."

Longarm's mouth went dry, but he left the rest of

his drink in his glass as he casually adjusted the hang of his .44. He had the picture, now. The gang had heard that the MacTavish girl was coming home from some visit, and at least two had hung back to— To do *what*?

Shut her up? That was crazy. They'd massacred her family at least three to five days ago. She hadn't been a witness to the killing of her brother and father, or to the brutal rape of her mother. Could they be after some hidden treasure of the family's? That wouldn't work. They'd had time to get it out of the poor woman tied to her bedposts. It must have been from her that they'd learned the girl was due back.

He frowned, as if thinking, and muttered, "MacTavish, MacTavish . . . it seems to me I've heard that name before."

MacAlpin said, "Auld Ian is a friend of mine. We used to trap together in the Shining Times."

Longarm hesitated. He figured he could explain his play to a friend of the murdered family, but the others were liable to do something silly, no matter how they felt about the late MacTavish and his homeward-bound daughter.

He took out a cheroot and said, "I'll smoke this out front. They stink like hell."

"Are ye waiting for ye're friends from Indian Mary's, then?"

"I ain't sure they're my friends. But if they aim to meet the stage, I'd best hang around long enough to make sure before I ride on."

He strode out and lit up, leaning against a post. The sun was almost down, but there was no sign of the arriving stage, or anybody else.

Longarm hated waiting as much as anyone did, but a lawman has to be good at it, since it forms such a large part of his job. He wondered just how many precious hours of his life he'd given away like this. A man could have a good meal or make love to a beautiful woman in an hour or so. Sometimes, waiting for a killer could get more tedious than herding cows in winter.

He'd finished his smoke and lit another before he heard the clop of pony hooves and saw two riders heading his way. The one on the dapple gray called out, "Howdy. Is the stage in yet?"

Longarm stepped away from the post and answered, "Nope."

The shorter one, who had to be Stubs, laughed and asked his partner, "What did I tell you, Ryan? You see, we did have time for a little fun!"

Longarm watched and waited as they reined in and dismounted. Gunning them right now was a tempting impulse, and the folks on the stage would be safer if they didn't arrive in the middle of a shootout. But, damn it, there were only two of them, and neither one was Canada Jack. If he attempted to arrest them as a U.S. lawman, his game was about over. If he simply gunned them with no explanations, the men inside would report it as murder to the Mounties, and he'd be no better off.

The one called Stubs was waving a tintype as he stepped into the light from the open doorway. He said, "Yessir, that is one pretty lady, and that's a fact."

Ryan muttered, "You're crazy. I must be crazy too, now that I've shot my wad in a squaw and had time to think about it. Let's head on east, Stubs. No gal on earth is worth it, and the others have a hell of a lead on us already!"

But Stubs said, "Nosir. I am a man in love and I mean to have my way."

He held out the picture to Longarm and asked owlishly, "Have you ever met a gal half as pretty as this, stranger?"

Longarm glanced at the tintype, saw that it was of a pretty blonde gal, and answered, "Not hardly. Is she your intended?"

Stubs said, "She sure as hell is. She just don't know it yet. She's due in on the stage and, wahoo! Here I am!'

Longarm blinked in surprise and gasped, "Kee-rist! Is *that* why you stayed behind? Because you found a picture of a gal you never even met and decided you wanted her?"

He realized at once that he'd said too much, but what the hell, he couldn't think of a better way. So as the two young owlhoots suddenly froze, eyeing him warily, he nodded and said, "That's right. I'm the law. You bastards do as you see fit, but if you want to live, grab for some sky."

As he'd hoped, they went for their guns as he crabbed sideways and drew. They didn't deserve less than a lingering death over a slow fire, but you don't gutshoot men at odds of two to one, with both slapping leather. He fired into Ryan first, since quiet men were usually more dangerous. But as he reversed his two-step, he saw that Stubs was just as good.

Their two guns went off at once. Longarm's aim was better. His slug spun Stubs around like a ballerina twirling on her toe, and since the son of a bitch hung onto his gun, Longarm fired again and put him on the ground. He stepped over and kicked the gun away, noting with disgust that it wasn't a Webley. Stubs was already dead, so he moved over to Ryan, saw that his gun was a Colt too, and muttered, "Shit."

Ryan opened his eyes and stared up in pain and wonder to croak, "Why?"

Longarm said, "Don't why me, you miserable shit! I saw what you did to the MacTavish family!"

A voice asked, icy calm, "What did they do to yon MacTavish, Yank?" Longarm saw that MacAlpin and the others had come out of the trading post. The old Scot held an over-and-under-twelve-gauge, but it wasn't trained on him, so Longarm said, "I found MacTavish and his wife and son, killed ugly at their spread. I buried them. These two were waiting for the girl."

"Are ye a lawman, then? Not that we doubt ye're word, ye ken."

Longarm holstered his gun and took out his wallet. Flipping it open, he displayed the federal badge pinned inside. He said, "I'm not supposed to be here in Canada. These two and the others gunned at least two people on my side of the border. I was trailing them when I found they'd butchered the MacTavish family. The woman had been—"

"Whist! Say no more, lad. The woman is entitled to respect, dead or alive!"

"Right. One of us is going to have to break the news to that girl who's due in any minute. I know it's a rough chore, but I'd like to get a head start on the Mounties."

MacAlpin stepped over to the dying Ryan, placed the muzzle of his shotgun against his ear, and fired both barrels, blowing his head to hash. Then he sighed and said, "Och, it didn't do a thing for me! What's this nonsense about yon Mounties, Yank?"

"The whole thing is going to have to be reported, ain't it?"

"Aye, we'd best drag these beasties out of the road before yon stage arrives. Then we'd best have a wee talk."

"Are you the law here, Mister MacAlpin?"

"No, but I'm the bullfrog of the town. Slade, ye and Jimbo get the litches oot of sight while the Yank and me decide how we're to deal with what happened. Come, Yank. We have to prepare our ainsels for a grim meeting with a bonny lass."

Flora MacTavish was twice as pretty as her stolen tintype, even crying like her heart would break.

MacAlpin had taken her and Longarm to his living quarters behind the trading post when the stage arrived, and at the moment, the girl, though full-grown and rather tall for a woman, was being held like a child by MacAlpin's wife, a motherly, moon-faced Blackfoot woman who answered to the improbable name of Bonnie.

69

The surviving daughter of the murdered family had hair the color of fresh-cut peaches and skin the color of clover-meadow cream. It was sort of hard to make out the color of her tear-filled eyes, but as far as Longarm could tell, they were that shade of amber a man has to think twice about.

Longarm told her his tale as gently as he could, and left a lot out. He saw no need to trouble her with grisly details he'd buried decent, and nobody in the room needed to know Claudette had been there. One of the townies had mentioned, while they were still waiting for the stage, that he'd seen a Red River cart leaving town like its pony had turpentine under its tail. The townie had had no idea where it was headed, and Longarm still felt sort of funny about it, like a man going through his pockets after a night on the town and wondering what was missing.

For some reason, Flora started bawling harder when he finished by mentioning that he'd marked the mass grave near the spread with a cedar shingle and a mason jar of buttercups. Bonnie MacAlpin took the girl over to a bed in the corner and made her lie down with a cold compress across her eyes. Every time Flora tried to sit up, the older Indian woman shoved her back down and crooned a soft, funny song he'd heard before. He didn't know what good a Blackfoot death song would do a white orphan, but it did seem to quiet her.

MacAlpin said something and Longarm switched his attention to the older man sitting with him near the fireplace. MacAlpin repeated, "We have no telegraph here, ye ken, but yon stage is headed for Fort MacLeod to the west. It will stop, this nicht, a wee ways up the river, so the Mounties won't hear of ye're informal justice too soon. But hear of it they will, and I'm a mon who canna lie."

"I understand, sir. If I knew for certain where the rest of the gang was, I could probably beat the Mounties to them. It's going to be a bitch following their trail and trying to leave none of my own."

"Aye, Slade and the boys found nothing in their pockets to tell us of their destination. You were right about me being hasty with my shotgun. MacTavish was my friend and I never thought of keeping the wee outlaw alive to answer questions."

Longarm shrugged and said, "I was too pissed off to be wearing a badge without a leash myself. The notion that grown men would be lurking to trifle with a gal for no reason but pure crazy lust threw my head off the track and I only studied killing."

"Ye say the one who left the Webley brass on MacTavish's floor is still running free like a mad dog?"

"Yep. I told you about their leader, John Chumley. The ones we got this evening were bad enough, but Canada Jack's the devil of them all."

"Aye, and ye told me how his family protects their wee black lamb. I can see how it will go in any Canadian court. The first thing they'll ask for is a change in venue. They'll hold the trial back east, where the judge will be some lickspittle who sits doon to piss and wags his tail at the London gentry."

"Well, if Canada Jack is packing that Webley when he's caught—"

MacAlpin waggled a hand disgustedly.

"Och, that's no evidence they'd hang an earl's brother on, lad. Aye, I can see him standing there in his Eton jacket and old school tie, wi' a brace o' expensive solicitors telling the judge how the poor lad fell in wi' wicked companions in the Wild West. The only eyewitnesses to his mad-dog killings are the mad dogs he rides with! They'll lie to save their ainsels. One or more will go to prison for a time, for being a wee bit naughty. Chumley's solicitors will se that nobody hangs, if they learn their parts well enough."

Longarm nodded and said, "That's why I've been sort of bending the rules up here, sir. Your own Mounties are good enough to round the gang up in no time. I'm sure they'd want to see them hang, too.

But the Mounties have some pesky rules about taking owlhoots alive."

"Och, fair is fair, lad. Those two out in the street resisted ye and were gunned fair. A Mountie would ha' done the same."

Longarm shook his head and said, "Had I been standing there in a fancy red jacket with gold stripes, they'd have given up without a fight. Your Canadian lawmen are sort of fancy-looking, but they have a rep for being tough, professional, and correct. It puts them at a disadvantage against a mad dog with a streak of sly."

MacAlpin nodded and said, "Aye, an outlaw cornered by the Mounties just gives up, if he has any sense at all. The Mounties never even pistolwhip a skunk, no matter what he's done. If he resists, they kill him. If he comes polite, they call him 'sir.' We know the gang ye're after has a canny leader. Ye've put me in a box, Marshal. We both know Chumley should be tried before a Yankee judge if he's no shot doon like a dog. I'd say the odds are even if you catch up with him first."

Longarm nodded and said, "I'd be pleased as punch to gutshoot the son of a bitch. But if I'm able, I mean to take him back to the States alive. In the long run, a killer suffers more if a lawman can control his feelings. No matter where you shoot a man, he dies in a day or so, if he don't get better. The long hours before a trial and after must hurt worse. I've been to a few hangings, and I've seen how the waiting wipes the smirk from a killer's face."

MacAlpin said, "Aye, Yank. We both agree it's best if you get to them first. Let's see what I'm to tell yon Mounties when they ride in to question everybody."

Longarm grinned and said, "I thought you couldn't lie?"

"I canna. I'm a loyal subject of the Crown. On the other hand, I'm getting a wee bit *old*, ye ken, and sometimes I forget things. I'm going to tell them the two litches were waiting for the stage with rape and worse in their minds. It seems to me I remember them saying as much when, for some strange reason, they drew on a buffalo hunter passing through."

"Some of the others must have seen my badge when I flashed it at you."

"Aye, but if yon Mounties don't ask if we saw a badge, I see no reason to bring it up. We'll have to tell them what ye looked like, to the best of our recall. Ye might have been a Yank, who's to say? I forget what ye're horsie looked like. It was ainly a horsie, ye ken. The bonny gray mare one of the outlaws rode drew all my attention in the half-licht. I'll recall ye did say something about hunting buff, and Slade told ye the herds were north of here, did he nicht?"

Longarm chuckled and said, "You're right. A man can sure bend things up without an outright lie. I thank you for everything, Mr. MacAlpin. You're a man I'd be proud to have for a friend."

"I told ye MacTavish was my friend, so there's noo need for sentiment. Do ye have enough money to see you haim to yon States?"

Longarm nodded and answered, "I cashed an expense voucher for silver and gold before I left Montana. But I thank you for the thought."

"Ye'd better take some shillings and pence along anyway. Ye drew a bit of attention wi' ye're Yankee money. Canada's starting to issue its ain coinage, but there's still a lot of English money in circulation up here, and nobody thinks twice about it."

"All right. You can change a few U.S. gold pieces for me before I ride out."

"Foosh! Ye've been listening to English lies about Scots, I can see! I told ye, damn it, MacTavish was my friend! Sit ye here and I'll fetch ye some coin of the Crown and we'll no discuss it further!"

The old Scot got to his feet and grumped out as Longarm lit a smoke, pondering his next move. So far, the gang had followed the old Hudson Bay network, and he remembered that one of the men he'd shot it out with had mentioned something about the others headed east. They'd follow the Oldman to the Saskatchewan, but there was more than one cutoff as the river trended north away from civilization. With luck, he'd cut their trail before they killed anyone else. The charade his friends in Petit Arc planned for the proper authorities might throw the Mounties off, but it might not. He remembered Crown Sergeant Foster as a stubborn cuss and a damned good tracker. It was a shame they couldn't work together, but every time they'd met, he seemed to rub Foster the wrong way.

The crooning in the corner had faded, and he assumed the Indian woman had rocked the heartbroken MacTavish girl to sleep. But she suddenly spoke, and when he glanced up, she was standing over him, red-eyed but determined-looking.

She said, "I've been listening, Mr. Long."

"You can call me Custis, ma'am."

"In that case, I am Flora MacTavish and I'm going with you."

Longarm shook his head and said, "Not hardly. How old are you, Flora? Sixteen?"

"I'm almost nineteen, and that's neither here nor there. I ride and shoot better than most men in these parts. I've bagged moose and I know the country. The Mounties will be looking for a lone rider."

He said, "I follow your drift and I understand your feelings, Flora. But you can't go with me. I don't mean to put you down as a girl-child. The best cowhand I ever met was a gal called Roping Sally. But I don't work with women. Sally was killed just being *near* me while I was on another case, and I've never forgiven myself."

Flora said, "We'll ride out to my spread together while I change my duds. You said our stock had been run off, but our ponies won't have gone far. Our water tank will have them grazing near. After I'm armed and dressed sensible, we'll put your saddle and possibles on a white Indian pony I broke, and you won't be riding a horse anybody's seen you on before. How do you like it, so far?"

Longarm grinned up at her and replied, "I'll take you up on the white horse. I aimed to escort you home in any case. Your spread was sort of wolverined by the gang, but I put things back in order a mite, and I'll show you where I stored your belongings. I'll give you a hand with your stock and I'll make sure you're safe there before I leave you. But leave you I must, Flora. I can't ride after killers with a gal tagging along."

Flora MacTavish said, "We'll talk on it on the way home." He saw that those amber eyes were dry now. Amber was a spooky color. It could look warm and loving, or it could look cold and hard. Flora's eyes were glittering like the sharp edges of a busted beer bottle she was fixing to twist in someone's face.

Chapter 5

The sun was rising as they rode into the dooryard of the MacTavish spread. They'd ridden most of the night under a hunter's moon, and it would have taken longer if the girl hadn't pushed her borrowed mount hard. Even in her visiting duds, she rode like a man, astride with the skirt pulled up, and the hell with whether Longarm liked her socks or not.

He tethered the lathered mounts and watered them cautiously while the girl explored her ruined home alone. Longarm was content to stay outside. He'd gotten rid of the blood-soaked mattress and other grim relics like the dead dog, when he buried the bodies.

By the time he'd rubbed the horses down with a fistful of straw, Flora had rustled up some clothes and reappeared wearing tight jeans and a man's hickory shirt. Her hair was piled up under a black Stetson, and he saw that she'd strapped on a sixgun. He remembered the holster and gunbelt as having been in one corner, empty. As if she'd read his mind, Flora said, "I had this Remington .32 with me on the coach. I noticed the buttercups you left on the grave. It was sweet of you, Custis."

He shrugged and said, "Roses would have been better, but I couldn't find anything but wildflowers."

She said, "I know. My father was a stern man and this was a working spread. Did you know my mother was only forty-eight?"

He looked uncomfortable and she said, "She was

76

always pretty, but I'll bet when you found her you thought she was an old lady."

He answered, "Well, I noticed she had gray hair, but I didn't study on it."

Flora sighed and said, "I loved them both, but life is hard on a woman out here. It's funny. Sometimes, when the light caught her right, you could see the young girl she must have been once."

"I saw she was a handsome woman," Longarm lied.

"I've noticed you keep ducking it, Custis. But tell me, was it . . . really bad?"

He'd been asked the same question before, so he knew she really didn't want the answer. He said, "There's no getting around the fact that they were murdered, Flora. But it must have happened sudden. I remember thinking, when I found your mother, that she looked sort of restful, like she was asleep."

"Where did they shoot her?"

"It's hard to say, Flora. I didn't examine any of them careful. It looked like none of them ever knew what hit them. The gang just jumped them, and it must have been over in a few seconds."

"Then why was the house torn up so bad?"

"They must have been looking for cash, ammo and such."

She shuddered and said, "Two of them were waiting to rape me. The tintype you got back for me used to sit on my mother's dresser."

"I know. They must have been drunk as well as crazy. Forget it. It's over."

She hesitated, set her jaw, and said, "I want to know. I want to know if they treated my mother as they meant to treat me."

Longarm looked away and said, "Hell, I told you I found the lady dead and looking like she was asleep, Flora. She never told me one way or the other."

"What about her clothes? Were they torn or anything?"

He answered quite truthfully, "I buried your mother

in a blue print gingham dress, Flora. It was buttoned up and it wasn't torn."

Flora murmured, "Thank God. She was sort of pretty and I thought—"

And then she was in Longarm's arms, with her head against his vest and crying fit to bust as he held her soothingly. They stood that way for a time, until she'd cried it out again, for now. Then she flinched, as if suddenly aware of where she was, and drew back, running her sleeve across her face as she sniffed, "I'm sorry. I don't know what came over me just now."

Longarm said, "What came over you was natural. I'd be more worried about you if it didn't show. You've been hurt and hurt bad, Flora. I wouldn't hold it against a *man* who cried at a time like this."

She shrugged and said, "I put some kindling in the range. It should be warmed up enough to cook on by now. I see you've chored the horses, so why don't we eat before we look for the rest of the stock?"

Longarm said, "I'll poke about while you rustle up some grub. There's a draw filled with crack willow over to the southeast. That's where I'd be if I was a stray pony."

"I'll go with you after we eat. I know the spread better than you, and the stock won't be as spooked by me." She looked away and added, "I don't want to go back in there alone, Custis."

He nodded and they went inside the soddy together. He saw that she'd fired the range and laid out some staples on the table he'd placed back on its legs before leaving the previous day. She motioned him to a seat and stood over the table, staring down like she was having trouble seeing things. She poured some flour in a mixing bowl and said, "I thought they'd taken more food than they had, but I see they mostly just messed things."

Longarm didn't answer. Before he'd straightened up the place, he'd found disemboweled bean bags and a gutshot sack of sugar. It had been Claudette's idea to put salvaged staples in empty cannisters and jars she'd found in the barn, and Longarm felt guilty about taking all the credit for a tolerable clean-up. Had Claudette not been a wanted rebel, he'd have given credit where credit was due.

He saw that Flora's hands were trembling, so he stood up and said, "Sit down, honey. I'll whip us up some flapjacks. You look like you've been dragged through the keyhole backwards. When's the last time you had some sleep?"

She sank wearily into his vacated chair and answered, "It seems like a hundred years. I was already tired from the stage, and the ride out here didn't help, but I'm not sleepy."

"Sure you are. You just don't know it. You've been handed an awful shock and you're running on pure nerves."

"What about you? You didn't get any sleep last night as we rode."

"Hell, I had a comfortable trip north and I'm a mite keyed up, too. Professor Edison says a man can get by on four hours' sleep out of twenty-four. He must be tougher than me, since I need about six when I ain't excited about anything. On a case, I can skip a night or two before I start snapping at folks and kicking little children."

She smiled wanly, and he started beating up a batter in the bowl as he continued, "Once I poison you with my Chisholm Trail flapjacks, I want you to stretch out for forty winks. I can see you're a cowboy, but I'll round up your stock while you nap. I'll use your roping saddle instead of my McClellan, and—"

"Custis, I don't ever want to sleep in this house again. It's haunted."

He went on stirring with a frown as he murmured, "I don't hold with spooks, but even if there are such things, the folks who used to live here were your kin. I'd be sort of pleased if my old mother and dad came to visit with me some night. They never have, but it would be a comfort to know folks *could*. I mean, we're all going there, some day. It'd be sort of nice to know in advance that we could come back if we wanted to. That's why I've never savvied why folks were afraid of ghosts. The idea that the dead stay put is a lot scarier, when you study on it."

She suppressed a shudder as she explained, "I don't mean the house is haunted by my father, mother, and Buddy. It's those others, the mad wolverines who tainted our home with their evil."

Longarm stepped over to the kitchen range and put a skillet on to warm as he said, "The gang is still alive. Most of them, anyways. The way I hear tell, folks can't haunt a place unless they died reasonably close. We're a good ride from Petit Arc and their unhallowed resting place."

She grimaced and insisted, "I'd like to burn this place and never see it again. I know you've been avoiding what you found here yesterday, but I can see it in my mind's eye. I probably see things worse than they were."

Longarm doubted that, but he didn't say anything as he greased the skillet and poured some batter in. Flora said, "My father had money in the bank. After we deal with the killers, I'm going to put the place up for sale. I'll never want to live here now."

He shrugged and said, "Yesterday was yesterday. After the hurt wears off, you'll have other memories. I saw the old swing your dad fixed for you out back. There was a homemade dollhouse and some other toys in the lean-to out back. Who made that wooden gun, your dad?"

"That was Buddy's. An Indian made it for him when he was little. Mom used to feed some Cree down the road from time to time. The times are out of joint for Indians, but they're proud about taking hand-outs. They used to split some cordwood or leave a basket or something. Buddy loved that old wooden gun."

80

Longarm didn't answer as he flipped the pan and turned the flapjacks over. If there were Cree nearby, they might know where Claudette had gone. He had to get this white gal settled down and move out before the Mounties came snooping about. MacAlpin would tell them about what had happened here, sooner or later, and any lawman would start his search from the scene of the crime.

He put the flapjacks on a plate and placed it on the table in front of Flora before starting two more for himself. She poured maple syrup over them, but toyed with the food more than she ate it. She said, "I don't feel hungry and I don't feel sleepy. I just want to get started. Where do you think we'll cut their trail, Custis?"

He frowned and said, "*I* might. *We* won't. I told you I'm riding on alone. It's broad daylight now, and if you don't want to stay here, I can't stop you from riding to some neighbor or back to town. But, while I mean to take you up on your offer of a fresh horse, I aim to leave here lonesome."

As he put his own breakfast on the table, he took out his Ingersoll watch, glanced at it, and added, "I can give you a couple more hours if you have any chores that only call for a strong back and a weak mind."

She smiled and said, "You already put in enough work here for two people. Mom didn't have her pots and pans over the stove that way, but you arranged them as neatly as any woman might have. You must have a wife and kids somewhere. You know how to keep house too well for a single hand."

He said, "I'm not married. I've studied on it more than once, but soldiers, sailors, and lawmen make terrible husbands."

Then he decided to shut up and eat. Women never asked questions like that unless they were interested in a man, and if they were, it was the first thing they wanted to know. Maybe he should have told her he had a wife and six kids. Both their lives were complicated enough already.

He ate his light repast and saw that she'd swallowed half of hers. When she refused his offer to wash the dishes, he got up and said, "I'll see where your stock ran off to. What am I looking for?"

She said, "We had a remuda of eight ponies in the corral and pasture out back. Our cattle are out ranging, of course. They'll drift in once the waters of that last rain dry out. We had some yard hens and a yellow dog, too. I wonder what's become of them."

He didn't answer. He knew they'd shot the dog and must have eaten the chickens. Twelve men living off the country tend to have big appetites. That could be the answer to the two in town having hived off from the others. Aside from wanting a crack at a helpless, pretty gal, they might have been getting tired of sharing with ten others. Things were even more spread out up here than in Montana. They had to be more careful too. He'd seen that Canada Jack hadn't mended his ways, but there might have been some worried discussion before and after. Canada Jack might think he had the law in his hip pocket, but some of the others would be wondering by now. The smartest lawyers on earth couldn't get you off if you just shot everybody. The Mounties were going to see at least one man hanged for the murders here. It wouldn't be anybody important, but some of the others in Jack's gang might not *feel* important.

He nodded and said, "I have to get cracking. If the gang splits up, I'm out of business."

He went out and over to the barn, where he took a double-rigged roping saddle from a saw horse and lugged it out to the tethered horses. He was resaddling his bay when Flora rejoined him, saying, "I'll show you where they like it in the willows. They might come quiet, once they see me."

He saw the logic in her offer, and waited while she got a throw-rope to use with her borrowed stock saddle. They mounted up, and Flora led off. It was a dumb time to notice, but Longarm had to admire the way those jeans fit her tomboy rump, and she sure sat a horse pretty.

It was only a short lope to the draw, and as they moved along one side, she pointed at a flash of white in the willows and said, "There they are."

She reined in and called, "Snowball, it's me! What are you up to, you naughty pony?"

The white horse nickered uncertainly and moved away through the brush. As they followed, Longarm's bay shied and he called out, "Hold up, Flora. There's dead horse in the air."

He rode up beside her and handed her his reins, saying, "Hold my mount steady. I'll have a look. We'll spook these horses too, if we ride any closer."

He dismounted and moved down into the brush-choked hollow. The bottom of the draw was sandy, and he followed his nose up it to where a dead roan lay bloated like a bagpipe, with two legs off the ground.

That answered a couple of questions. The owlhoots hadn't taken the MacTavish stock because the shooting had spooked them into busting loose. He couldn't tell if the dead horse had been hit by a stray round or if a frustrated owlhoot had fired at it as it ran off. From the condition of the bloated horse, it had lived a day or more longer than its owners. That's why he and Claudette hadn't seen any stock the day before. After keeping company with a dying stablemate, the remuda didn't have much use for strangers.

He called up to the girl, "One of your critters is dead and the others are spooked. Maybe I can drive them out of this brush on foot. We'll never get near them mounted, down in these willows."

She yelled back something that sounded like an agreement, and Longarm moved toward the nervous ponies up the draw. They moved too, dancing just ahead of him and cussing him with unhappy whinnying.

He saw that the brush opened up some, ahead, and the six or eight horses didn't like that much. A big white gelding got between him and the others, as if he meant to protect them. Longarm said, "Easy, Snowball, I'm on your side."

Snowball pawed at the sand with his forehooves and said something terrible about him in Horse. Longarm took off his hat and charged, yelling, "All right, let's wrestle! Powder River and let her buck, you mule-headed son of a bitch!"

As he'd expected, the startled remuda exploded in every direction. He chased Snowball up the bank, yelling like a Comanche, and as the white gelding broke cover, he was running in the general direction of Flora. Longarm saw that Flora was moving to cut Snowball off as he aimed between her and a corner of the corral. The girl had shaken out a loop, but the gelding was big and running flat out. Longarm called, "Don't try it! He'll pull you down!"

But Flora had her loop swinging, and he swore softly as she threw. The borrowed mount she rode was way too light for a tie-down catch, and he knew he'd have to pick them both up when that big white brute hit the end of the rope with all that weight and speed.

But Flora knew what she was doing. Before the spooked gelding took up the slack of her throw, the lean and graceful girl had leaped off with the coil in her hands. She landed like a cat and dug in her heels as Snowball hit the end of the line. She couldn't stop him with her hundred-and-twenty-odd pounds, of course, but she stayed on her heels as he dragged her. Longarm ran forward to help, but saw she didn't need it, and walked to collect their grounded reins before the mounts they'd started out with joined in the general confusion.

Flora rode her heels like she was on ice skates as she walked up the rope hand over hand, talking to the frightened gelding. He finally started dancing sideways, looking her over as he slowed to a stationary tap dance. She walked the rope up to him and patted his neck, saying, "You naughty boy, I've a good mind to send you to bed with no supper!"

Snowball suddenly came to his senses and nuzzled her free hand as she let him smell she was someone he knew. As Longarm led the other mounts over, Flora said, "The others will come in now. Snowball's the one who always starts the mischief. We'd better let him simmer down before you saddle him, but you can see how he can throw anyone looking for you off."

Longarm patted the nervous gelding and said, "Yep, he's a handsome big brute. The Mounties will be expecting an ordinary bay or chestnut. Won't you sort of miss him, though? I'll leave the army bay here, but it won't be a fair exchange."

"I'll ride the bay. That way, I'll wind up in the end with Snowball, and you'll be able to return the bay to your army."

"Flora, I keep telling you, I mean to ride alone. What's the matter with your ears, girl?"

"Pooh, I can ride as good as you. Do you want me to show you how I shoot? Let's put some cans and bottles on the fence and—"

"Honey, I ain't after cans and bottles. Aside from ten guns ahead, I'll have the Mounties behind. You're a Canadian. They'll be sore as hell if you aid and abet me any more than you have."

"To hell with the law. Those sons of bitches killed my family!"

"I know. You still can't tag along. I ain't asking you. I'm telling you."

"How are you going to stop me?"

He'd been afraid she'd think of that. He smiled and said, "You're too pretty to shoot. Maybe I'll just spank you."

She said, "I dare you to try!" and there was something in her eyes that made Longarm's heart skip a beat and told him he was on the wrong tack. The girl was exhausted and mixed up, and couldn't know the kind of smoke signals she was sending with her wide amber eyes. She looked like she wanted him to kiss her, for God's sake. She needed a night's sleep to clear her head.

They put the horses in the corral, and he led her back inside. She hadn't eaten much, but such food as she'd put in her tired body might help. He got them both to a settee in the main room and lit a cheroot as he tried to make small talk. He agreed they'd talk about who might be riding with whom later, and switched the subject to cows. He could see she was wondering why he wanted to discuss her cows and other cows he'd known, but her eyes were a mite glazed, after all that exercise on top of a rough night. He'd never told anybody much about coming West after the War and starting out as a green cowhand. He'd never told it because it was tedious as hell. He could see she was trying to be polite as he droned on about rogue steers, dogies eating larkspur, or what a hand did about a cow bloated on clover. He knew she knew all about cows, and that he was boring her. That was his intention. The rules of polite society said women were supposed to act interested when men talked about themselves, but he'd often suspected they found it a chore. Flora's eyes were getting sort of glazed by the time he got to punching cows up the chutes at the railhead, leaving out the parts about the saloons and card houses at the end of a drive. She brushed a hair out of her face and suddenly leaned into him. Then, as she found her head on his shoulder, she woke with a start and said, "Oh, I'm sorry. What happened?"

He put an arm around her and snuggled her back with her head resting comfortably against his tobacco-brown tweed. He moved the hat off her curls and let it fall to the cushions beyond as her breathing steadied.

She sure felt nice, sleeping against him like that. He felt a tingle and moved his legs slightly to get some air to his confounded crotch. He glanced down at her denim-clad legs snuggled next to his, observing that she sure fit against a man nice. The top button of her loose shirt was open, and if he moved his head a mite, he'd have been able to get a better view down inside. But he didn't move his head. He stayed put, smoking with his free hand as he let her settle into an exhausted sleep.

He could have used some sleep himself, but he'd worry about that later. He willed himself to finish his smoke and snuff it out before he moved a muscle. Then, slowly and gently, he slid out from under her and lowered her to the cushions without waking her. Her hips were at an awkward angle, so he gently took her booted feet and moved them up to leave her reclining comfortably. He didn't think he could remove her gunbelt without waking her, but it was dangerous to toss and turn with a .32 against your hip, so he picked up her hat and carefully disarmed her. He put the hat and gun on the nearby table and turned back to see if there was anything else he could do to make her comfortable before he tiptoed out. Flora's face looked tired but still troubled, and as he watched, she put her hand against the fly of her jeans and started slowly rubbing herself.

He felt like he'd been caught peeping in a lady's window. That was the trouble with having a nosy job. A lawman saw people when they weren't on their best behavior, and it sometimes gave him insights into just how proper his fellow Victorians were. He'd found pornographic pictures in the home of a murdered preacher, and one time he'd found a shocking gadget in the carpetbag of a nice old lady murdered in a stage holdup. He'd thrown the realistic dildo away as evidence hardly related to the case, but he'd sure wondered some about that little, dried-up-looking spinster's private life before they killed her.

The sleeping girl was still playing with herself in her sleep when he left her. It gave him a whole new insight into what he'd assumed was a virgin tomboy.

But what the hell, maybe she *was* a virgin. What she did to her own body was her own business, and he supposed even spinsters had feelings. At least her dream wasn't a nightmare about her dead folks. She'd have them too, he knew. But there was nothing he could do about it, except to pay the killers back for what they'd done to a nice kid and her kin.

He went out and saddled Snowball with his army rig and possibles. The big white gelding didn't like it much. Longarm figured they might have a noisy party as they got to know each other, so he led Snowball out across the prairie for a quarter-mile before he tried to mount.

Snowball didn't like that notion, either. So Longarm braced a boot and hip firmly, twisted the bridle, and spilled the gelding in the grass. He leaped aboard as Snowball struggled to his hooves and tried to get the bit in his teeth. Longarm hauled his muzzle down against his own off-shoulder and sighed, "Sorry, I ain't got time to play fair. You notice I'm seated good and have a heel dug in for keeps on either side. I don't mean to fan you, and since nobody's watching, I'll be hanging on to the swells with my free hand. You just do what you have a mind to, you son of a bitch."

Snowball's answer was to start bucking. Few fancy bronc-busters could have stayed aboard, but Longarm rode him dirty. There was nobody there to cheer, and the only prize would be staying aboard. It took a while for the gelding to understand this. Snowball crow-hopped and Snowball sunfished. He tried turning end-for-end in midair, and he tried pretending he was going to come down upside-down.

But Longarm was a big man and had a strong hand on the reins, so, despite his threat, he didn't even have to grab leather. His improper grip with his heels was advantage enough, and Snowball found that it hurt to keep trying for the bit with his head pinned so awkwardly. Being a sensible horse despite his frisky streak, Snowball just suddenly stopped fighting.

Longarm heeled him into a lope, saying, "Let's get it all out while you get used to my balance, Snowball. The day is young and I've time for just a mite more foolish exercise. After you settle down to acting sensible, we've got some work to do."

He rode at random, out of sight of Flora's spread. When he felt that the horse was tired enough to behave, he reined him to a walk while they got their bearings.

He knew where the town was, but that was not where he intended to be when the Mounties rode in. He was southeast of Petit Arc, and MacAlpin would tell the Mounties he'd last been seen headed north. The Canadian lawmen would know he hadn't gunned the MacTavish family, so, while they'd want to question him, they'd save serious tracking for the gang of killers.

Longarm doubted that the gang had left any notes pinned to trees, but he knew they were trending east with the grain of the land. It was hard to read sign on the thick sod of open range. A pony turd was only a pony turd, with nothing to say whose pony dropped it.

There'd be hoofprints along the trails or near the river, but there'd be too many of them. He'd just have to head the same way and ask folks he met if they'd noticed ten men in a bunch. That was the thing to worry about. Folks noticed large parties. If the gang had split up, who was going to be able to tell him some hunter or cowhand drifting by was a wanted killer?

The Webley might help. Most folks just thought a sixgun was a sixgun, but some might notice an unusual sidearm. The thought cheered him and he said aloud, "Overconfidence is going to do you, Canada Jack. Anybody with a lick of common sense would have shucked that gun and started riding alone, behaving himself, by now. You just keep thinking you're the bee's knees and I'll get you, you son of a bitch."

Longarm had never figured out why so few owlhoots seemed to have common sense. Time after time, he'd found a wanted man wearing the same duds and riding the same mount everyone had said he'd last been seen with. That damned fool, Jack McCall, had made it clear to Colorado when he started buying drinks all around and bragging openly about gunning Hickock in the back. They'd lynched McCall, of course, but the others never learned. Sometimes he thought they read too many of those Ned Buntline magazines.

Longarm headed northeast to cut the riverside trail as he played the game with himself that had cost so many owlhoots their lives or freedom. Longarm was better than most lawmen at putting himself in his prey's boots. He hunted men the way the Indians hunted game, not by sniffing at a cold trail, but by considering where the critter he was hunting might be aiming to get to, then heading him off. He was pretty sure Canada Jack would be making for the action farther east. The advantage the bastard had was that Longarm didn't know the country. He was sort of riled about Claudette and her Red River cart taking off like a bird to Lord-knows-where, but he'd make better time on this gelding, once he figured out where he was. The trouble with open prairie was that it all looked the same. He wasn't lost—not yet—but he was starting to see why folks followed rivers and trails up here.

He topped a rise, reined in, and muttered, "Shit," as he sat his mount, morosely surveying the next draw.

It was full of trees—skeletal tamaracks that looked like half-starved Christmas trees. They were only good for telegraph poles, and grew in liquid mud. He could see how it had happened. The glacier ice they said had been here, once, had scooped out a hollow without bothering to arrange any drainage. The draw had once been a prairie lake, but now it didn't know what the hell it was. You couldn't paddle across, and you

90

couldn't ride to the other side. The long, skinny swamp stretched out of sight around bends, both ways.

He looked up at the sun to get his bearings, and decided northwest was his best bet. It would take him out of his way and edge him back at Petit Arc, but at least the river was up there. There was no telling where he'd wind up, riding southwest and likely into more of the same.

As he turned Snowball and clucked him into a walk, Longarm spied another rider heading his way from the west. He kept on as if he hadn't noticed. The approaching rider was mounted on a bay, and wore jeans and a hickory shirt. Longarm glanced the other way at the tamarack swamp to his left and said, "You sure picked a mean place to be, God damn you."

He considered making a run for it, but that was silly, on open prairie. She knew he wasn't going to shoot her, so what the hell.

Flora MacTavish loped up and reined in beside him, saying, "That wasn't very nice of you, Custis."

He said, "I wasn't trying to be nice; I was trying to be alone."

"That's what I figured when I woke to find you and Snowball gone. I knew this swamp would hold you till I caught up. Where are you headed?"

"Around this fool swamp, of course."

"You're riding the wrong way. It stretches almost to the stage road near Petit Arc. The Mounties and you should arrive about the same time."

He reined in and asked, "How would you get across, then?"

She said, "You can't, on a horse. It peters out five miles to the southeast, and we can ride around."

"I'm trying to meet up with the river trail, not too close to the town."

"I know the way. The Mounties will ride out to our spread, first. I left them a note saying I'm going back to my cousins in Medicine Hat with some friendly Cree. That's two days down the valley, and they won't

91

be anxious about me. They'll poke about the neighborhood all day, and probably start down along the river about sunrise tomorrow."

Longarm turned his mount to let her lead him, but he said, "Look, you have kin two days off the way everybody's headed. If I let you tag along, will you promise to stay in Medicine Hat when we get there?"

"Well, we've a long ride ahead to talk on it, Custis."

"No, we don't. We have to settle it right here and now. I'm pretty sure the gang has ridden on past Medicine Hat by now, so I'm willing to risk your guiding me that far. Lord knows, I need a guide. But you have to promise me Medicine Hat is the end of the line for you."

She asked, "What if you change your mind?"

He said, "I won't. I'll see you to the safety of your kin and we'll part there sensible. Otherwise, I mean to take you in to Petit Arc and let the MacAlpins spank you."

"You'll get caught by the Mounties if you go there."

"Maybe I will and maybe I won't. Do we have us a deal?"

"Oh, all right. But I hate Medicine Hat. It's such a dinky little town, and my cousins are so stuffy."

"Maybe when you grow some, you can run off to join the circus."

"I'll have you know I'm almost nineteen, sir."

"I stand corrected, and you are of legal age to make a fool of yourself. But it won't be around *me*. If it's a small town, there may be something you can do to help in Medicine Hat. Before we split up, we can ask around. Folks in small towns remember strangers, but they don't answer questions strangers ask."

"My cousins can tell you if the gang rode through. But, damn it, I sure wish I'd been born a man."

"I noticed. But we have to make do with the cards the good Lord dealt us. So behave yourself."

They rode on for a time, following the lay of the

land. Flora seemed to be hesitating about something on her mind, and after a while she said, "Custis?"

"Yep?"

"When I woke up, I saw you'd sort of put me on the settee and, well, I was sort of unbuttoned."

He said, "I took your gun away. I never messed with your duds. You must have done it in your sleep."

She looked away and murmured, "Oh. I had the funniest dream . . ."

He didn't ask her what it was, but she told him. She said, "I thought you were . . . being fresh."

He said, "I wasn't. I don't roll drunks, either."

"Have you ever, well, done anything to a girl while she was asleep?"

He shrugged and said, "If you're asking if I've ever seduced a lady in her sleep, the answer is no."

"I'll bet you've been tempted. I know the way men are."

He shook his head and said, "You ain't talking about *men*. You're talking about boys, of any age. You mustn't judge the rest of us by the way those owlhoots acted in Petit Arc, honey. Most folks, men and women, are sensible."

She lowered her eyes and blushed and, like a damned fool, he asked her what she was so upset about.

She said, "I dreamed it if you say so, but it was so *real*."

"Everybody has those dreams, honey. They're nothing to be ashamed of."

She turned a deeper shade of rose as she answered, "I wasn't ashamed. When I suddenly woke up and found you weren't really doing it, I was mad as hell."

Chapter 6

They reached the Oldman late that afternoon, and Flora said they were near its junction with the Bow, where it turned into the Saskatchewan and started getting serious. He asked again about the town of Medicine Hat, and she said it was about fifty miles downstream. They cut the wagon trace and headed along it to the east. The river ran in oxbows, lined with alder, crack willow, and other brushy growth. So, since the trace ran straighter, they rode over dry and soggy stretches in turn. As they rode, Longarm kept his eyes on the rutted roadbed, but there'd been too many hooves, going too many ways, for him to pick out a sign.

The sun was low as they approached a brush-filled draw running into the river to their left. Longarm reined in and said, "Stay here. There's smoke above the treetops, yonder. Looks like a campsite."

"It could be Cree, or just some traveler."

"I know. Stay here anyway."

Longarm handed her his reins and dismounted with his Winchester. He walked up the trace a few yards as he eyed the treeline, then he moved left, toward the river. Any guards posted would be watching the road and high ground away from the river. The river ran white and treacherous along this stretch, so they might not be set for an amphibious attack.

He bore left into reeds and mushy footing as his boots started soaking through. The alders grew thick along the shoreline, and he had to step in running water more than once, but if he couldn't see *them*, they couldn't see *him*. He shifted his rifle to his left hand as he swung himself around a slippery trunk, and when he was back on solid ground, he saw he'd come to a sandy flat where the draw drained into the river.

A horse stood on three legs, tied to a sapling on the far side of a campfire. The man at the fire was dressed as a cowhand, and hunkered by the fire with his back to Longarm.

Longarm shifted his Winchester back to a more serious position and said, "Howdy. What happened to your pony?"

The man jumped up and spun around, his hand undecided near the holstered S&W on his hip. Longarm said, "Don't. You'd never make it."

The man relaxed and said, "You sort of spooked me, neighbor. Do you always walk on water?"

"Just when I'm calling on folks I don't know. My name is Long. I disremember who you said you were."

The man smiled boyishly, and Longarm saw that he was only about twenty, despite a week's growth of beard. He said, "I'm called Lucky. I ride for the MacLean spread, over near Petit Arc. As you see, my mare picked up a stone. I got it out, but her frog's cut all to hell. I figured to rest here for the night."

Longarm looked him over as he tried to think up something tricky to say. Then he decided they'd sparred around enough and said, "I want you to un-buckle that gun rig, let her drop, and step clear before we talk about your pals."

"Are you crazy, mister? I don't have enough on me to make it worth your while, if you're a road agent."

"You know who I am, you son of a bitch. Shuck that gun and do it sudden. I won't say it twice."

The stranger unbuckled his belt and let it fall, but he insisted, "You got no call to treat me like this, mister. When I tell the boss about this, he'll have the law on you."

"Aw, shit, kid. I've heard this same tale until I'm wore out hearing it. If it'll save some time, I'll spell it out for you. Your hat has a Texas crease in its crown, and your pony is packing a brand I know. The Running W spread is right outside Switchback, Montana. Your Canuck accent leaves a lot to be desired, too."

"Hell, I admit I'm a Yank, like you. That don't mean I can't ride for a Canadian outfit, does it?"

"Give the man a cigar for hitting one out of a half-dozen. What happened, Lucky? Did they ride on without you when your mare went lame?"

"I don't know who you're talking about."

"It won't wash. Stubs named you to the Mounties when they caught him last night in Petit Arc."

It didn't work. Lucky's eyes flinched, but his lying mouth kept grinning as he answered, "Stubs? I don't know anybody named Stubs."

"You're going to meet him in hell, directly, if you don't start telling me true. How much of a lead does Canada Jack have on me?"

Lucky shook his head and said, "You have the wrong man, pard."

Then a circle of rope settled down around the startled owlhoot, and as Longarm shouted, "No!" the loop snapped shut around his leg below the knees, and Lucky started moving in a hurry, on his face and screaming, as Flora dragged him at a dead run!

Longarm swore, "Son of a bitch!" and followed on foot as the man vanished through the trees in a cloud of dust. He didn't know where she'd left Snowball, so he just kept running until he cleared the trees. She'd dragged Lucky back the way they'd come, so he found the big white gelding tethered to a sapling as he followed the trail of dust in the evening light. He swung himself into the saddle and lit out after them, yelling at Flora to stop.

She didn't. She dragged the killer over a mile before her noose slipped off his ankles, and as Longarm reached the dragged owlhoot, Flora was over him with her gun. She fired and missed his head by a hair. Long-arm rode into her and slapped the gun from her hand, shouting, "I wanted to talk to him, damn it!"

Having disarmed her, Longarm dropped down to kneel beside the man she'd dragged. Lucky hadn't been lucky. It looked like he'd caught something that could tear off on every stone along the trail. Longarm rolled him over and slapped his torn-up face, saying, "Come on, where's Canada Jack, God damn it!"

Lucky whimpered, "I'm kilt! Keep that crazy woman off me!"

"You talk, or I'll let her drag you back to Texas. Where are the others headed, and what do they mean to do when they get there?"

Flora had climbed down and come over. She hissed, "I loved my mother, you son of a bitch!"

Then she kicked him in his bloody face.

Longarm said, "I wish you wouldn't do that, Flora."

Lucky sobbed, "Keep her off me! Chumley and the others said something about Moose Jaw and Jesse James. That's all I know!"

Longarm snorted, "Hell, the James boys never held up anything north of Minnesota, and they got shot up *that* time! Are you sure Canada Jack wasn't thinking along the same lines? He might have meant a railroad job."

"Mister, I can't tell you what Canada Jack might be thinking. He don't know, himself. I think he's crazy."

"I can see we're reaching common ground at last. You didn't just drop out because your pony went lame. That murder on this side of the line has made some of you thoughtful, right?"

"He's loco," Lucky mumbled, his swelling lips making it hard to follow his words as he complained, "He says the law can't touch him, but what about the rest of us?"

Flora stamped her foot and demanded, "Ask him which ones killed my family!"

Lucky muttered, "Honest, ma'am, it wasn't me. It was

97

Jack and Shamrock as done most of the shooting. The rest of us was just along for excitement."

Longarm knew Flora didn't know her mother had been gang-raped, so he withheld comment. He'd heard *this* tale before, generally just before a hanging.

He nudged the owlhoot and asked, "Who's Shamrock? Is that his last name, or just what he's called?"

Lucky didn't answer. He couldn't. Longarm glanced up at the girl and said, "I figured he was busted up on the inside pretty good. I know he had it coming, but killing him was a poor notion."

"Is he really dead? I'm glad! I wish I could have killed him twice."

"I know. It's sort of a let-down, ain't it? That's the trouble with revenge. They only let you kill an enemy once, and sometimes ten times won't do nothing for the pain."

He grabbed Lucky's ankles and started hauling him to the riverbank. Flora tagged along, asking why.

He said, "We don't have time to bury him, even if he deserved it. I aim to let the current have him so he won't be found near here."

He dragged until the ground felt mushy under his heels, then rolled Lucky into the river with his boot. As the bloody mess swept down the river through the white water, he said, "It's almost dark, and we have to study about holing up. I'll untie his pony and get rid of his gun and such. Then we'll move up the draw at least a couple of miles. I want a couple of rises between us and the wagon trace, in case anyone comes by."

She looked uncertain. Then she licked her lips and and said, "I've never spent the night alone with a man, Custis."

He said, "I figured as much. You could still head for home."

"I don't want to go home, but . . . can I trust you?"

He shrugged and said, "Most men are as much a gent as the lady they're with is a lady. I don't aim to leap at you, but I've never fought a good-looking gal off with a club, either."

She blushed and said, "I see. How you behave will be up to me."

He nodded and replied, "It always is, in polite society. Let's move out before we have unwanted company in red coats."

Crown Sergeant William DeVerrier Foster was a clean-cut man about Longarm's size and age. He never explained why he rode or walked with what seemed to be a ramrod up his rear, and there was something about the set of the Mountie's jaw that precluded asking.

He stood at sundown on the steps of MacAlpin's trading post in Petit Arc as his four-man patrol waited silently for him to make up his mind.

They'd been out to the MacTavish spread, and Foster had filled a jar with bits and pieces of what might have been clues or belly-button fluff. The others assumed they'd be riding back to Fort MacLeod. It seemed obvious that the killers had crossed the line into Saskatchewan Territory by now, and it was the business of the troop in Regina to set up a trap for the desperadoes. The formal pecking order of the spit-and-polish organization frowned on crossing jurisdictional lines unless absolutely necessary, and if there was one thing they all knew about Foster, it was that he was spit-and-polish.

As their patrol leader talked with MacAlpin, the bored and weary color rider allowed his guidon to droop a bit. Foster glanced at the Mountie pennant, and without turning his head, snapped, "As you were, Grogan!"

The abashed color rider snapped his staff straight, and a vagrant breeze rippled the little flag. Foster insisted that his colors be carried straight.

He was almost ready to call it quits, for the moment. He had no description, and hadn't wired for permission to ride farther east.

He'd taken statements from everyone, and was going over his notebook one more time because that was the way he was supposed to do it.

He noticed that a couple of curious townies had joined him and MacAlpin, but he ignored them as he pursed his lips and said, "I would have liked a word with that buffalo hunter who shot it out with two members of the gang, but I'll take your word that he was more or less drawn into the affair innocently. You say he was a tall man on a horse that might have been black or brown?"

MacAlpin said, "Aye. It was dark, ye ken. I'm sure he wasn't wi' them. For he'd been inside, buying supplies, when they rode in and just threw down on the mon."

"Hmm, he was either lucky or damned good. If he comes back this way, tell him we'd like a signed statement from him. Can't have chaps just riding off after a shooting, eh?"

One of the townies said, "He won't find no buff where he's heading. He was traveling light for a hunter, too."

MacAlpin shot the blabbermouth a withering look, but it was too late. Crown Sergeant Foster snapped, "Did you get a good look at him, sir?"

"Sure. He was a tall cuss on a bay gelding. He wore a flat hat and rode a McClellan saddle, like the Yank troopers ride."

Foster snapped his notebook shut and muttered, "*Longarm!* I might have known!"

MacAlpin said, "He didn't give that name, Sergeant." But the Mountie wasn't listening. He walked stiff-legged to his horse and swung up into the saddle. His horse was as stiff-necked as he was, and stood like it was expecting to be cast in bronze as Foster snapped, "Corporal Dobbs, take the point. We're riding east."

The corporal stammered, "East, Sergeant?"

"If I'd have meant west, I'd have said west, Corporal. We're riding until the moon sets. Then we'll bivouac until dawn and ride on. Are there any further questions?"

"Uh, one, Sergeant. You seem to be taking us into Saskatchewan Territory."

"I know. If need be, I'll lead you to the Atlantic and beyond."

"Well, I know that gang is pretty ugly, Sergeant, but—"

"Gang?" Crown Sergeant Foster said with a frown, as if he'd just heard of them. Then he said, "Oh, right. The gang of murderers. We'll take *them*, too, if we're able."

The other Mounties exchanged worried glances as Foster smiled wolfishly and added, "Murder is only murder, after all. This case has suddenly become *personal*. What are you waiting for, man? Take the point and move out at a regulation trot!"

The point man wheeled out on the wagon trace and headed east, with Foster and the colors abreast, and the other two bringing up the rear.

MacAlpin turned to the man who'd spoken out of turn and said, "I've been meaning to talk to ye about ye're overdue account, ye big-mouthed son of a bitch!"

Flora sat cross legged on the moonlight-silvered grass and asked, "Aren't you going to build a fire? It gets cold out here on the prairie at night."

Longarm finished wrapping a sliver of jerked beef in raw sourdough, and handed it to her along with his canteen. The fool girl had lit out after him without provisions, and he only kept a small emergency ration in his possibles. He said, "It ain't my falult it gets cold up here at night. I never asked you folks to build your country so far north."

She took his improvised sandwich, felt it experimentally in the semidarkness, and said, "Who ever heard of eating sourdough *raw*?"

He answered, "It won't kill you if you don't overdo it. A little goes a long way if you eat it before it's been

101

baked. The water will help it cook inside you. Couple of bites will hold you half a day, once it swells some."

"Oh, my God."

"Well, don't eat it, then."

"But I'm hungry, Custis."

"That's what I carry a sock of sourdough for. It ain't supposed to please your palate, it's supposed to fill your gut."

"Don't you ever bake it?"

He shrugged and answered, "Sometimes, when I've time and a fire. I don't build too many fires with owl-hoots out in front and Mounties behind."

The girl nibbled at it and said, "It's disgusting. The only thing I can think of that might be worse would be sucking a raw egg."

He chuckled and said, "I know. Some folks *like* to suck eggs, but it ain't my notion of dining at Delmonico's. One time the Mimbres had me cornered up a canyon for a couple of days, and all there was to eat was these eggs I found in a buzzard's nest. The buzzards had lit out and I couldn't tell how fresh their eggs were, but—"

"Custis, you're making me sick to my stomach. I'd rather hear about Delmonico's. Did you ever really eat there?"

"Nope. Never been to Paris, either, but I know it's there. I reckon the fanciest restaurant I've ever eaten in would be the Palmer House in Chicago. Boy, that sure was fancy. If you spilled gravy on your vest, you'd walk out with a dollar's worth of stain to brag about."

She took a gurgle from the canteen before she sighed wistfully and said, "I've never been to a big city. My cousins in Medicine Hat have been to Toronto, and they said the main streets were paved and all the houses were painted."

Longarm didn't really care, but he wanted to tire her with food and conversation before they got around to the delicate matter of turning in, so he said, "You keep talking about your cousins, but you never mention aunts, uncles, and such. What are your cousins, orphans or married up?"

She swallowed some raw sourdough with an effort, sipped more water, and explained, "They're really my mother's cousins. I suppose you'd call them old maids. They're twins, and sort of old. They must be over thirty."

"That's pretty old," he answered dryly.

Flora said, "They run a saddle shop my late uncle left them. I think they own some shares in a business in the old country. Anyway, they have money to gad about, and sometimes I think they're sort of odd for spinsters."

Flora handed back the canteen, saying, "There, it's all down and I'll probably swell up and burst. What are we to do about the bedrolls?"

He sighed and said, "You know we only have one, thanks to your sudden desire to light out after me without packing."

"I know, but I don't mind sharing. I used to sleep with Buddy when we were little. Mom said it looked funny for a girl to sleep with her brother, once they were half-grown."

Longarm said, "Your mother sounds like a reasonable woman."

"Oh, for God's sake, there's nothing wicked about sleeping with your own brother."

He didn't feel like arguing the point. He said, "I ain't your brother. I know I'm supposed to be gallant and let you have the roll alone, but I'm overdue for a good night's sleep, and you're right about how cold it will get between now and sunrise."

"Well, then, why don't we go to bed and snuggle up?"

He got up and walked over to where he'd piled the saddles of their hobbled mounts. He unlashed his roll, brought it back, and spread it across the grass, moving the slicker, clean socks, and other things rolled in with the blankets to one side. He sat down again and said, "You turn in if you've a mind to, Flora. I'll sit and smoke a while."

She crawled over to the bedroll on her hands and knees. Then she sat on the tarp and started hauling off her boots. She said, "Oh, dear, my feet are swollen. Could you give me a hand, Custis?"

He muttered under his breath and stood up again. He turned his back to her, reached down, and took one of her booted ankles to brace between his knees. He got a firm grip and said, "All right, shove."

She put her other boot against his butt, and between them, they popped the boot off. It felt better taking off the second, with her stocking foot against his buttocks.

He sat down again as she reclined on one elbow on the roll. Flora said, "I don't like to sleep in my jeans, but I'm not wearing underthings."

He said, "Leave your jeans on, damn it. I know you're just a kid, and I pride myself on self-control, but we're drifting from common courtesy into ridiculous. You're not wearing anything under that shirt, either, are you?"

"No, but how could you tell?"

"Never mind. You just turn in and try to go to sleep."

"What about you, Custis?"

"I told you I feel like smoking, damn it. I'll crawl in when I've a mind to."

Flora pulled the tarp and top blanket aside, and emptied her pockets to put their contents in her hat, by her coiled gunbelt nearby. She slid in and drew the covers up, saying, "Oh, it's sort of cozy. But we might not have much room between us."

He said, "I know. It's a one-man roll."

She giggled and said, "Maybe one of us should sleep on top."

Longarm closed his eyes and muttered, "Lord, give me strength." Then, in a louder tone, he said, "Go to sleep, girl. It's past your bedtime."

"Why are you treating me like a child?" she pouted, adding, "I'm a woman grown, and today I killed a man!"

He said, "I reckon that's *one* sort of virginity. I've got enough on my plate without further initiations. I'm trying to be a gent, Flora, but you've got a sassy way of talking, for a maiden. Someday, when you know more about the facts of life, you're going to remember this night and be amazed as hell."

She murmured, "Are you saying you . . . want me, Custis?"

He shrugged and looked away at a star on the horizon as he answered, "I wanted a silver-mounted saddle and a Parker shotgun once upon a time. It didn't kill me that I never got them. There's some things the Lord just don't plan for us to have, Flora. Go to sleep."

She said, "I can't. I feel wide awake, all of a sudden. I just don't understand you men at all. I thought men were just mad about virgins, and you're acting like I just broke out in spots."

He pounded his fist against the sod and snapped, "Now that's just about enough out of you, missy! You're getting past curiosity into teasing. You know you're pretty and you know I'm a man. You must know you're skating on thin ice, too."

"I wouldn't mind if you raped me, Custis."

"Oh, for God's sake, who said anything about rape?"

"Don't men rape girls when they fall in love with them?"

He laughed a bit wildly, "They don't even rape them if they just *like* them, savvy? The term is seduction."

"Then what's rape?"

"Seduction without salesmanship. Against a gal's will."

Flora's voice grew tiny as she said, "Oh, then I guess what I want is seduction."

"Honey, you don't know what you're saying," he said kindly.

"I don't know. I'm sort of scared and full of butterflies, but I think I'm willing, if you are. I've been thinking about it ever since we met, and I'm curious as hell."

"Curious? You mean you want to throw away your virginity because you're *curious*?"

She nodded and said, "That's another thing I'm curious about. How can a girl *lose* her virginity?"

"Oh, for Christ's sake, nobody can be *that* innocent!"

"That's what I mean. Innocent is not having any notion about something. You don't lose ignorance when you learn to read and write. You don't lose anything worth having when you learn a new song. What can you lose by knowing or feeling something you've never known or felt before?"

He chuckled and said, "You know, I tried that argument on a gal when we were both sixteen? It didn't work worth a damn."

Her voice grew older and wiser, with the timeless wisdom of womankind, as she suggested, "Try it on me, Custis. I don't think I'll put up much of a fight."

He muttered, "That does it. There's a limit to any man's common sense."

He stood up and shucked his outer garments before he slid into the bedroll with the girl. His heart was pounding and his mouth was dry.

As she snuggled close to him, the clothes between them seemed somehow obscene, and he started to unbutton her hickory shirt as they kissed for the first time. She wrapped her arms around him and responded warmly to his lips, but then, as his hand slid over her breast, she drew back and gasped, "I don't know! I'm scared!"

He stopped moving his hand, but held her breast cupped in his palm with the erect nipple between two fingers. He could feel her heart, and it was pounding like a trip-hammer.

"Easy does it," he said. "There's something you have to study on about me, Flora. I want you so bad I ought to be horsewhipped, but I'm not the marrying kind."

"I didn't ask you to marry me."

He grinned and put his lips to hers as he ran his hand down her torso to the waistband of her jeans. As he unbuttoned them, she started squirming and he thought she was going to ask him to stop, so he left his palm against her firm belly, the tips of his fingers touching the first pubic hairs below her navel. She crossed her legs but kept kissing, and then she suddenly took his hand in hers, opened her thighs, and moved his hand farther down. He kept kissing as he began to stroke her gently. He could tell she was hot, but he knew a clumsy move might freeze her, and it would be best to bring her around with his fingers once, before trying to get those damned jeans off. She moaned and started moving her hips to take his fingers deeper, and her free hand groped at his fly until she had his erection in her moist palm. She left her lips against his as she squeezed experimentally and murmured, "Oh, dear, I didn't think it would be so big. I don't think I could take anything that big inside me!"

He said, "Just keep playing with it. There's more than one way to skin the cat."

She giggled and began to stroke him as she relaxed and opened wider to his two exploring fingers. She murmured, "Deeper. I think I'm . . . oh, yes, I want the other in me now!"

He knew better. He'd never had a violin lesson, but he knew you could snap a string by changing the tuning too suddenly. He got his two fingers in as far as they'd go, and worked until he felt her contracting as she kissed him wildly. As she shuddered in the afterglow, she asked, "Could we do it some more, and maybe go a little further?"

He said, "These duds are sort of in the way. What do you say we get out of them?"

"Well, I'll take the jeans off, but I can't take off this shirt. I'd be naked."

He didn't argue. Some gals were like that. He'd met a lady once who wouldn't take off her socks for some reason. So, as Flora raised her hips, he peeled her jeans off, and somehow his own pants seemed to evaporate. He didn't remember shucking his boots, but he must have, for he was suddenly bare from his shirttails down.

He kissed her some more before he rolled atop her. Flora said, "No, wait . . ." as her thigh opened to welcome him. As she felt him entering her, she protested feebly, "I've changed my mind. I'm scared." But then she was arching her spine to take it all in, and the next time she came up for air she gasped, "Oh, God, that's ever so much nicer than Cousin June said it would be!"

He braced his weight on one elbow and unbuttoned his own shirt, and as her nipples rubbed against his bare chest, she sighed, "Oh, it does feel nicer naked! Take it off. Take everything off. I want to do it all. I want to do all the wicked things they told me about."

He was eager to oblige a lady, but he decided to try and keep it simple the first night.

The next day at noon, they stopped under a cottonwood by the trail to brew a quick pot of coffee. A Red River cart came along, heading west, and the Métis family in it stopped to ask if they could swap some tobacco for some coffee. Longarm figured they just wanted to jaw, but he accepted the swap anyway. The old Métis and his full-blood wife looked poor and proud. Their two kids looked hungry, so Longarm was pleased to see Flora putting extra sugar in the cups she filled for the kids without being told to.

After they finished discussing the weather, Longarm

asked the Métis if they'd met up with any large mounted parties on the trail. The man sipped at his tin cup as he thought. Then he said, "By Gar, *non*, and I will burn a candle for it, me. The Mounties told us to look out for a most bad gang. We did not think the two of you could be them."

Longarm tried to sound disinterested as he asked, "Mounties? I didn't know any were about."

The Métis nodded and said, "Most big patrol of five, them. Most times *les* Mounties ride alone. This gang, she is very big and *tres formidable, non*? The Mountie patrol passed us a few hours ago. They were riding for Medicine Hat and the telegraph."

Longarm turned to Flora, who was looking like butter wouldn't melt in her mouth. He said, "Medicine Hat is this side of the Saskatchewan line, ain't it?"

She nodded and said, "Less than a day's ride, as the crow flies. If they follow the river beyond the town, it'll be more like two days to the border."

She reached out to tickle one of the half-breed kids as she added, "We'll likely meet the nice Mounties coming back, unless they push on."

He nodded as if nothing could please him more as he observed, "Right. They're a few hours ahead of us. Say they spend them talking to folks in Medicine Hat . . . Yep, we'll get to see if they're Mounties we know, just this side of town."

She said, "We'll have to avoid a shortcut I know, if you don't want to miss your old friend, Sergeant Foster. He was the one you told me about, wasn't he?"

He grinned fondly at her and said, "Yeah, I'd hate like hell not to meet him if he's in the neighborhood. I'm sure he'd be pleased to see me, too."

The Métis looked puzzled and asked Flora, "Are you not M'selle MacTavish from near Petit Arc?"

Flora sobered and said, "Yes. My folks were killed by that gang the Mounties are chasing."

The Métis blanched and removed his battered hat as he crossed himself. Then he said, "*Eh, bien*. I understand, me. At such times, politics seem unimportant. On this occasion, let me join in wishing the Mounties good hunting!"

He was eyeing Longarm warily, and Flora said, "This friend of mine, like my father, is a friend of Louis Riel."

The Métis gravely held out his hand to Longarm and said, "I am Pierre Colbert, me. You may mention me as a friend, should the need arise."

Longarm shook the fellow's hand, feeling a little guilty. He didn't have time to explain his position on Canadian politics. So far, he'd liked every Métis he'd met, but it wasn't his fight, and he felt sort of bad about using it as a means to another end.

He tried to explain when he found himself alone with Flora again, after they'd said their goodbyes and ridden on. He said, "Old Sergeant Foster is sore at me, but I bear him no ill will. He was just doing his job, the time we tangled. He's a hell of a tracker, and so honest it makes me sick."

Flora said, "I've met his kind. What's your point?"

"My point is that I'm not up here to overthrow your government. I just have a job to do for Uncle Sam. How the hell did you Scotch-Irish get mixed up in the Métis rebellion, anyway?"

Flora frowned and said, "Bite your tongue. My father was a loyal Canadian!"

"Well, forgive me, but he sure had a funny way of showing it. The Métis underground considered him a safe white to confide in."

"He was. That didn't make him a rebel against the Crown. Prime Minister MacDonald is the rebel, if anyone is. It wasn't anyone, red, white, or in between, who wanted things changed out here. A rebel is somebody who wants to make things different. Men like my poor father and Louis Riel just wanted things to stay the way they'd always been."

Longarm thought and said, "That's funny. Sam Adams and John Hancock took pretty much the same position in another time and place. King George said they were rebels anyway. How many other whites out here do you reckon Riel can count on, if push comes to shove?"

Flora shrugged and said, "It's hard to say. Poor Louis Riel is his own worst enemy when he gets excited. You see, there's no doubt his people are being mistreated, and any fair-minded person, red or white, thinks that's a shame. But if Riel is serious about stirring up the full-blood tribes . . . "

"I follow your drift. Fair is fair, but an arrow through the parlor window makes most folks nervous. You've never had much trouble with the Plains Cree, have you?"

"Not like you've had in the States. But the Cree don't look that much different from Cheyenne or Sioux, and while a civilized Métis getting robbed is one thing, smoke-talk and feathers is another."

"I know. I've had this conversation with a Métis. Being part Indian, they can't seem to understand the gut feelings of a pure white when the talk shifts from petitions to tom-toms. What are your feelings on the Northwest Mounted Police?"

She pursed her lips and thought before she answered, "I reckon they're caught in the middle. Mounties must think like any other Canadians: some for, some against. If there's ever an all-out shooting fight, they won't be *allowed* to think for themselves. The government will order them into the field, and they'll do what they have to."

Longarm shook his head wearily and observed, "It seems to me it would save a lot of fuss if you fair-minded white Canadians changed the laws so the Métis had equal rights."

Flora nodded, and answered, "I'd like it if *women* had the vote in the British Empire, but they don't. How about down in the States?"

"Not hardly. There's been a lot of yelling and bent umbrellas on the subject, but so far, the red-blooded

111

men of America have defended their right to elect criminals and idiots."

She didn't know how to take that, so she said, "Right now, I'm more interested in finding those outlaws who murdered my family. What did that one we killed mean about the law not being able to touch Canada Jack?"

Longarm might have pointed out that *they* hadn't dragged Lucky to death, but if it made her feel more comfortable, he was willing to share the blame or credit, whichever. He said, "I thought I told you why I was being so cross-grained about the one called Canada Jack. The Mounties will likely hang any of the others they catch. That's why I want you to behave if we stumble over any more of the gang. I aim to *talk* to them and leave justice to the Crown."

"What if we catch Canada Jack? Can I kill him?"

"Nope. *I* don't aim to kill him, either. I mean to see him sweat for a time in a U.S. federal prison. He's started to purely *rile* me, and I'll be damned if he's going to get any favors from me."

"Favors?" She blinked, "Do you call gunning a man a favor?"

He nodded and explained, "Yep. The more I follow his career, the surer I am that Canada Jack has something twisted loose inside his head. I know it sounds loco, but he's *trying* to get killed. He don't know it, of course. He keeps telling himself he's a big, bad desperado. The boy is sick as hell."

She frowned and said, "That's silly! Why is he fighting so hard to get away from everybody, if he wants to die? Why doesn't he just shoot himself, or turn himself in?"

"He hasn't got enough sand in his craw. He likely thinks he's fighting to stay alive, with the part of his brain he talks to. But deep down inside, he's been committing suicide all his life. He was born with money and position. He could have anything he wants with-

112

out harming a fly. But the poor ornery bastard just can't help himself."

"My God, you sound like you feel sorry for him," she said, astonished.

"I feel sorry for a mad dog, too. That don't mean I want one running around loose."

He could see that she didn't much like what he was saying, so he added, "I know you want revenge, kitten. But believe me, taking him in alive will hurt him worse than anything you could come up with, even with an Apache squaw advising you."

She grimaced and said, "I don't know about that. Since you first told me what had happened at our spread, I've thought up some lulus."

He shook his head and said, "They wouldn't help your hurt enough to matter. Yesterday, you killed one of them ugly. Do you miss your folks less today?"

She looked fixedly at him for a moment, then said, "You're right. Let's talk about something else."

"What do you want to talk about, Flora?"

"What we did last night. That did a lot more for me than dragging that damned outlaw."

He laughed and said, "There you go. Making friends beats whupping enemies, every time."

Chapter 7

There were two places known as Medicine Hat. One was a dot on the survey map where, Lord willing, the C.P.R.R. intended to have a railway station. The other was a little trail town where real folks lived. It was closer to the river than the railroad builders considered proper, because an early Hudson Bay *voyageur*, in his ignorance, had found a good place to put in with his trading canoe. The Plains Cree had once swapped buffalo robes for salt and blankets there. By the time of Longarm's visit, the buffalo had given way to beef in the wake of the Big Kill of the seventies. Paddlewheelers had replaced the birchbark river craft of yesteryear, winter ice and summer slackwater permitting. Most travel this far west was still a matter of walking or riding. The rails wouldn't reach Medicine Hat for a few more years.

Longarm and Flora MacTavish didn't ride in by way of the well-traveled wagon trace. Thanks to her visits to the prairie town, she knew of an old buffalo trail, overgrown with new grass, but still visible in the moonlight. Approaching from any direction in broad daylight would have been risky with the Mounties unaccounted for.

She led Longarm to the back of her spinster cousins' shop and frame house. It only took her a few moments to duck inside and enlist her older kinswomen in their plot against the Crown. They were twins, both somewhere in their thirties and, while attractive, looked severe and prim. Both wore black dresses with high lace collars, and wrapped their dark hair in tight buns.

Their parlor was furnished with lace curtains and Boston ferns. While Flora told them about the massacre, the one called May started crying, and Cousin June sat tight-lipped on a horsehair chair, muttering suggestions of revenge that would make some Indians blanch. She said, "I knew they never should have settled so far from any neighbors. If white outlaws hadn't done it, they'd have probably been done in by the damned breeds your father messed with, Flora."

Longarm shot Flora a wary glance as he perched on the edge of the chair they'd offered him. Flora understood and said, "June isn't keen about Louis Riel, but she's mad at MacDonald's Tories, too."

June nodded and snapped, "The whole damned country's gone to the dogs since Hudson Bay stopped running it. There's no trade to speak of out here anymore, and the crazy railroad they keep promising us is bogged down somewhere in Saskatchewan."

Flora said, "You said something about the Mounties when I first came in, June."

The spinster nodded. She said, "They arrested some rascal this afternoon. He was drinking in the saloon."

"Do you think he was a member of the gang who killed my family?"

"I don't know. The damned Mounties never tell us anything."

Longarm asked, "Do you know if they've headed back to Fort MacLeod yet, ma'am?"

She said, "Call me June. You don't look young enough to call me ma'am. As for the Mounties, I don't think they went west when they rode out. The men in town think they were headed across the line into Saskatchewan. They sent a telegram somewhere, then lit out, stiff-necked as ever, waving their damned flag. They never tell us anything."

He asked, "What about their prisoner?"

"I suppose they left him with the town law," June

replied. "We have a constable here in town, but he's a worthless drunk. I suppose they'll pick up the man they arrested when they pass through again on their way back to MacLeod."

"Then there are no Mounties in town tonight, right?"

"Of course not. The damned government gets us set to face a Cree uprising, then spreads the Mounties too thin to be of any use to anyone. Would you like for me to snoop about a bit for you? It's still early."

He thought and replied, "No thanks, uh, June. I reckon it's safe to do my own snooping, and I ought to send a telegram of my own."

Flora looked startled and asked, "Won't you give yourself away by sending a wire to the States? There's no direct line south, and any wire you send will be routed east, the long way around."

June nodded and added, "The damned Tories read our mail. They say it's because of the Métis and Fenians, but that's just an excuse."

He said, "I don't aim to sign my right name. I just want to let my boss know I'm still alive. This trip has taken longer than we figured, and he's likely to be mad at me for being here in Canada, but at least he'll get some sleep tonight."

Cousin June seemed to brighten a bit as she said, "Speaking of sleep, you and Flora will be staying here tonight, won't you?"

Cousin May stopped crying and chimed in, "Goodness, I have to put something on the stove and make the guest room ready."

He noticed she said "room," singular, and wondered how they'd figured out his relationship with Flora so suddenly, but he didn't ask. He stood up and said he'd be back directly. Cousin June said she'd leave the back door open.

Flora followed him out, saying she'd stable and rub down their horses. As soon as they were alone, she murmured, "Hurry back, dear. I've never done it in a feather bed, and I'm curious as hell!"

116

He asked, "What about your cousins?"

"What about them?" she asked in reply.

"Don't you figure they'll ask questions?"

"Oh, I'm sure they'll be happy for me. June always said dying a virgin was a fate worse than death."

He laughed and said, "You'd sure never know it from looking at them."

"I know. They're sort of sneaky. You go on about your business and I'll explain things delicate. They won't mind."

He shrugged, kissed her, and left by way of the alley, then cut around to the main drag and asked a townie where the telegraph office was.

He passed the town lockup a few doors before he reached the little Royal Post and Telegraph establishment. He went in and asked for a blank. As he stood at the counter composing a coded message to Billy Vail, the clerk left him to attend to an incoming message. The clerk cut in with his own key, asking for them to start over. Since Longarm had caught a name he knew in the first burst of Morse, he snatched up an extra blank, turned it over, and took down the code he was listening in on.

The incoming message was aimed at Sergeant Foster from Regina:

SUPERVISOR REED FINDS YOUR CROSS-
ING BORDER MOST IRREGULAR AND
DEMANDS EXPLANATION AND CLEAR-
ANCE FROM OTTAWA STOP THIS TROOP
PERFECTLY ABLE TO DEAL WITH ANY-
ONE YOU MIGHT HAVE THE DECENCY
TO DESCRIBE STOP ARE YOU AWARE
THIS TROOP HAS SENIORITY QUESTION
MARK

Longarm chuckled and balled up the transcription as the clerk took down a few more acid comments and the signature. When he rejoined the tall American at the counter, Longarm was innocently finishing his own wire. It was addressed to Vail's home in Denver and read:

HAVING A WONDERFUL TIME WISH YOU WERE HERE AND I WAS THERE STOP COUSIN JANE SENDS LOVE STOP SIGNED LOVING SON

The clerk read it over, told him how much it would cost, and Longarm paid and left.

He stood on the boardwalk outside for a moment as he pondered his next move. He could pick up gossip in the barber shop or the saloon, but gossip went both ways, and he wasn't sure he wanted to be remembered in Medicine Hat.

He noticed a man sitting on a chair in front of the jail, with a shotgun across his lap. He walked over to him, smiled, and said, "Howdy. I hear you've got a mean one in there tonight. Are you expecting his pals to try and bust him out?"

The Canadian lawman glanced up and answered, "Hell, he ain't got no friends, this side of Saskatchewan. It's just stuffy inside, and I'm tired of listening to him."

"He's the cussing kind, huh?"

"Whimpering is the word you're looking for, mister. I didn't catch the name."

"Oh, I disremembered my manners. My name is Hank, and I swap horses for a living. I'm headed down to the saloon, and I could bring a bucket of suds by on my way back to my hired rooms, if you'd like."

The deputy constable glanced up the street, directly away from the twins' place, and said, "Staying at the Pronghorn Hotel, eh? Well, I thank you for the neighborly thought, but I'd better pass on the golden opportunity. I'm on duty."

"I can see you're a man who takes his job seriously. You say the gent you arrested is whimpering?"

"Pshaw, we didn't arrest him. The Mounties done it.

He was riding with a gang that killed some folks up the river. He denies it, of course. But Crown Sergeant Foster says he has him dead to rights. The whimpering is over hanging. Foster says he'll hang for sure, once they send someone to fetch him."

Longarm nodded and said, "I think I know Sergeant Foster. Big, tight-lipped cuss with a poker up his ass, right?"

The deputy chuckled and said, "You sure described him to a T. He ain't a bad lawman, though. The one inside was pretending to be someone else, but the Mounties nailed him to a stump and pushed him over backwards with a couple of trick questions."

Longarm laughed and said, "Yep, old Bill Foster's pretty tricky. Maybe I'll see you on my way back to the hotel, if I don't meet somebody prettier."

The Canadian laughed back and said, "Good hunting. But you'll have a rough time getting laid in this town. It's dead as hell between paydays."

Longarm said goodbye and moved along the storefronts in the dim light, until he found a handy slot between the buildings. He sidestepped in and moved to the alley behind the buildings fronting on the street.

He glided down to the rear of the jail, found a barred window, and softly called, "Hey, pard. You in there?"

There was a long delay before a sullen voice called back softly, "Of course I'm in here, you silly son of a bitch. Who are you, and what's the play?"

Longarm warned, "Keep it down. Chumley sent me."

The jailed owlhoot gasped, "No shit? I thought old Jack was sore at me for running off."

"Well, he ain't tickled pink about it, but we can see you learned it's no safer riding alone. You can call me West Virginia."

"I'm Kid Sullivan."

"Hell, don't you think I know that? Listen, I think I can get you out, but I'm not sure Shamrock will be waiting where I left him. Do you have any notions where the gang means to hole up, closer to Regina?"

119

The unseen owlhoot's voice grew wary as he demanded, "Don't you know? How did you get in on this, anyway? I don't remember Shamrock saying anything about any West Virginia."

Longarm snorted in disgust and said, "Suit yourself and stay where you are, then. I've got Mounties all around me and I don't know you that well, either. I'll just tell Shamrock I couldn't get you out."

He shuffled his boots in the alley grit, and Kid Sullivan pleaded, "Hey, don't run off on me! I don't have no fucking brother in the House of Lords, and I'm facing the gallows tree for sure!"

"I know. But I don't aim to join you if I can help it. There's no sense busting you out unless I'm *going* somewhere with you. The Mounties don't have my wild oats down next to a good description, but the minute I'm caught with you, we both get to dance on the end of a rope. Our only chance is a beeline to Jack and his boys."

"Well, you know about the train."

"Sure. I only threw in when Shamrock told me the game was getting interesting. Frankly, I've better things to risk my neck for than gunning Indian agents and raping old ladies."

Kid Sullivan sighed and said, "I know. That's why I left. I thought killing that woman the way Jack done it was getting past hard-boiled into just nasty. She was a nice old gal and a pretty good screw. I don't know why the hell he wanted to shoot her the way he done."

Longarm swallowed the green taste in his mouth and insisted, "The train—where will they be holed up waiting for it?"

"Hell, you know about Canada Jack's hideout in Moose Jaw, don't you?"

Before Longarm could answer, he heard a door slam inside the jail and another voice calling out, "Stop that infernal talking, damn it! Don't you know folks go crazy talking and playing with themselves?"

Longarm left too suddenly to hear any answer the jailed killer might have offered. He didn't figure he'd have gotten much more, in any case. The man had been too frightened of his impending trial and hanging to think too straight, and if he'd deserted the gang, knowing as much as he did, it was a safe bet they'd change a few plans. They were heading for Moose Jaw. That was enough, for now. Foster wouldn't be tearing into another troop's territory if he hadn't gotten as much by more direct methods.

The map told him to head due southeast. His growing understanding of the country told him to stick to the river as far as Claudette had said to. Common sense said to start right now. Flora had guided him as far as she really knew the way, and from here on, she'd just be extra trouble. But the horses were at the twins' place, he was tired, and what the hell, he'd never had Flora in a feather bed. He'd take some time to sort his plans and get an early start while she was still asleep. It was his favorite way to say goodbye. Few sleepy, naked ladies chased a man down the road.

He made sure the horses were all right, then he tapped on the back door and opened it without waiting to be let in. The house was dark, although he could see well enough by the moonlight streaming through the lace curtains. He moved into the front parlor and found it unoccupied. He felt sort of awkward as he went back to the central hallway and softly called out "Flora?" to the doors in general.

A muffled giggle came from behind the nearest door. He tried the knob carefully and opened the door. By the silvery, dappled light, it was hard to figure out just what was going on at first. He hadn't seen many gals wrapped together in any kind of light, and the tangle of naked flesh was confusing. He figured they wanted to be alone when one of them gasped, "Faster, faster. Don't stop!"

He closed the door gently and, having placed the twins in his map of the house, felt free to open doors at random until he saw a naked lady reclining on the covers alone, and slid in to shut the door behind him as he muttered, "I didn't know which room they'd given us. The Mounties have lit out and all's right with the world, and for some reason I've got the damnedest hard-on."

As he threw his coat and Stetson over the back of a chair and began to unbuckle his gunbelt, June said, "I'll be pleased to take care of your poor little critter, for I'm hot as a locomotive myself."

He hesitated, shrugged, and hung the gunbelt over a bedpost where he could get at it. As he unbuttoned his vest, he said, "I can see you ladies are free-thinkers, but I'm sort of surprised about Flora. I've met willing virgins before, but she purely takes the cake for enthusiasm."

June laughed deep in her throat, and explained, "I guess she got tired of waiting and started without you."

As he peeled off his shirt, she added, "You must be good, and I *like* those shoulders!"

He liked what he saw too, as his eyes adjusted to the dim light. Out of her severe spinster's dress, June was upholstered more lavishly than the boyish, younger Flora, and her unbound dark hair fell in a mass of ringlets over her shoulders and upper torso. Her large but firm-looking breasts played peek-a-boo among the flowing tresses as she waited, propped on one elbow with her free hand either covering her groin modestly, or playing with it. This sure was a confusing household.

Longarm sat on the bed to shuck his boots, and she started kissing his spine as she reached around to unbutton his pants, saying, "Let me help you."

Then she moved her hand and gasped, "Oh, did I say poor *little* critter?"

They were both still laughing as he exploded out of his pants and rolled into the bed with her. He kissed her and started running his hands over her moonlit curves, but she muttered, with her lips on his, "Don't play games, cowboy. It's time you mounted up and rode!"

He said, "Hush," and started posting as they galloped

to glory. One small, sane part of his mind was always amused at the rest of him as he decided this was the best he'd ever had. The thing he liked most about women was that each one seemed to be the best he'd ever had. It couldn't get a man in trouble unless he forgot to consider that there might be something even better down the road ahead.

Longarm rode Snowball along the riverside trail, knowing he ought to be ashamed, but feeling a little pleased with himself.

The U.S. Army remount service would make a fuss about his returning a white gelding to them instead of their regulation bay, but Snowball was a better mount, and they could probably find some officer who liked to ride pretty. Flora had to ride something, and the Mounties wouldn't be looking for a woman riding a bay.

He'd sneaked out of the house before sunrise, and by now, it was shaping up to be a fine, sunny morning, without a cloud in the sky. The prairie grass was still partly green, and quick-rising wildflowers smiled up at him. It felt good to be alive, and he wondered why men like Canada Jack had to be so ornery to a world that could be friendly, if only you gave it a chance.

He was beyond the last cattle spreads in the neighborhood of Medicine Hat, but he assumed the dots on the horizon up ahead were cows, at first. Then, as they came nearer, he muttered, "Oh, shit." The morning stopped grinning at him.

The two riders coming his way were bright scarlet above their black britches, and nobody dressed that fancy but the Mounties. He knew they'd seen him, but they weren't acting excited. To them, he was just a stranger on a white horse, Nobody but old Bill Foster knew him on sight, and the stiff-necked sergeant couldn't be *everywhere* in his red coat.

Longarm said, "Just act natural, Snowball," as he rode to meet them.

The Mounties reined in as he approached, and he knew he was expected to stop and jaw for a while. So he waved a greeting and joined them, saying, "Howdy. Ain't it pretty out, this morning?"

One of the Mounties wore a corporal's stripes on one sleeve, but he smiled anyway as he said, "Good morning. We just rode up from Cypress Hills. Have you come from Medicine Hat, sir?"

Longarm nodded as he scanned the mental map he'd worked out. The Cypress Hills police post lay right on the Alberta-Saskatchewan line, somewhere down to the southeast that Claudette had warned him to avoid without a guide. He said, "I'll bet you boys are going to fetch that prisoner our constable's holding for you, right?"

The corporal pursed his lips and said, "No, he's Fort MacLeod's arrest. Do you have any idea whether Crown Sergeant Foster's patrol is still in Medicine Hat, sir?"

Longarm shook his head and said, "You just missed him. My pals at the jailhouse said the boys from Fort MacLeod headed east after that owlhoot's side-kicks."

The two Mounties exchanged glances, and the corporal swore softly under his breath before he said, "That jumped-up son of a bitch."

Then he saw the smile in Longarm's eyes and quickly added, "Forget I said that. We wash our own linen."

Longarm asked innocently, "Did old Bill Foster do something wrong?"

"Are you a friend of his, sir?"

"Not hardly. I know him to say howdy to, but it's hard to swap jokes with a man who walks about with a poker up his ass."

The two Mounties tried not to laugh, and the

corporal said, "You *do* know Foster, don't you? How far east would you say he and his men might be?"

Longarm shrugged and replied, "A day's ride or more. I didn't see them leave Medicine Hat, just heard about the arrest and such from friends who'd been there."

The corporal asked his friend, "What do you think, Mike?"

The other Mountie said, "The hell with it. That other bunch coming down from Battleford might intercept them, and they have a man with the tapes on his sleeve to back their bitch. Why don't we ride on into town, wire the supervisor that the prick crossed the line, and have a drink before we ride home?"

The corporal nodded, and Longarm thought he was home free. But then the two-striper smiled and asked, "Do you have any identification on you, sir? It's just a formality, but . . ."

Longarm nodded and took out his wallet. He'd long since removed the badge and federal ID card he usually carried in it, of course. As he started to hand it over, the Mountie corporal said, "Please hold onto your wallet and any bills you may have in it. Anything with your name on it will be quite enough."

Longarm fished in the wallet until he found a club membership card he'd gotten in Denver that didn't have his official title next to his signature. He didn't think he'd better show them his railroad pass.

He handed over the club card, asking lightly, "What do you figure I'd be best as, a Fenian or a Métis?"

The corporal smiled thinly and said, "You don't have much of a brogue, but neither did the last Fenian I arrested. I see you're American."

"Yep. Came up for a look-see at the open range Queen Victoria's trying to unload. Our Homestead Act got started earlier, and most of the best range down home is wired up fierce."

"I thought you were a cattleman. God knows, we've got plenty of open land up here to file on. This says you're a member in good standing of the Larimer

Street Marching and Chowder Association. Isn't Denver pretty far from the sea for chowder?"

"We use mountain oysters," Longarm answered dryly.

The Mountie chuckled and handed the card back. He said, "We castrate steers up here too. Mountain oysters are a little rich for my blood, though. I'm sorry we had to detain you, but you understand it's our job to be inquisitive. Where are you headed now?"

"Over to Regina and the railroad. I wanted to take a look at country a little more convenient for shipping beef. Is there some rule I'm busting by riding across a state line?"

The corporal shook his head and said, "No. Neither Alberta nor Saskatchewan are organized provinces, yet. You're free to go anywhere you want up here, as long as you abide by British law. Welcome to Canada, Mr. Long."

"I thank you for being so neighborly, but I couldn't help noticing you boys acting like old Bill Foster has you riled. I know it's none of my business, but if anyone up here is free to come and go as he pleases, what's the fuss?"

The Mounties exchanged glances again. Then the corporal said, "It's a matter of departmental courtesy, sir. Nothing for you civilians to concern yourselves over. I apologize for any inconvenience we may have caused you, and I wish you a safe trip to Regina."

They both waved and rode on, as Longarm fought to keep from laughing. As a lawman who'd gotten in the same trouble more than once, he understood what Foster had done. A lawman who worked another lawman's territory had to give a damned good reason if he returned empty-handed. He wondered if there was some way he could share credit with Foster when he caught up with Canada Jack. It seemed ornery to keep stealing arrests from the poor cuss, but he'd learned, the last time they'd tangled, what a mule-headed man Foster was. It was hard to make a deal with a gent who thought he'd written the rule books personally. Foster was good, damned good, but he'd never learned that one hand washes the other in the real world.

As he rode on, he wondered how Foster managed to ignore the fine print when it got in his way. For a man who insisted that everyone else obey the rules as if they'd come down from Mount Sinai, carved in stone, he could bend the hell out of them when it suited his own purposes.

George Armstrong Custer had been like that. Longarm had heard all the second guesses of both sides, since Little Big Horn. And, while he took the charitable view that Custer had just had rotten luck that day in June, it had surprised him to read the army manual that Custer had written on the subject of the Plains Indians. The army still used Custer's bible, because it was a damned good book, written by a man who knew his Indians. It had just about everything there was to know about Mister Lo in its dry, factual pages. Custer had warned of the traps used by different tribes, and he'd repeated over and over that it wasn't safe to underestimate fine cavalry just because they weren't wearing army blue.

Then he'd led his troop into a boiling hornet's nest he couldn't have handled with a full brigade. Men like him and Foster sure were hard to figure.

Longarm knew he himself was a human being who could make mistakes; that was probably why he survived the ones he made.

Chapter 8

Longarm wasn't sure just when and where he crossed the imaginary line between the unorganized territories, but as he drifted northeast into Saskatchewan, the country changed some. It was still rolling prairie, away from the river, but the river ran quieter with a wider, marshy flood plain, and the trail tended to lose sight of it for hours at a time as it cut across oxbows and tried to keep its feet dry. In places, swampy draws running into the mainstream at right angles forced big detours, and even following the trail could turn a man's head around if he didn't keep his eyes open. Some of the hairpins were almost figure-eights.

A few afternoons after he'd ridden out of Medicine Hat, Longarm noticed that the wind had circled to the east and the sky was turning to slate. He'd passed few travelers along the way, and had circled wide of the occasional lonely spread he'd passed. But if that sky meant what it said, it was time to look for shelter. "Rain from the east lasts three days at least" on the northern prairies, as the saying went. Longarm didn't know too much about codfish, or he'd have known that Canadian and New England fishermen agreed on a wetter sea beyond the horizon.

He had a slicker in his roll, of course. But three or more days of steady drizzle would soak him anyway, and the horse was in greater danger. A man can survive a head cold; stuffed nostrils are fatal to any horse, because it can't breathe through its mouth.

As he rode across the swells, searching the horizon

for signs of a homestead, Longarm smelled smoke. He reined in and thought about that a mite. The smell of burning grass can mean danger on the summer prairie.

But what he smelled was burning cow chips. Without the acrid fumes of burning grass stems, that meant a campfire.

Longarm clucked Snowball slowly up the next rise as he drew the Winchester from its boot and casually rested it across his thighs. He topped the rise and spied a prairie schooner down in the next draw. It was a family of nesters; a man and woman with four kids were hunkered around their cow-chip fire, having supper.

The man spotted Longarm and stood up, so Longarm waved and rode in friendly, letting the man see him putting the Winchester away for now.

As he reined in near the fire, one of the kids called out, "Coo, are you a cowboy, mister?"

"I ain't an Indian," Longarm replied, adding, "I've some sugar I'll swap for a cup of that coffee I smell, folks. My name is Long, and I'm headed for La Coteau."

"We're the Morrisons," replied the man in a friendly Cockney accent. Then he added, "You're turned around mate. La Coteau is east of here, and you're heading west."

Longarm glanced around, frowned, and dismounted to rummage through his possibles for the sugar as he answered, "I don't reckon I'm that lost. Where are you folks headed?"

Morrison pointed northeast and said, "Medicine Hat. We've filed on a quarter-section out that way."

Longarm got the sugar, hunkered down at the fire, and handed it to Morrison's shy-looking wife before he said, "You might find Hudson Bay in that direction, Mr. Morrison. But I just came from Medicine Hat; it's over that way."

The greenhorn looked bewildered and said, "Are

you sure? I could bloody swear that's the way we just came from. It jolly well *looks* east!"

The woman suddenly sobbed, "I told you we were lost, Father! Oh, what are we ever to do?"

Morrison looked almost as worried as his wife as he tried to soothe her, saying, "Now, Mother, this Canadian knows the way, so it's all right."

Longarm glanced up at the sky and said, "I can see you were thrown off by the darkening and the wind shift. Why don't I show you something while your lady finishes brewing that pot?"

He stood up and led the bewildered Cockney away from the fire. When one of the kids tried to follow, Morrison said, "Stay with your mother, Willy. This is grown-up talk."

As they drew out of earshot, the greenhorn sighed and said, "All right, mate. I know you think I'm a bloody fool, but how did I get us lost?"

Longarm said, "I generally don't call a gent a fool unless I know more than he does, Mr. Morrison. You could probably show me around your own country pretty good. How long have you been on this side of the water?"

"About a month. We took the train to Winnipeg and bought the covered wagon and supplies. The brochure thay gave us in Liverpool said it was easy to get to the western provinces from there, but I don't know. We've been having a ruddy awful time finding anything but gnat bites, and the kids eat more than we allowed for."

Longarm hunkered down and said, "You're almost there. Let me show you something."

As the Englishman knelt beside him, Longarm fingered a clump of grass and explained, "The prevailing winds out here are from the west. Never mind what it's doing now. You see the way the seed heads of this grass line up? The tassles always grow away from the prevailing wind. There's a sort of *brushed* look to the grass, if you know what to look for. If you sort of squint as you ride or drive over the prairie, it looks like somebody's combed the grass in one direction."

Morrison looked around and hesitated a moment before he grinned and said, "By George, I *see* it!"

"Sure you do. Another thing to watch for is the way wildflowers face out here. Nine out of ten blossoms open to catch the morning sun. So if buttercups and such are grinning right at you, you're looking northwest."

"Oh, I did read something about sunflowers following the sun, and—"

"Back up. It ain't true. I've been hearing that for years, but most sunflowers I've met up with face south. Some seem to swing southwest as the day wears on, so I generally don't trust them. Watch the *little* flowers, they're less inclined to fib. Closer to the river, you'll notice that the trees lean away from the west wind. Evergreens look straighter, but they point their tops at the morning sun, too."

Morrison laughed and said, "You know, I remember my old Dad telling me some of this when I was a lad?"

"Mine too. Living in the city tends to make folks forget what we all knew a while back. There's no magic to finding your way without a sign on every corner, you just have to remember there *ain't* any."

"It was jolly decent of you to draw me aside before we had this chat, mate. I'd heard you frontier lads liked to have a bit of sport with newcomers."

"Well, some old boys don't know any better, I reckon. Mean is mean, no matter where. I've heard of city mice having fun with their country cousins, too. It's easy to look smart at another man's expense, when you forget that nobody knows everything."

Morrison grinned sheepishly and asked, "Can I act the mighty trail blazer with Molly and the kids, now that you've shown me how to keep from getting turned about on this perishing road west?"

Longarm smiled back and said, "Sure. You're the man of the family, ain't you?" Then he added, "As long as you aim to be Dan'l Boone from here to Medicine Hat, would you hold still for a few more pointers?"

"God strike a light, of course!"

"Well, when you finish supper, you'd best move your wagon to higher ground. This draw might be a lake by morning. You don't want to camp on the crest, either. That's where you catch all the wind, and sometimes lightning."

"I can see that, once you point it out to me. But how do I know just where to draw the line between being flooded or blown away?"

"Ant piles. These little red prairie ants have been camped out here longer than the Indians. They don't make their nests where they figure to get drowned. Mind you, don't camp *near* an ant pile. The little bastards bite like fire. Just line up as high on a slope as the ant piles and, by the way, they build the entrance to their pile to the southeast, too. They don't like the west wind kicking dust in their faces as they rise and shine."

Morrison's wife called out to them, and as they headed back to the fire, the nester said, "I shot a jackrabbit this morning, but there didn't seem to be much meat to it. I fear we're serving bread and beans this evening."

Longarm shrugged and said, "I've never found a jack worth wasting a bullet on unless I was starving. The Indian kids snare some for the hell of it, but rabbit don't stick to your ribs. Not enough fat in it. If you take the time off to hunt out here, try for pronghorn in the open and mule deer in the brush. There used to be a mess of buffalo, but you'll be lucky as hell if you find meat like that for the taking, these days."

As they rejoined the woman and children, Longarm got some pemmican from his saddlebag and hunkered down to carve off slices for everyone, saying, "This stuff looks awful, but it's pretty good with bread."

One of the children took a chunk, trustingly, and started to chew. Molly Morrison eyed her own share dubiously, and asked what it was. He explained, "Indian rations. It's pounded dry beef, cuet, and berries."

"Cor, you can't mush fruit up with meat!"

"Well, the Indians don't know that, ma'am. They put flour in their coffee and salt in their tea, too. Some tribes look sick when you ask them if they'd like some fish. It's all in the way we were brought up, I reckon. I met some Chinese gents who thought eating cheese was plain disgusting. I generally *try* things before I decide whether I like them or not."

Morrison said, "Now, Molly, when in Rome and all that . . ." He tried his own pemmican, grimaced at the unfamiliar texture, then nodded and said, "Not bad, really. You say you can buy this from the Indians?"

"I'll have no dealings with ruddy redskins!" His wife announced firmly, as one of the little boys chimed in, "Blimey, I want to see an Indian! Can we have an Indian, Dad?"

Longarm noted the worried look that passed between the nester and his wife. He nodded and said, "Yeah, you'll meet some Cree by wintertime. They generally send a squaw to your door with a basket or rabbit pelt for sale. She's looking for a handout, of course. But some of them are proud."

Morrison asked, "What if we turn them down? We've little enough for ourselves, and they told us the Cree had been tamed."

Longarm shrugged and said, "It's up to you. I doubt they'll scalp you, this late in the season, for being less than neighborly. On the other hand, you never know when a friend might come in handy."

"Phaw! What good is a shiftless Indian, even if he wants to be your friend?"

Longarm didn't answer. He'd shown the idiot how to keep from getting lost again or flooded in the coming northeaster. He didn't have time to lecture him on

Christianity. He knew that a lot of folks who went to church every Sunday felt the same way about the folks who'd been out here first.

He could have told them about sides of venison or corn-husk dolls dropped shyly on a soddy doorstep by a grateful Indian who'd gotten through another spell of poor hunting with a little help from a friendly settler. He could have told them tales of Indians warning friendly whites when the war drums started tapping thoughtfully. But he knew it was a waste of time. Any good he did would just be undone by some know-it-all settler farther west.

Longarm took out his watch and said, "I'd best ride on as soon as I finish this coffee, folks. I figure we'll have cats and dogs coming down by nightfall."

Morrison said he was welcome to spread his roll next to theirs, under the wagon, but Longarm said he didn't want to crowd them.

He finished and thanked them as quickly as he thought polite, and mounted up, cussing himself for giving them part of his rations. He'd meant to mosey over by the river and see if he could bag a sunset deer for them, but he was just as glad he hadn't offered.

Longarm wasn't a sentimentalist on the subject of Indians. He'd swapped shots with too many Indians to consider them noble savages, and smoked with too many to think of them as subhuman primitives. He knew a Cheyenne from a Sioux, and would never make the fatal mistake of taking an Apache for a Papago. But he would have been the first to admit he didn't know a hell of a lot about the Canadian Plains Cree. That was probably why he was so pissed off at a man who knew all about Indians but couldn't tell east from west.

The cluster of sod buildings under the daisy windmill lay on the lee slope of a rise, facing away from the river. Longarm might have ridden on by if he hadn't spotted cattle on the skyline and, knowing a spread had to be near, searched for it as night was falling.

As he rode toward it in the gathering dusk, a dog yipped and the yellow square of a doorway winked open. A woman's voice called out, "Is that you, Tom?"

Longarm called back, "No, ma'am. My name is Custis Long, and I'm headed for La Coteau. I'd pay you for a place to put this pony for the night."

The door slammed shut.

Longarm reined in and sat there quietly. Something ticked the brim of his Stetson and he muttered, "Damn."

If he hadn't been shit on by a bird, it was starting to rain.

He considered riding on. The gal in the house seemed spooked. If "Tom" was her husband, she figured to be alone in there. Finding another spread in rain and darkness was going to be a bitch, but he understood her position. He dismounted and got his slicker from his saddle roll as it started doming down harder. He put on the yellow oilcloth and buttoned the top, leaving the waist open as always for a quick draw, should the need arise. As he remounted the nervous Snowball, the door opened once more and the same voice called, "It's fourteen miles to the next spread."

He called back, "Yes, ma'am. I ain't taking this personal. I can see the fix you're in."

As he clucked the gelding into motion, she called, "Wait. I can't let you ride into the storm, but—"

He reined in and suggested, "What if I was to pull into your barn over there, ma'am? You could bar your door and be no worse off. Your dog would yap if I came pussyfooting across in the rain, wouldn't he?"

She laughed, relieved, and said, "All right. My husband will be back any minute, and maybe then we'll invite you in for a bite, if it's not too late. Forgive me, I can tell by your voice you're a gentleman, but—"

"Say no more about it, ma'am. I know what your man told you before he rode off. I'd have told you the same. Me and Snowball will bed down over here, and

I thank you for letting us get out from under that mean sky."

Without waiting for an answer, Longarm rode over to the sheds and barn, dismounted again, and led Snowball under the overhang. Across the yard, the door closed, more gently this time, and the only light from the house was that from a beer-bottle window in the thick sod wall.

Longarm removed his saddle and harness, and hung them over a rail before putting Snowball in a stall with a rear bar of lodgepole. He hadn't asked for oats, so he didn't search for any. Snowball had grazed while he supped with the nesters, in any case.

It was really pouring now, but the roof was dry, so he took off his slicker. He struck a match for a quick look at the almost pitch-black interior, and had the position of everything important memorized by the time his light went out.

The barn was little more than a large one-story soddy with a pole-and-turf roof. There were no other horses. The end wall was piled with hay almost to the ceiling.

Longarm unlashed his bedroll and carried it over, unrolling it atop the pile as, outside, there was a flash of lightning. They'd just about made it too late. The rain was coming down fire and salt, now. If "Tom" had ridden to the nearest town, he'd probably lay over for the night if he had any sense. That was probably why his wife was spooked, alone in the house across the way.

Longarm climbed up on his roll and unbuckled his gunbelt, but it was too early to sleep and nobody with a lick of sense smoked on a pile of dry hay. The only good thing about it was that he'd have been even more uncomfortable outside.

Something bit him on his leg, inside his pants and above his boot top, and muttered, "I might have known."

Hay piled at ground level was like that. The bug

bite itched and tempted him to scratch it, but he steeled himself not to. Whatever it was—hay mite, tick, spider, or no-see-um—it would have company before morning. Scratching just made it worse. Damn "Tom" and whatever had taken him off. Bedding a stranger down in buggy hay was plain uncivil.

Despite the rain, the air in the barn was muggy and warm, so he left his clothes on as he lay atop the tarp, hoping to spare himself at least a few bites from whatever he was sharing the hay with.

He tried to relax. No man was ever fatally injured by a few hours of extra shut-eye, and he had a long ride ahead, if it ever stopped raining.

He lay back with his eyes shut and listened to the rain on the roof. It seemed to help, and he'd almost dozed off when he heard the sound of hoofbeats and rose on one elbow, muttering, "Welcome home, Tom."

But there was more than one horse, and they were riding in hard. That seemed reasonable. Nobody figured to *walk* his horse on a night like this.

Then a harsh voice called out, "We know you're in there, honey!" and that didn't seem reasonable at all.

As Longarm quietly sat up and put his hat and gunbelt back on, a second voice yelled, "Hey, come on, Martha. We're getting wet as hell out here!"

Longarm slid off the haypile and moved on the balls of his feet toward the Winchester on his saddle. He heard the woman in the house call out, "Go away! My husband will be home any minute!"

The first rider yelled back, "Bullshit! We all know he's bedded down at the doc's with that infection! What do you think we rode out here for? Open the goddamn door!"

Longarm figured the lady didn't aim to. He could hear them hammering on it now. It sounded like they were kicking as well as using their gun butts.

The woman's voice sounded muffled as she yelled, inside the sod walls, "Go away! I have a gun!"

"Aw, shit, we ain't afeared of that old muzzle-loader

137

we know about, Martha honey. You only got one shot, and then where would you be? Come on, let's keep it friendly. There's only three of us, and we'll be gentle if you will!"

Longarm had his Winchester now, as he stood in the overhang, trying to make them out. The woman inside had doused the light. The three riders and the ponies they'd dismounted from were shifting inkblots in the dark downpour.

There was a flash of lightning, and for a split second he could see the three of them. They were bunched up by the door. While the sod walls might stop a .44-40 slug, the door wouldn't and there was no telling where, inside, the woman was.

Longarm levered a round into his chamber. The sliding click of the breech was audible above the sound of the rain and one of the roughnecks gasped, "Hey, did you fellows hear that?"

Longarm said flatly, "What you just heard was a rifle getting ready to go off if you sons of bitches don't vacate the premises, sudden!"

A blossom of muzzle-flash answered what he'd considered a reasonable suggestion. Longarm fired at it and crabbed to one side, staying in the shadows as a voice gurgled, "Oh, Christ!"

Another gun flashed. Longarm knew there was blank wall behind it as he fired back, jumped the way he'd come from, and fired at still another flash aimed at where he'd just been.

The sky ripped open in a chalk-white flash and he spotted one man still on his feet, moving in a dead run for their horses. He led with Kentucky windage, fired, and the next time the lightning flashed, he saw that the man was down in a rain puddle.

It was quiet as hell for about a million years. Then he heard a window creak, and the woman's voice called out, "Have they gone?"

Longarm said, "Not hardly. Stay put. If you'd like

to help, shove a lantern out on a broomstick so we can have some light on the subject."

A voice groaned in the darkness, "You'll pay for this, stranger. Who asked you to butt in?"

Longarm didn't answer. After a while, a lantern seemed to float out from the wet sod wall, and as he watched its swinging puddle of dim light, he saw he had all three desperadoes on the ground.

He called out, "I'm coming in to see how bad I hurt you boys. If one of you moves enough to notice, I'm going to get purely testy."

There was no reply. The one who'd protested his joining the party was still breathing, but unconscious now. The other two were dead. He didn't bother to roll the one with his face underwater over to make sure.

The door popped open, and the woman ran out to throw herself against Longarm, sobbing, "Oh, my God, I was so frightened! If you hadn't been here, and after the way I treated you—"

He said, "You're getting wet, ma'am," and half-led, half-shoved her inside the nearby door. A little fox terrier growled at him from where it trembled in a corner. Longarm saw a chair and table near the fireplace and said, "Sit down and let's study our next move, ma'am."

He saw for the first time that she was quite beautiful, and her wet shift, clinging to her body, left little to the imagination. Her dark hair was plastered to her fine-boned skull by the rain.

He said, "You'd best dry off while we talk. I was hoping those men outside were some I was looking for, but I can see they were some of your local admirers. What's this all about, uh, Martha?"

The girl picked up a towel and stepped behind a screen as she said, "A few days ago my husband stuck himself with a pitchfork and it festered. He's been in town, trying to save his leg. Those men you just fought were the Duncan brothers. I knew they didn't like Tom, but I never expected them to go *this* far!"

"The way it turned out must have surprised them, too. What were they, outlaws or just town bullies?"

"A bit of both, I think. They've been accused of stealing stock and worse, and most of the men around here are afraid of them."

She stopped, stared wide-eyed over the top of the screen at Longarm, and added, "I should say, *were* afraid of them. How will we ever explain what happened to the law?"

He smiled crookedly and said, "I am the law, sort of. Let's eat the apple a bite at a time. Did I get the whole gang, or have I started something serious?"

She thought and answered, "There were just the three of them, though three was more than enough when they rode out here from Manitoba a year or so ago. My Tom wasn't afraid of them, but he was the exception in these parts. I wasn't there, but they say Tom backed the oldest one down one day in town. He was the meanest one. They called him Rufe. Tom never told me what they were arguing about, but I think it might have been a remark Rufe passed about me."

Longarm said, "That would be a fairly educated notion, Martha. I reckon I have a handle on it now. They knew your man was laid up at the doc's, figured you were alone out here, and came calling, ugly."

As she stepped back into view, wearing a dark kimono, Martha grimaced and said, "They must have been insane. How could they have hoped to get away with it? Tom and the other men would have killed them afterwards!"

Longarm felt better about the shooting now, as he nodded and said, "That's true, if they'd left you alive to tell on them. Tom figured to come home to a burned-out shell and not much of you to talk with. They might have figured the Cree would get the blame. On the other hand, they might not have thought too hard at

140

all. Gents who fire at a rifle, holding pistols, ain't the smartest kind you meet up with."

She sank weakly to the chair and sobbed, "My God, it's worse than I imagined, and I was already trying not to scream!"

Longarm nodded and said, "Just set a spell and let me see if there's anything worth doing for the one still breathing."

He stepped outside, leaned over in the rain to feel for a pulse, and came back in, even wetter, to announce, "They can stay where they are, for now. I'll haul them out of the way when and if it stops raining so."

She said, "You must be soaked!"

He said, "I sure am, but I don't have a kimono to change to. I'll be all right, it's warm in here."

"I'll make you some hot chocolate. Whatever must you think of me? First I chase you into the barn, and now I'm dithering around, not knowing what to do next, with you wet through and through after saving me!"

He looked uncomfortable and said, "Chocolate would be fine, ma'am. Uh, would you mind fastening that robe a mite better?"

She glanced down at her exposed nipple, flushed, and hastily wrapped the kimono tighter, gasping, "Oh, Lord! You must think I *deserve* to be raped!"

He said, "No, ma'am, nobody deserves that. I can see you're sort of mixed up. You've probably never worn that thing in front of anyone but your man, and you just don't have the hang of it yet."

She laughed a trifle wildly, and turned away to putter with her pots and pans on the baked-clay hearth. As she knelt with her back to him, he noticed how thin the cheap imitation silk was, and he sort of wished she hadn't fastened it so tight, after all. Now that she had her front well-hidden, it looked like her rear was about to bust out at him.

He tore his eyes away and tried to think of something else as she did whatever on the cow-chip coals.

Martha was the neatest thing to look at in the soddy. Everything else was sort of worn and shabby. He could see that she'd tried to keep the dirt floor tidy and the plain plank furnishings dusted, but it was still sort or gritty and mud-colored everywhere he looked. There was a brass bedstead in one corner, with a patchwork quilt thrown over the sheets. The little dog was watching from under the bed, and the mattress sagged in the middle, like the springs were tired, or had been getting pounded beyond the usual call of duty. He could see why those three who were going stiff in the rain outside had wanted her across that bed. She was a cut above pretty, and had a dangerous way of moving. He didn't think she was a bawd. She acted like she didn't know the effect she had on men. Her husband's abuse of those bedsprings probably set with her as true love. He wondered if it would help her and Tom if he told her she ought to wear more underclothes and maybe pin up her hair in a bun. He decided he'd keep the notion to himself. The trouble with telling a pretty gal she was giving you a hard-on was that she tended to take it personal.

He asked if it was all right to smoke, and she flinched at the sound of his voice before looking back over her shoulder with a smile and saying, "Of course. The chocolate will be ready in a minute. Would you like something to go with it?"

He said, "I supped back up the trail," and fished out a cheroot. It was a mite damp, but he'd thought to soak his sulfur matches in hot wax, so he had no trouble lighting up. She joined him at the table and said, "Mmm, that smells good. Tom smokes trade tobacco in his pipe, and sometimes it gets a little rank."

He nodded uncomfortably, and said, "I can see you're having a time making a go of things here. How many head are you grazing?"

She sighed and said, "Less than a score. We only have one pony and no money for hired help. Tom says the price of beef is rising, but until the railroad comes this far west, well, it gives us something to *do*, I suppose."

"Who put up all this sod? It's a lot of work for just a couple."

"Oh, Tom's a good worker. Sometimes I think that's all he wants to do. Before he hurt his leg, he was at it like a beaver, day and night. I *told* him he'd hurt himself if he kept pushing himself when he was tired, but some men are just like that, I suppose."

She hesitated before she asked, "Do you have time to run your wife to town once in a while, Mr. Long?"

Longarm started to say he wasn't married. Then he thought better of it and said, "I didn't, when we were first starting out. How long have you kids been married up?"

She thought and said, "Almost two years. Tom says we're at the dangerous stage where— Why on earth am I telling you this?"

He blew a smoke ring and replied, "Because we're strangers, and because you've been alone out here with nobody but your man to jaw with."

"I know. It's not that we don't get along, you understand. I mean, I think we have a good marriage, all things considered, but—"

"I know you have a good marriage, ma'am. You're pretty, and your man is a hard worker, so you've got it half-licked already. I've got a few years on you, so I know what's eating you. You love your man, but you're lonesome for other company."

She looked away and protested, "I've never looked at another man since I married Tom, sir."

He nodded and said, "I can see that. I didn't mean you've been hankering for forbidden fruit. I was talking about plain, ordinary talk with someone you didn't jaw with morning, noon, and night. Men and women cooped up too long get a mite windy when they get a chance to talk to anyone new."

"I'm not sure I like the way this conversation is drifting, sir."

"There's a point to it, ma'am. I'm starting to see what happened just now. Those poor idiots who rode out tonight didn't understand you like I do. You don't know how to handle yourself in conversation with strange men, so you go a mite flustered and, well, it could be taken as flirty."

She rose, her eyes blazing and her kimono fell partway open again as she flared, "That's not true! I never gave the Duncans any reason to take me for a wicked woman!"

He sighed, "You're doing it again. Don't you have something less exciting to put on?"

She glanced down, gasped, "Oh!" and ran behind the screen, crying. Longarm saw that the chocolate was burning, and got up to hunker down at the hearth and stir it as he called out soothingly, "I told you I was a sensible cuss, but maybe now you get my meaning. If I was your man, I'd see you got to visit more with the neighbor ladies, and I'd buy you a corset. I know you don't need one, but it might save a heap of misunderstandings in the future. You see, gals are sort of rare out here, and pretty ones are scarcer than hen's teeth. Those three brothers must have talked about you, pro and con, for some time before your man gave them a chance at you alone while they were drinking lonesome."

She stepped back into view, wearing a print Mother Hubbard, and asked, "Is this any better?"

He nodded and said, "Yep. I wouldn't smile like that when you ask a man for his approval, though. You've got a pair of eyes a man notices across a smoke-filled room. You're going to have to study lowering your lashes some. I read smoke signals pretty good, but as we just learned, some men don't have a lick of sense when a pretty gal looks at them without cussing."

She laughed and sat down as he poured out the chocolate. Her face was flushed and she brushed a strand of drying hair from her forehead as she said, "I've never met a man who could flirt so innocently, and I ought to send you back to the barn, but you know, I *like* it."

He resumed his own seat, took a sip of the warming drink, and said, "That's why I'm doing it. Every pretty lady should get flirted with polite from time to time. Like the fellow says, it's good for a lady's complexion. There's no harm in a pretty married gal wanting to be told other men still notice her. You've got to be careful about casting sidelong glances at the wrong sort of men, though."

She looked horrified and asked, "Are you suggesting that what happened here tonight was my fault?"

He reached across to pat the back of her hand as he soothed, "No, I'd have had to stop them if they'd been threatening to kick in a parlor house door. What they got was what they had coming for a long time, most likely. I'll say no more about the hows and whys of it all. The next thing we have to study is what you want me to do with the bodies."

"What *I* want you to do with them?"

"Yes, ma'am. It's your land they're laying dead on. Their ponies have run off. They'll likely head for home, so sooner or later the Duncans will be missed. How serious do you reckon anyone will look for them?"

"I don't know. Nobody liked them, but won't the crime have to be reported?"

Longarm grimaced and said, "The *crime* never happened. I shot the bastards before they could get at you. I reckon the Mounties would be interested enough, if anyone reported anything to them."

She looked bewildered and asked, "What do you mean, *if*? Aren't you going to stay here with me until Tom gets back?"

"Not hardly. I mean to move on as soon as it's dry enough. I have reasons of my own for not wanting to meet you with your Mounties, but I can stack those boys in your smokehouse if you feel the need to report what sensible folks might consider the usual end to such matters."

145

"Oh, my God, I might have known you were on the run!"

"Calm down. I ain't an outlaw, exactly. Let's say I'm traveling incognito."

She smiled wanly and said, "That's funny, I thought the Prince of Wales was fatter and had a beard. What do you suggest we do?"

"If it was up to me, the three of them would just sort of never come back. I could drag them over to the river and lose them pretty good."

"I'd have to tell my husband when he comes back."

"Well, sure you would. I know better than to ask a gal to lie to her man. Tom can report it or not report it. There ought to be some money to go with their guns, and he can report that too. Meanwhile, they won't be here, and neither will I. How do you like it so far?"

Martha frowned down at her chocolate and replied, "I don't know. You're a strange man. One moment I'm afraid of you, and the next . . . Why are you even asking me these things? You know I can't stop you, no matter what you mean to do!"

He shook his head and said, "That's not true. Us incognito princes ain't much for explanations, but I'm on your side. I want you on mine when I ride on. Unless I let you have some say in things, you're likely say or do all sorts of things I wouldn't want you to."

Her eyes widened and she started to ask something. Then she shuddered and said, "You do what you think best. I don't want to question it. I'm not sure I want to *know* about it!"

He nodded, put down his cup with half the chocolate untasted, and got to his feet. He said, "Lock up after me, and don't open to anyone but your man, if he comes back tonight."

"Are you leaving now?"

"Yes and no. I'm already wet, so I may as well get rid of those corpses. You're right, there's no need to jaw about where and how. I'll come back and rub myself and Snowball down in the barn. If it's still raining hard

146

at sunup, I may stay until it lets up. If I'm wrong about the weather and the day dawns clear, this'll be good-bye."

As he turned to go, she suddenly leaped up and came around the table to him. She wrapped her arms around him and pleaded, "Please don't kill me! I'll do anything you say!"

He stood stock-still, frowning down at her fright-ened face as he asked, "Where'd you get such a fool notion, girl? I told you to lock up after me."

She hung on, sobbing, "I know what you said. But I just remembered how you said the Duncans meant to make sure I never talked! I swear, I'll never tell a soul you were here!"

He laughed and said, "You ain't thinking straight, ma'am. If I was that sort of gent, I wouldn't be going to so much trouble to cover my tracks. Hell, I could have just laid low and let the Duncans do whatever!"

"But if you're not a wanted killer, why can't you tell me who you really are and what you're up to?"

He chucked her under the chin and said, "I thought we had that all worked out. I'm the Prince of Wales, traveling in disguise. I'll be saying *adios* for now, ma'am. Make sure you bar the door after me."

He stepped out in the rain, went to the barn, and saddled Snowball, saying, "Sorry, pard. We have to find some rope and maybe an old tarp. The grass is slick, and it won't be a hard drag for you to high water. I promise you some oats and a dry rub after we tidy up this mess."

Chapter 9

Longarm's eyes opened in the gray light of the barn as he stopped breathing while he tried to figure out what had awakened him. He slid a silent hand under the saddle blanket he'd been using as a pillow, and as he touched the cold brass of his derringer, Martha's voice called out, "Are you still here?"

He sat up and said, "Morning. I ain't dressed or I'd stand up."

She was standing there barefoot in her cotton shift, holding a tray. She said, "I brought some flapjacks and coffee out, in case you hadn't left yet."

He propped himself up on one naked elbow and said, "It's still coming down by the bucketful, but we may see some clearing by noon. I thank you for the neighborly thoughts about breakfast. Any sign of your man yet?"

She joined him, kneeling in the hay, as she placed the tray between them and said, "No. I doubt if the doctor will let him ride in weather like this, even if he's better."

She glanced up at the clothes he'd hung to dry and said, "You should have stopped by the house when you came back, and let me dry those things by the fire. Was it . . . bad?"

He reached for a fork and asked innocently, "What are you talking about, ma'am? I disremember hearing or seeing anything bad since you were kind enough to let me hole up here out of the rain."

She nodded and said, "That's right. Nothing happened. I guess I must have had a bad dream."

He took a forkful of flapjack, tasted, and said, "You're a good cook, ma'am. By the way, I found a mason jar with fifty-odd in coins in it as I was rubbing down old Snowball. It's on the shelf above his manger. You folks ought not to leave your egg money out here in the barn."

She gasped, "Fifty dollars?"

He said, "Some dollars, some shillings and pence. I didn't tally it, since it's yours."

He ate some more, saw that she seemed to be waiting for something, and said, "I'd be obliged if you'd leave me alone to dress, ma'am. It'd look sort of funny if anyone rode in right now to see you jawing with a naked stranger."

She blushed as she lowered her eyes, but said, "Nobody will be riding by on a day like this. The draws are full of running water, the prairie is fetlock-deep in mud, and it's still raining. We're as cut off as if we were marooned on a desert island."

He nodded and said, "That may be true enough right now, but the rain always stops and the trails to reality can dry out sudden. I'd like to get dressed now. I'll bring this tray over directly."

She left, looking confused. He finished breakfast, hauled on his damp boots and britches without bothering about wet socks or underwear, and went to the doorway, still stripped to the waist. He stared up at the sky and muttered, "You'd better cut that out or give me some strength, Lord."

It was almost nine, so he'd overslept, and that helped. But he still faced a long, soggy day with no place to go. Martha had been right about traveling conditions on the surrounding prairie. The mud on high ground might not stop a determined rider, whatever his mount thought about it, but every low spot would be deep enough to swim in. The only bright side was that neither the gang he was after nor the Mounties would be moving, either.

He put his slicker on over his bare skin, and found a pair of gum boots and a straw hat hanging on pegs in the sod walls. He figured that as long as he was stuck here, he might as well be doing something useful, and he could see that the chores had gotten ahead of the injured Tom and his woman.

He picked up a pitchfork and the tray Martha had brought, and stepped out in the rain. He legged it over to the house, set the tray on the doorstep, knocked, and turned away for a look-see at the yard in the cold gray light. The teeming rain had washed away any blood there may have been in the trampled mud. One hoof or boot mark looked pretty much like any other, and all of these were smoothing out nicely. He found his own spent Winchester brass and stomped it under the mire. The unfortunate Duncan brothers had fired revolvers and had ejected no brass. He'd had second thoughts on the subject of the spoils of victory, and everything but their untraceable pocket money was bobbing down the swollen Saskatchewan right now. Folks who surfaced after rolling along a riverbottom for a while tended to be messy, and there was a good chance anyone who found one or more of the men he'd had to shoot would bury them as flood victims. A rain like this one usually took a few careless plainsriders along with a mess of livestock.

He didn't notice any of Martha's stock nearby. They were bunched rumps-to-the-wind somewhere, or they were bobbing like apples down the river. Nobody would be able to tally stock for a day or so.

He found that a manure pile behind the barn had been spread some by a rivulet off the roof, and that gave him something to do for a time. He ditched the pile and covered it with fresh straw to keep the flies down when the sun came out, then he went back in the barn and dried off some as he tidied up the tools and tack. Folks got careless about sod walls and mud floors

150

between rains, and he figured to save them some rust and mildew by putting things back in order. He found some driftwood Tom had likely hauled up from the riverside brush, and used his knife to whittle pegs and hooks. A wet day was the time to drive things into the sod walls without making a dusty mess. By noon, he had the barn as neat as it was ever likely to get, and Martha called across the yard that she'd been cooking again.

As Longarm started across the yard in the straw hat and slicker, fork in hand, he blinked in surprise at an apparition riding in from the west. It was a lone Mountie. The scarlet tunic was hidden by a military rain cape, but the hat and monogrammed saddle pad gave him away. He and his chestnut looked half-drowned, but he was sitting tall in the saddle, as if he were on parade.

Longarm had his derringer and watch under the slicker, but he was glad he'd left his gunbelt in the barn. The young mountie was good. Nobody but a fellow lawman would have noticed the way he automatically patted down everyone he met with a head-to-toe sweep of his friendly eyes. The Mountie pulled up between Longarm and the house, touched a gauntlet to the brim of his dripping hat, and said, "Good day, sir. This would be the Wilson spread, wouldn't it?"

Longarm thought Martha might have said their name was Wilson, so he nodded, wishing he had a straw between his lips to go with the old straw hat and muddy gum boots.

The door of the soddy opened before the Mountie could get too interested in Longarm. He turned in the saddle as Martha called out, "We were just about to set down to table, sir. You're welcome to join us."

Longarm could have kissed her. He could see that the Mountie had them sized up as husband and wife, now. If the girl could just play it without coaching . . . But *would* she? They hadn't agreed on any line to take in front of unexpected visitors. They hadn't *expected* unexpected visitors. Nobody ever did.

The Mountie ticked his hatbrim to Martha and said, "Nothing would give me greater pleasure, mum, but I'm on Her Majesty's business. You folks haven't by any chance seen a band of Indians passing, have you?"

Longarm saw that it was his turn, so he shook his head and said, "Not hardly. What sort of Indians are we talking about?"

The Mountie said, "Chippewa. A band of young renegades."

"Ain't we kind of far west for Chippewa?"

"We are, and I mean to chide them for it when I catch up with them. We've received a complaint from the Cree that they've stolen two ponies and a young squaw. They seem to be young braves trying to revive the ancient customs. Rather silly, what?"

Longarm shifted his weight on the grounded pitchfork and observed, "I notice you're riding alone. Ain't that sort of unusual, against a band of hostiles?"

The Mountie shrugged and answered, "Oh, I'd hardly call them anything so dramatic, sir. They're probably just rowdy kids. I understand there are no more than a dozen or so."

Longarm didn't argue. He'd heard the Mounties thought they were sort of tough. He said, "Well, I wish you good hunting, but you're going to have yourself a time getting anywhere in this rain. Every draw will be running stirrup-deep."

The Mountie nodded and said, "I know. I've been fording some. The storm seems to be letting up, though. It's my hope the renegades will have made camp between here and La Coteau to wait it out."

He swung back to Martha where she stood in the doorway, ticked his hat again, and added, "Let me thank you once again for your hospitality, mum. But I really must be going."

The Mountie spurred his wet horse, rode across the yard, and headed east at a mile-eating trot.

As Longarm followed Martha inside, he opined, "That boy is either good or crazy. There's nothing harder to predict than a gang of kids, red or white."

Martha took a pot of stew from the hearth and began to serve them on tin plates as she said, "Oh, our Mounties aren't afraid of a few Indians."

Longarm nodded and answered, "That's what I just said." Then he cocked his head and, yes, he heard it again. A horned lark was singing.

Martha smiled across the table and agreed, "The rain seems to be letting up."

Longarm nodded but didn't answer as he chewed. Martha was a good cook, considering that she and her husband were living close to the bone here. The stew meat was smoked past common courtesy, and the vegetables had been mummified past preservation into tastelessness. He'd noticed they had no hogs or hens. Tom was probably waiting until they had some kids to hand the small chores of a homestead on to.

He finished fast and, like most countrymen, saved the small talk for after he ate. Martha apologized for having no dessert to go with the coffee, and he said a smoke would do him as well. So he lit up as she cleared the table.

Outside, the rainwater still dripped from the eaves, but the sun was out and birds were foraging in the wet grass for half-drowned bugs. The afternoon sunlight through the beer-bottle window played naughty tricks on Martha as she puttered about in her thin cotton dress, and he couldn't help feeling annoyed at the cruel shark that men called Time.

He knew what a few more years of mud, dust, and cow-chip smoke in her hair were going to do to the gal. Frontier living seemed to tan and toughen a man into a critter that looked healthier than its pallid Eastern counterpart. But maybe women were supposed to stay pale and perfumed. By the time Martha was thirty, he knew she'd look older than most Eastern gals of forty. It was a crying shame, but it wasn't *his* fault she was stuck out here on this bleak prairie homestead.

She finished stacking the wiped-off plates, and rejoined him at the table with a wan smile as she brushed a strand of hair from her brow and said, sort of wistfully, "I guess the water in the draws will be going down now. How soon do you figure it will be safe to ride cross-country again?"

He shrugged and said, "I don't know. If that Mountie doesn't come back pretty soon, we can figure he's been able to ford the next couple of draws. Ought to be a mite muddy for *sensible* folks for a while. I misdoubt we'll see serious traffic on the trail for another twenty-four hours."

She murmured, "Twenty-four hours . . ." softly, like a prayer. Then she said, "This is going to sound crazy, but I keep having this funny feeling that I've been asleep and dreaming."

He said, "Yeah, being cooped up by the weather, with the chores thrown out of kilter, messes up your sense of time."

"That must be it. It seems like you rode in a week or more ago, and I can't remember a time when I didn't know you."

He blew a smoke ring and didn't answer. She stared at the blue smoke in the shaft of sunlight between them and mused, "It's crazy. My common sense tells me the Duncans came out here only last night, and I know you fought them, but it feels like it was all a dream. I keep having this crazy notion that I'm about to wake up and you'll be gone, and I'll never be sure if you really existed or if I made you up."

"Do you make folks up much, Martha?"

"Of course. God knows, there's not much else to do out here. It's bad enough when Tom is home, but since he's been in town with that infected fork wound—well, I'd heard hermits and sheep herders got sort of odd out on the prairie with only the wind for company, but I've only recently begun to understand it."

He said, "When the water's down, I'd be proud to ride you into town. You could see how your man is, maybe buy yourself some ribbons, or a book to read."

But she shook her head and said, "No. I promised Tom I'd stay and mind the little we have. He'll either be coming home or sending word in a day or so."

Again he didn't answer, so her face was sort of flushed as she suddenly blurted, "Damn it, are you staying another night, or aren't you?"

He said, "I've been studying on it. If the wind shifts around to the west before sundown, we can figure the storm is over."

"It's still going to be awfully muddy for a few days."

"Yep, but the westerlies will dry the grass on the rises in no time, and I've a waterproof groundcloth. I'm used to living with the country as I find it."

"In other words, you're anxious to be moving on."

He smiled wistfully and replied, "I wouldn't say I was all that anxious. I just have a tumbleweed job."

She laughed. "I remember. You're the Prince of Wales, traveling incognito."

Then she stared across at him to add, "Do you realize I'll never know who you were, or where you've ridden off to? An hour after I watch you ride over the horizon, it will be like you were never here."

He didn't answer.

She lowered her eyes to her work-worn hands on the table between them, and said, "I don't think I'm going to tell Tom about you or the Duncan boys when he gets home. It would only worry him, and it's not as if there's anything he needs to know. I think I'll just pretend I was out here alone while they doctored him. In a day or so I'll probably think it was all a dream, anyway."

Longarm blew another smoke ring as he decided not to argue with a lady. He knew she'd tell her husband everything. Old Tom wasn't going to think the brownies had done his chores and left fifty dollars as a gift from Fairyland. Besides that, he'd met few women who could resist telling a man more than he really wanted to hear. Considering how gals fought to save themselves from shame and degradation, they sure spent a lot of time talking about any men who drifted their way. He'd had gals who wouldn't kiss him spilling all sorts of secrets he'd never asked a word about. His eyes must have twinkled as he thought back to that redhead on the train who'd apparently been used and abused by every white man west of the Mississippi before they met up, and he was still sort of wondering what she'd thought was wrong with *him*.

Martha caught the look in his eyes, but got it wrong, as she blushed and said, "You see right through me, don't you?"

He shook his head and lied, "Nothing to see worth a blush, ma'am. We ain't done or said a thing your man or friends could fault us for."

She reached over to lay her fingers on the back of his free hand as she asked, "How could they? I mean, nobody will ever know you were here!"

He said, "We'd know it. That's the trouble with secrets. At least two people share most secrets worth having second thoughts about. What we keep inside our heads is easier to live with. Sometimes I get notions I ought to be horsewhipped for thinking of. But I've never had much trouble living down the terrible sins of my imagination."

"Custis, I've never had the chance to do anything *worth* having to live down."

"I figured as much. If you quit while you're still ahead . . ."

"Damn it! What's the matter with you? Don't you think I'm pretty?"

He snubbed out his smoke, took her hand in both of his, and stared soberly into her eyes as he replied, "You're one of the most beautiful gals I've ever met, but you're married and—"

"Custis, Tom and I—" she started.

"Hush, I ain't finished. I was about to say you're

156

also a lady I respect and admire. Right now, you're sort of caught in a web of fairy dreams left over from your girlhood. You've been saved from the ogres by, well, a passing Prince Charming. You're trying to make the story come out right with a fairy-tale ending, and I'm tempted as hell to play out my part, like a fairy-tale hero."

She laughed and said, "All right, what if I am? Hasn't every girl the right to be the princess saved from the ogres, at least once in her life?"

"It don't work that way, Martha. In the stories, they ride off to a castle in the clouds and live happily ever after. In the cold gray light of the grown-up world, folks wind up feeling soiled and foolish."

She tossed her head defiantly and said, "I guess I know a thing or two about my own feelings. I'm not a teenaged virgin, damn it!"

He got to his feet, saying, "You're a respectable married lady, Martha. If I didn't know that better than you, we wouldn't be having this dumb conversation without clothes on. I'm going out to air my saddle and such in the afternoon sun. We've both got some thinking to do, and jawing just confuses a subject after you've circled it more than once."

As he turned away and stepped outside, she called after him, "I think I hate you!"

He didn't answer. He was probably going to hate himself too, some night alone and wondering. He went to the barn and led Snowball out to sun himself, as the warm breeze from the south stirred the wet grass and rippled the puddles in the mud. He left the big white gelding in the corral and hauled out his saddle, possibles, and damp clothes from the musty barn. He spread his things to dry on the corral posts, and saw that there was already enough reasonably dry dirt between the puddles to take off the borrowed gum boots and hang them with the straw hat where he'd found them.

He perched on the corral gate in his pants and

undershirt, letting the sun soak the dampness from his bones as he cleaned and oiled his guns. He did this more to kill time than because he'd let rust get a head start on him. It was his habit to keep his hardwear covered with a thin film of oil at all times, in rain or shine.

From time to time, he cast a wary eye along the skyline all around, but though the wind was shifting ever to the west, nobody seemed to be riding out there yet. He saw some calico cows grazing on the next rise over, so the couple's stock had made it through the storm. If Tom meant to come home this afternoon, he'd had time to study on it by now. If nobody came by sundown, they'd hardly risk a treacherous, muddy ride later on. The moon wouldn't rise before ten.

Longarm swore softly and began to put his guns and cleaning kit away. He put on his shirt and vest, arranging the derringer and watch on the chain they shared across his chest. Putting on the shoestring tie would have been silly, so he left it in the pocket of his frock coat.

He spread the groundcloth on the damp grass and put the blankets, slicker, and other possibles in place inside it before he rolled it, lashed it, and tied it across the rear skirts of his saddle. Then he hefted the bridle, climbed over the fence into the corral, and chased Snowball into a corner.

He had his mount saddled and ready, and was putting on his coat and hat when Martha came out to join him, protesting, "It's not three o'clock yet!"

He nodded and said, "I know. That Mountie never came back and the wind is from the west. I doubt if we'll see another drop of rain this side of autumn."

"Won't you even stay for supper?"

"I'd like to. Can't. There'd be no sense riding out after supper with only an hour or two of light left."

She said, "I know. But you're welcome to spend another night."

He didn't answer and she quickly added, "In the barn, if you're afraid of me."

Longarm reached out and took her chin in his hand to raise her face as he said soberly, "I ain't afraid of you, I'm afraid of me."

She closed her eyes and he leaned forward to kiss her gently on the forehead. Then he stepped away, vaulted into the saddle, and was riding away as she stood there, blinking in surprise.

Longarm didn't look back as he and Snowball rode off at a lope. The girl bit her lip as she stood there staring after them, wondering if she should call out to him, and what she could call out, and if it would do any good.

It took a long time for a horse and rider to vanish on the prairie horizon, but Martha stood there watching until the distant dot winked out of sight and, as Longarm had foreseen, reality was riding in from the other side, even before he'd ridden out of her life forever.

Martha turned back to the house with a wistful little sigh, but by the time she'd reached her door, she was smiling as she told herself, "Someday, when I tell this story to a granddaughter, she's probably going to think it was more romantic than it was."

And then Martha laughed aloud as she added, "But damn it, I'll never get *anyone* to believe he was actually riding a white horse!"

That first night's camp after the rain was soggy, and he couldn't get any cow chips to burn, so he turned in with cold pemmican in his gut as well as a cold butt on the damp ground. The sun rose a million years later and got back to work, but the draws were filled with ground fog most of the morning. By the next evening, the west wind had dried the grass, and chips would burn with plenty of paper kindling and some cussing. The next day dawned hot, and by noon the blackflies were eating him and Snowball alive. He tried to trend away from the river to avoid the bugs hatched by the rain, but, off the trail, wet sloughs and tamarack swamps popped up in the damnedest places, and the blackflies followed anyway. There was nothing to do but smoke furiously under the kerchief he'd draped over his hatbrim, and bull on through to La Coteau.

It was midafternoon when Longarm heard gunshots off to his right. A mess of gunshots. He'd been in enough firefights to know it wasn't anyone hunting. A carbine was having a serious discussion with at least four sixguns, and that occasional, deeper roar could only be a ten-gauge scattergun.

Longarm heeled Snowball through a muddy draw and up the next rise to just below the skyline before he reined in. He slipped his Winchester from its boot and tethered Snowball to a clump of burdock before legging it up the rest of the way for a look-see.

He crawled the last few yards, and as he cautiously peered over into the next draw, he saw a miniature Little Big Horn, with the Mountie he'd met at Martha's playing the Seventh Cav, solo.

The Mountie's horse was down and dead, with the Mountie crouching behind it and not in much better shape. The wounded man in the scarlet tunic was trying to hold off a widely scattered band of Indians, dancing just out beyond point-blank range. Longarm could see four other ponies and a couple of Indians stretched out on the grass between the Mountie and his attackers. It seemed likely that that was what they were yelling about.

The Mountie wouldn't have held out this long against a war band that knew what they were doing. But the Indians looked young and they were wasting a lot of taunts and ammunition trying to scare the white man to death instead of working around to take him from the flanks and rear. Longarm saw a couple of tipis and some horses being held a quarter-mile up the draw. It looked like the Mountie had ridden in

160

openly, and been dismounted by a fusillade before he could get around to telling them about Queen Victoria's views on raiding.

Longarm sighed and muttered, "This is sort of dumb, considering I ain't supposed to be here, but what the hell."

Then he stood up and headed down the slope, calling out, "Hold your fire, Mountie! I'm with you!"

The wounded Mountie looked back over his shoulder, nodded, and went back to sniping over the flank of his dead horse. The sight of a second white man with a rifle didn't spook the Chippewa as much as Longarm had hoped it might. One of them yelled something awful and danced nearer, shaking his sixgun like a fist.

He wasn't close enough for Longarm's Winchester, but he'd wandered unwisely into the Mountie's range. The wounded Canadian's carbine cracked, and the Indian staggered with a surprised look on his face before he keeled over and stayed put. Longarm knew he was dead. Men didn't fall that limply, even unconscious, with a spark of life left in them.

He ran over to the Mountie and flopped down behind the horse at his side, saying, "Nice shooting. How bad are you hit?"

"Thigh, hip, right side, just under the ribs. I don't think they hulled any vital organs, but my vision's not what it used to be. What time is it?"

"About two-thirty or three. We've got plenty of daylight left. Does anybody know you're here?"

"No, and it looks like evening. Aren't you Tom Wilson? I talked to you the other day, right?"

"We'll get to the introductions after we see if we get to keep our hair. How many would you say are in this band? I can see they have some reserves up behind them tipis."

The Mountie grimaced and replied, "I think I took care of the really dangerous ones before you got here.

161

What's left seems unwilling to charge. If only I can keep my damned eyesight a bit longer . . ."

Longarm said, "Put your head down and let some blood flow to your brain. I've got them covered for now. I can see you've done your serious bleeding, if you'll try not to move too much."

The Mountie shook his head and said, "They're *mine*! They fired on Her Majesty's uniform in cold blood, and I don't mean to let them get away with it. I was riding in with my free hand raised in greeting and my guns in their holsters, when—"

"Try not to ge excited. I can see what happened. We're forted up pretty good, and it's a bitch to circle *two* men. I figure they'll ride off after some more hollering about our mothers. If they'd started losing interest in one shot-up white, before I got here . . ."

"Damn it, Wilson, that's not the point! They still have the squaw and ponies they stole!"

Longarm soothed, "Easy, old son. Let's eat this here apple a bite at a time. The first thing we have to do is get you to a doc. You've sobered the shit out of them, and the other Mounties can deal with what's left after we drive them off."

The Mountie tried to sit up, gasped in pain, and insisted, "No, God damn it! That's not the way we do it in the Northwest Mounted Police! Those sons of bitches resisted *my* arrest, and it's my job to finish the job or die trying."

Longarm saw a Chippewa getting within sassing range and fired, bouncing a keyholing slug off the ground to civilize him in the left shin. As the screaming youth limped off, leaving his gun behind, Longarm told the Mountie, "I can see you're trying to die just fine, but I'm going to have to overrule you. I've got a horse on the other side of that rise. If I cover you, do you reckon you could crawl that far?"

"Not without the kidnapped girl. She's up in those tents."

Longarm muttered, "Aw, shit." Then he saw that

another Indian was making a rush for the gun his comrade had dropped. They were kids, all right. The poor little rascal was filled with tales of the Shining Times and wanted to show everyone he was a true brave.

Longarm braced his muzzle, judged the windage, and waited until the Chippewa dropped to one knee to grab the gun in the grass before he fired. The would-be coup-counter died with everyone in agreement as to bravery and damn-foolishness. As the boy fell on his side, Longarm swallowed the green taste in his mouth and muttered, "Old men who fill kid's heads with bullshit should be horsewhipped."

"Did you get another?" asked the Mountie, weakly.

Longarm said, "Yeah. Hang on, I suspect his pals are a mite riled at me about it!"

The ragged line of Chippewa were advancing, shooting wildly, and this time they didn't stop at taunting range. Longarm nodded and said, "This one's for keeps."

Then he was too busy to give the wounded Mountie a running description of the skirmish. He fired, levered another round as his target dropped, and got another. As he swung his muzzle on the nearest target, another creased his Stetson with a lucky shot from his flank. Longarm jackknifed the one he was aiming at, swung the muzzle, and blew the face off a wildly screaming youth coming in at a dead run. They were all well inside his Winchester's killing range now, and charging in a wide arc. Longarm snarled, "So be it!" and rose to his feet, pumping a fan of lead from side to side as he fired from the hip.

The survivors wavered and began falling back, but Longarm jumped over the dead horse to chase them up the draw. He nailed one through the spine and hit another in the back of the neck before the remaining three or four were out of range and moving like they'd just met up with the devil and hadn't liked it much.

Longarm saw that he had them on the run, and he

aimed to keep it that way as he followed as far as the tipis. The ragtag remnants of the band were mounted and riding off by the time he got to the tents.

He stopped to thumb more ammunition into his Winchester before he used the muzzle to poke open a tipi flap. There was nothing interesting inside. The second tent held a naked girl, bound hand and foot with rawhide thongs, and lying on her side on a blanket.

He ducked in and said, "Howdy," as he fished out his knife to cut her loose. She was as copper-colored as a new penny, but had the features of an Irish colleen tucked between her raven's-wings of smoky black hair. She watched him soberly as he cut her free, and snatched for a tattered cotton skirt nearby to cover her nakedness before she sat up and said, "I am grateful, but Turtle Claw will kill you for this."

He stood up and offered her a free hand to join him on her own feet as he replied, "I think I just ran Turtle Claw and his sidekicks to Montreal or maybe Nova Scotia, but I'm sure glad you speak English. I don't know enough Cree to mention."

The girl got up, holding the tattered cloth to her breasts as she exclaimed, "I am not Cree. I am Chippewa. My name is Dancing Eyes, and when they told me I had to marry Turtle Claw, I ran away to be with my sister, who'd married a Cree."

Longarm said, "Come on. There's a Mountie down the draw who'll be interested in your family troubles. I might have known it was a domestic situation. More damned lawmen have gotten killed getting between fighting in-laws."

"Are you not a Mountie? Why did you come to take me from the young men that Turtle Claw sent after me, if you are not a Mountie?"

He answered, "Because I'm a born fool. Come on, let's let Queen Victoria sort things out. I've got other fish to fry."

As he led her down the draw, Dancing Eyes asked, "Why are you angry with me? It wasn't my fault the

164

old man refused to take no for an answer. Did my sister's Cree husband tell the white men that the young men from my village came to take me back?"

"I reckon he was sore because they stole his ponies, too. I ain't mad at you, honey, I'm mad at me. I don't know what else I could have done, but I never came up here to mix in Indian troubles, and it's sort of tedious to keep getting sidetracked."

As they joined the wounded Mountie and the dead horse, the girl said, "I think he is dead." But Longarm knelt to feel the unconscious man's carotid artery and shook his head, saying, "Just weak from loss of blood. Do you know where the nearest settlement is?"

She shook her head and said, "No. We were riding east, avoiding the whites. They had me tied on a travois, most of the way."

He said, "Well, we've got one horse, if Snowball hasn't run off. You stay here and watch the Mountie while I fetch the brute."

"What if the others come back?"

"Pick up that carbine and do the best you can. I don't expect they will. I'd like to stay and jaw some more about it, but we've got to get this old boy across a bronc and to a doc before he gets done bleeding to death."

Chapter 10

There wasn't a doctor within forty miles, but they found a Métis settlement just two bends down the river, and one of the ex-trappers said he knew a little about gunshot wounds, so what the hell.

Considering past differences with Her Majesty, the half-breeds were gentle as they carried the unconscious Mountie inside and stripped him down for rough surgery.

The young Canadian had been right about where they'd hit him, and the Métis trapper decided not to dig for the slug in his side. He bandaged the Mountie tight and said he was still carrying a couple of bullets in his own hide that only bothered him in damp weather.

One of the Métis women gave Dancing Eyes a freshly laundered cotton frock and some moccasins. The woman seemed insulted when Longarm offered her a half-crown. She sniffed indignantly and said, "*Mais non, m'sieu.* We are Christians."

Longarm tipped his hat gravely and said he understood. It was funny how poor folks seemed to remember things like that more than fancier folks he knew of who drove up to a handsome church in a coach-and-four. It seemed likely that was the reason so many better but less fancy churchgoers stayed poor. The villagers wouldn't even let him pay for the meal they served him and the Indian gal. But he did manage a fair swap when it came to horses. Horse-trading and Christianity had nothing in common, anywhere.

He exchanged the handsome Snowball for a pair of runty but tough-looking Indian ponies. This was partly to help Dancing Eyes get wherever, and partly to throw off any description of a strange rider on a big white gelding. The time to change mounts was before you knew you had to.

The Mountie never recovered consciousness during any of this, and, since there was still some daylight left, Longarm decided it would be a good idea for him not to be around when the Mountie sat up to ask foolish questions.

Knowing the man he'd saved was in good hands, he forked one of the runty pintos and headed east. He was sort of surprised when Dancing Eyes seemed to be tagging along. He waited until they were clear of the village before he said, "If you're still trying to run away from your Chippewa boyfriend, you're headed the wrong way."

The girl said, "Turtle Claw is not my boyfriend. I have never let him touch me. He is old and fat and smells of firewater."

"Yeah, but the Chippewa still live east of here, and, as you might have noticed, that's the way I'm riding."

"You said you wanted to go to Moose Jaw. I have a cousin who lives on another reservation over that way. If those young men who kidnapped me don't kill us, I will be safe from Turtle Claw there."

"Do you know the way from La Coteau to Moose Jaw?"

"Of course. Those young men will expect us to ride northeast for La Coteau. If we cut due east from here, we may get through. It's very treacherous country in spots, and they think I'm only a woman."

He laughed and said, "I wonder where they got that notion. It's none of my business, but I did find you sort of beat up and naked, and I was sort of wondering . . . Never mind."

She shook her head and said, "They were not sent

to rape me. Turtle Claw would kill any man who touched me before he did."

"I begin to follow your drift. What is Turtle Claw, a big muckety-muck? I thought Queen Victoria discouraged Home Rule among Irish, Hindoos, Chippewa, and such."

Dancing Eyes laughed and said, "Turtle Claw is not a chief, as you people mean it. He is a medicine man—much more feared than any treaty chief would be. I think he gave those young men something to make them leave me alone and act crazy in other ways. I tried to get them to let me go by offering to be nice to them. But they yelled and hit me. They kept drinking something from a bottle, but it didn't smell like trade liquor."

He nodded and said, "Yep, it all falls into place, and that Mountie was lucky as hell. You must not be exactly dead set on sleeping with Turtle Claw if you were willing to—whatever—to get out of it."

She shuddered and said, "I'd make love to a sick dog first. It's not just that he's old and ugly. He's evil and . . . he's my uncle."

Longarm whistled softly and said, "That would put most gals off their feed, wouldn't it? I thought every tribe except maybe the Crow considered incest a mite less respectable than cannibalism. You say the old man's a religious leader?"

She grimaced and said, "He's a devil. Everyone knows it's wrong to even flirt with a boy who shares the same totem. I was once in love with a beautiful boy from another village, and he loved me, I knew it. But we were both turtles. The Great Spirit would have cursed us with bad hunting and two-headed babies for four generations!"

Longarm nodded understandingly. He was modest about his Indian lore, but he knew that Indians were more moral, in some ways, than the whites who often snickered at them. He knew some considered it only right and fitting to share a wife with a friend, and what many a white man had considered prostitution was an Indian's notion of fair service for some needed grub, or even firewater. On the other hand, no Indian he knew of would fool with another man's wife and daughter and brag of it at his club. They weren't as proddy about virginity as whites were, but the rules they followed were just as meaningful to them, and they carried the notion of incest past common sense. A white man could marry a cousin, while most tribes forbade any possible relationship between such a couple. An Indian who'd loan you a squaw for a bottle of redeye would throw up if he found he'd kissed a lady who's great-great-grandmother had belonged to the same lodge as his own great-aunt's cousin twice removed. He wondered if there were any folks, anywhere, who lived with *no* rules. He'd heard the Sandwich Islanders ran around naked, screwing and eating one another all the time, but he'd read where they made up for it by having all sorts of foods they *couldn't* eat, and places on their dinky islands where they were forbidden to set foot. Sometimes it seemed as though the human critter needed Sin, even if he had to study hard to find it.

He decided he hadn't ridden all the way to Canada to jaw about social customs, so he asked the Chippewa girl, "What's the story on this shortcut to Moose Jaw? The Métis tell me you have to follow the river as far as La Coteau before you cut away from it."

She said, "They travel by cart, like other whites. There are many streams to ford, many swamps. Although lately, settlers have begun to drain some of them. On a pony, you can get through, if you know the way. Do you want me to show you the old buffalo trail I traveled as a child?"

"Just hold on; I'm thinking. I'm trailing some other whites. They ain't Indians, so they'll likely follow the regular trail, and they're God knows how far ahead of me. How many days' travel would we save by taking your shortcut?"

169

"Oh, almost one of your weeks."

"I'm starting to like it better already. Do the Mounties patrol the old buffalo trails?"

"Of course not. Why would they want to? The buffalo are no longer hunted in these parts, and no whites travel that way. I doubt that we'd meet anyone a day's ride this side of Moose Jaw."

He fished out a cheroot, lit up, and mused, "Hmm, if I could be waiting when Canada Jack gets in from riding all over Robin Hood's barn . . ."

"Can I have a smoke?" she cut in, adding, "It's not polite to smoke in front of people unless you have enough to share."

He said, "I'm sorry, I disremembered my manners. Most of the ladies I know don't smoke cigars."

He reined in and handed her a cheroot. She steadied his hand with her own as he lit it for her. She took a deep drag and said, "Oh, that is very nice tobacco. I suppose most of the women you've made love to have been white, eh?"

He heeled his pony forward before he answered, "It sort of works out that way, if you spend most of your time with your own kind."

She took a drag and observed, "I've never made love to a white man. What's it like?"

He laughed and said, "I'm damned if I know. That's one experience I've never been curious enough to try."

She frowned, then smiled as she followed his meaning, and said, "I meant what's it like to sleep with a white person? I've heard some very odd things about white women."

He shrugged and said, "Funny, they've told me some whoppers about Chinese girls, but I never noticed anything that different when— Uh, never mind."

"Oh? You've been with a Chinese woman? How about Indians?"

He said, "Like I said, there ain't that much difference. I mean, there's differences among women, praise the Lord, but you can't say one *breed* of gal is better than another. That'd be as dumb as saying all Texans were brave, or all Mexicans were afraid of them. I reckon folks are folks. Some good, some bad, and most of us sort of in the middle."

She said, "I heard white girls hated men and put sand inside themselves to discourage them."

"That'd sure discourage *me*, but the last time I heard that tale, it was Navajo gals who did it."

He took a thoughtful drag and said, "Let's talk about something else, for Pete's sake. It's broad daylight, and this fool saddle ain't comfortable when a man gets to dwelling on such subjects."

"Can we talk about it when we make camp, then? I know you think I'm forward, but I'm only trying to learn. I haven't had a chance to talk about lovemaking with many white men. The missionaries on our reservation are Jesuits, and they seem to have hell confused with the subject."

He nodded and said, "You take the point, and try not to steer me into a swamp right off. We'll discuss the differences between red and white gals tonight, if you've a mind to."

Then, as she trotted around him to lead, he shot an appraising glance at her bouncing rump and added, half to himself, "I sort of misdoubt there's a hell of a lot I can teach you, though."

She grinned back archly over her shoulder and asked, "Will you tell me to go to hell if I ask too many questions?"

He shifted his weight in the McClellan and muttered, "Not hardly. I figure them poor priests have prayed over you about as much as is likely to do any good."

Dancing Eyes made love like they were both slated to be shot at dawn and one night was all they were ever going to get. There'd been no sense in shilly-shallying around as they made camp at sunset. The pretty little squaw had been teasing him for hours with her saucy remarks and rollicking rump. So when

171

she started to strip as he rolled out the blankets, Longarm just shucked off his duds to take his comeuppance like a man.

She was made out of some copper-colored substance too soft and smooth to call muscle and too firm to call anything else. Her breasts were as firm as most men's biceps, and when he first took her in his arms to kiss her, she rolled him on his back and got on top, saying, "That hair on your face tickles, and there's no need for all that silly hugging and kissing."

She forked her thighs across him, reached down between them to guide him into her and gasped, as she settled down, "Oh, there *is* a difference!"

Then she started pounding like a tom-tom, eyes wild and teeth bared like a she-cougar in heat. He tried to help her, but she didn't need it. She moved her hips faster than a high-school boy could have moved his own fist, and he came almost before he had time to get used to the idea. If she noticed, she didn't change the rhythm. She was panting and starting to sweat, and he wondered how anything human could keep going like that. He was about to caution her to slow down and make it last when she gasped, *"Heyanahena!"* and started moving even faster.

This time they got there together. Dancing Eyes stopped, shuddered as if she were being electrocuted, and suddenly collapsed on him, gasping for breath. He ran a hand up her spine, murmured something nice, and wondered, when she didn't answer, if she'd fainted.

Then she opened her eyes, brushing the lashes against his throat, and giggled. She said, "I thought I'd killed myself."

He laughed and answered, "You damn near killed us both."

She rubbed her nose against his chin and said, "I haven't made love for many moons, and you have a very exciting body. I'm still twitching."

"I noticed. Would you like to try it with me on top?"

"Not just yet. I told you I was curious about the

things the priests said were mortal sins. I'd like to experiment with other things I heard some white women liked."

He frowned but said, "Well, there's such a thing as common courtesy, and I'm game if you are."

She giggled in delight and said, "Good. I want to try kissing."

"Uh, you mean on the mouth?"

"Of course, where else would you want to kiss me?"

He laughed and took her buttocks in his cupped hands to pull her up so they were face to face. He kissed her, felt her responding like a little girl, despite the way she moved the other end, and said, "Pucker up and close your eyes, honey."

She made a little rosebud mouth and he kissed her again, feeling her insides contract as he put the tip of his tongue between her tightly pursed lips. She felt her own responses too, and began to gyrate her hips teasingly as she purred, "Oh, that is nice. Put it in deeper. Your tongue, I mean."

He knew what she meant. There wasn't anything else he could get much further inside her, at the moment. Dancing Eyes began to suck his tongue as she started moving faster, and he spoke into her open lips as he said, "Slow down. Let's make it last, this time."

He saw that, whatever her spirit might be willing to try, her flesh wasn't about to slow down or skip a beat, so he rolled her over on her back and took charge. As he started moving his own way, she gasped, "How did you do that without taking it out?" and he said, "Don't be so damned technical. This ain't supposed to be an acrobatic lesson."

"But I like to be in charge."

"I noticed. If you want to find out what it's like to do it like a white gal, the first thing you have to learn is that we do it this way, most of the time."

She moved her legs out to get some purchase on the firm ground with her bare feet, thrust herself coyly up to meet him, and asked, "Is it all right if I do this? It feels silly to just lie here."

He kissed her ear and murmured, "Now, *that* is what I had in mind."

"Do I do it as good as a white girl?"

"Honey, you do it better than most Indians, and I'll throw in the Fiji Islanders as an educated guess. Lesson number two is to shut your pretty little mouth and just float with me to the stars."

"It doesn't seem to be slowing you down. Don't white people talk while they make love?"

He sighed and said, "Too much, sometimes. Just hush and let yourself go."

They started kissing again as she learned to respond his way, and when she wanted deeper penetration, she signaled, silently, by digging her nails into his buttocks and arching her pelvis. He decided this time he had it perfect, and wondered why a feeling so good had to end. But, of course, it had to if there was to be any point to moving at all, and moving was what Dancing Eyes was good at.

As he came up for air, Longarm said, "Thank you, Lord. That was considerate as hell of you and all the angels."

Dancing Eyes started to cry. He held her gently for a while before he asked her why. She said, "Someday we are going to get old and die. Have you ever thought of that?"

He frowned and answered, "Sure, but it ain't my favorite topic of conversation. What in thunder made you think of it at a time like this?"

"It bothers me most when I am enjoying life. Just now, I asked the Great Spirit why the good things last such a short time and the bad things take so long."

He chuckled and agreed, "Yep, it's an hour for lunch and six hours between. But maybe pleasures wouldn't mean as much if we knew they'd never end."

He started to roll off for a smoke, but she gripped him passionately with her firm thighs and insisted,

"I never want to stop. I don't think it would be possible to get tired of this if only we were strong enough to do it and do it forever."

He moved experimentally, not wanting to be impolite to a lady, and decided his back wasn't broken after all. Thrusting slowly, he said, "I reckon I'm good for one more, but we've got to study on getting some sleep before sunup. We've got a long day ahead of us in the saddle and, well, this ain't delicate, but it's uncomfortable as hell to ride with tender privates."

She sort of growled deep in her throat and said, "I want you to raise blisters between my thighs! I'm so glad those young men sent by Turtle Claw didn't do this with me. Isn't it lucky I was able to save all this for you?"

He laughed as he started moving faster. Then, as she responded in kind, he said impishly, "Oh, I don't know. Had those poor braves been less polite, me and the Mountie might not have had to fight them. You'd have likely crippled the whole bunch by the time we came along."

The Indian cutoff to Moose Jaw was deceptive. After all he'd heard about the country being impassable, Longarm was surprised, at first, by how open and gentle the rolling prairie seemed. On the first day's ride into the uncharted hunting grounds, they crossed wagon traces and spotted settler's windmills here and there. There were hundreds of pathways southeast from the Saskatchewan, but none of them really went anywhere. Each rutted road ended at some cattle spread or an abandoned trapper's cabin by some placid prairie lake. Dancing Eyes explained that once upon a time, the fox and beaver had extended far out across the prairie in the connected web of pond, swamp, or timbered draw between the wider expanses of buffalo grass. The cutoff lay in a never-never land between horse and canoe country. Farther west it was mostly high and dry and, in the Shining Times, the Cree and other Horse Indians had lived "fat cow" on the "Sea of Grass." Farther east, it was the country of the first *voyageurs* and their Canoe Indian comrades, who could paddle endlessly from one lake to another if they portaged over a watershed divide here and there. But these central prairies were neither fish nor fowl. The waterways were too far apart to pack a birchbark canoe. The saddle trails kept ending in low ground too soft to ride across and too dry to use a raft or boat. The trick of getting through was to wander as the hunted-out buffalo had, not trying to head anywhere in a straight line, but simply following the grass that grew on dry land. Longarm was sure, as he watched the sun, that the little Chippewa was lost. But she kept telling him she knew the way, so he followed her pony's rump in what he was sure more than once were complete circles. It would have been all right if he hadn't been in a hurry. He'd come West after the War, when the Shining Times were a rapidly fading memory, but this uninhabited stretch of prairie hinted at what it must have been like to the Indians and first explorers west of the long trench occupied by the Mississippi, the Red River, and Lake Winnipeg.

It wasn't virgin prairie now. Old campsites, and an occasional spent rifle shell, turning greener than the grass it lay in, told of whites who'd passed this way before him. Once, as they topped a rise, Dancing Eyes got off her pony to rummage in a clump of Russian thistle, and, as he reined in beside her, he saw she was crying again.

The Chippewa girl lifted a sun-bleached buffalo skull from where it had been nesting among the alien weeds from some white wheat farmer's spread, and held it up to the sun, as if she were offering it to the sky.

She said, "It's not considerate to leave Brother Buffalo with his eyes facedown in the dirt. Some white hunter must have killed this one. No Indian would have been so inconsiderate."

Longarm looked around at the empty horizon and said, "Yep, the hide hunters had fat cow, while it lasted. But they sort of overdid it. What are you aiming to do with that skull, honey?"

She walked to the highest part of the rise and placed the skull gently on the grass with its hollow eyes raised to the sun. She said, "I am letting its spirit out. The Jesuits say animals don't go to the sky when they are dead, but they say a lot of foolish things. I think, somewhere, the buffalo still gather in the spring to be hunted by the grandfathers who've gone ahead of us."

He said, "That sounds as reasonable as squatting on some cloud with a harp, but I'm sort of anxious to get to Moose Jaw. So if you've made that critter comfortable, what do you say we move on?"

She nodded and mounted her own pony, saying, "We must ride to the south for a time, now."

He stared the way they'd been headed, saw nothing to the east but grass, and asked, "How come? I don't see a pond or swamp within a good three miles."

She explained, "We could ride more than ten miles that way, but it's a trap. There's a long finger lake full of tamarack beyond the meeting of land and sky. This ridge leads around it in a big horseshoe, if one has patience."

"What about that rise ahead of us? It looks like it trends the same way, and a small circle is less than a big one, ain't it?"

She said, "No. This ridge runs in a smoother curve. As you get closer to the swampy ground they lie around, the ridges wrinkle. The path along each one winds more and more, with gullies breaking the crests in places. I *told* you I followed the herds here as a child."

He nodded and said, "Lead on, then. I sure hope you remember your childhood, though. How long has it been since you were hunting buffalo, kitten?"

She thought and said, "Ten summers, maybe. You

won't believe this, but once these hills were brown with buffalo as far as one could see."

He said, "I believe you. By the time I came west after the War, the south herd had been pretty well shot off, but I remember the north herd. It lasted until just a year or so ago, in places. It's sort of spooky when you study on it. I'm well on the comfortable side of forty, and I already feel like an oldtimer. I get to talking with a greenhorn in a saloon, and if I mention something I saw more than a year or so ago, he looks at me like I'm an ancient Roman."

She said, "I know. I am only twenty-four, and my world has changed so much I have trouble making children believe my stories. Just before I was kidnapped, I was telling my sister's children how I used to help my mother skin out buffalo until my hands were raw, and they looked at me like I was a grandmother. When I said I remembered when there were no Mounties, they whispered to their mother that I was very ignorant. My sister's children are Christians, and they've forgotten the name of the Great Spirit. This makes me very sad."

He didn't want her to start crying again, so he said, "Well, I know plenty of Indians who still keep to the old ways. Besides, I thought you said you were a Christian. Didn't you learn English from the Jesuits?"

She nodded, but said, "My father was wise. Before he died, he said we had to take what was good from the white man and keep what was good from our grandfathers. I think reading and writing is good to know. I would like to have a sewing machine, if I ever get married. But I don't like all this talk of hell and sin, and your idea of working six days a week, whether there's anything important to do or not, seems very silly."

He laughed and said, "I reckon I must have an Indian grandfather I don't know about. I sure go along with you on working from dawn to dusk, if it can be avoided."

She peeled off her cotton shift and adjusted it under her bottom as a saddle cover before she asked, stark naked, "I've been meaning to ask you about that. You say you are not a Mountie, yet you keep talking about someone you are hunting. What sort of a white man's job *do* you have?"

He said, "Calling me a hunter is close enough. How come you just took off all your duds? It's a mite after high noon, and you're naked as a jaybird."

She shrugged and said, "It's getting hot. Why should I wear that Métis woman's dress when I don't want to? Don't you like to look at me this way?"

He grinned and said, "It's interesting as hell. I just ain't used to ladies riding about in broad daylight in their birthday suits, I reckon."

She glanced back over her shoulder and said mischievously, "Why don't you take off all that stuffy wool they make you wear? I've never understood why you people think it's so important to cover yourselves so. When I was young, I thought white people must be hiding something hideous, but now I know some of you have nice bodies. You make love as much as we do. What on earth are you trying to hide?"

He laughed and said, "Damned if I know. Maybe folks just get used to the way they were brought up. I know some Indian tribes who dress up more than most whites. Others run around bareassed in the winter."

"They are both being silly," Dancing Eyes opined firmly. "It is just as silly to wear no clothes when it's cold as it is to be all wrapped up in wool on a hot day like this one. I think you would be more comfortable if you rode my way."

He gazed at the way her copper-penny spine swayed in time with her pony's gait, and muttered, "Not hardly. I've a strong suspicion we'd have to stop and spread the blankets on the grass if I was to shuck these tight britches."

She swung her left leg around to face him, and rode

179

backwards as she smiled invitingly and said, "That's a good idea. Why don't we stop for a while?"

He lowered his eyes from her sunlit breasts, but saw that his eyes were getting him in even more trouble, and settled them on her pretty face as he said, "I'd like to, but there's only so many hours to a day, and we've a lot of ground to cover before we make camp for the night. You're making this trip pleasant as hell, but we'd better save the loving for the hours we can't ride."

She complained, "It will be hours before the sun goes down. Would you be willing, if we didn't have to stop and dismount?"

He said, "Sure, but we ain't traveling by steamboat or rail. If I had you in a stateroom or a train compartment, there'd be no nicer way to let the miles slip by."

She giggled and said, "You could undress without dismounting, if you really wanted to."

He smiled back and said, "Sure, but that would still leave you on that pony and me on this, and—" His smile turned to a look of puzzlement. "Are you serious?"

"Why not?" she asked roguishly, adding, "Your pony looks strong enough to carry two of us."

Longarm glanced uncertainly around the skyline. They were absolutely alone on the vast expanse of buffalo grass, and her suggestion had him breathing sort of heavy, so what the hell.

Feeling like an idiot, he started taking things off and lashing them to his saddle. Getting out of the pants without dismounting took some doing, but she reined in beside him to help by steadying his mount as he stood in one stirrup. She took his boots and lashed them to her own saddle swells before, still holding her own pony's reins, she transferred to his saddle, facing him.

He held her waist steady with his rein arm as she wriggled into place with a thigh over each of his hips

180

and her spine braced on the hornless swells of his McClellan.

He said, "It's no use, it's too tight a fit."

And then he gasped, as she moistly made a liar of him.

He tensed his bare buttocks on the saddle leather to thrust, but there was almost no play between them and she said, "Let the pony do it for us."

He relaxed as he felt what she meant. The saddle of a walking horse moves in a circle, in a series of gentle jerks. With the girl's weight balanced on his hipbones and braced by the saddle swell against her tailbone, the results were interesting, but sort of teasing. He couldn't get in all the way, and the motion wasn't fast enough. He said, "Hang on," and as she wrapped her arms around him tightly, he kissed her and slammed his bare heels against the pony's flanks.

The pony started trotting, with the other trailing on the lead in the girl's clenched fist. Hoping the brutes would have sense enough to follow the path along the crest of the swell, they abandoned themselves to the thrills of the wild ride. The motion was that of passionate lovers, seasoned with occasional unexpected bounces and a complete lack of effort. Dancing Eyes laughed wildly and gasped, "Faster, faster, make it lope!"

He followed her suggestion, yelling, "Powder River and let her buck!" It was interesting as hell, at a full gallop.

As Dancing Eyes felt what was happening, she pleaded, "Don't stop! I want to ride like this forever!"

But the pony had less energy than she did, and dropped down to a jogging trot, which aroused him all over by the change in rhythm. He sensed that they were on the side of the rise now, going who-knows-where, and what did it matter?

The pony jogged downhill, the new angle of the saddle offering new opportunities as he suddenly found himself hitting bottom with every bounce. There was the sound of splashing, and he glanced over the girl's brown shoulder to see that they'd ridden into a water-filled slough, but that was the pony's problem, for he was otherwise occupied.

The pony suddenly stopped, and they looked down to see that their mounts were standing knee-deep in water. The one they were on lowered his head to drink, and the unexpected pitch threw Dancing Eyes off balance.

He grabbed to keep her from falling, but she laughed and said, "No, fall with me!"

And so, laughing like a maniac, Longarm followed her off the saddle to splash down between the ponies in the cool, clean prairie pond.

The water cushioned their fall, and they sat up together, laughing like kids in a swimming hole. She splashed water in his face, and he kissed her to make her stop. Then he picked her wet, slippery body up and waded to the marshy edge, where he threw her down and finished having her in the soft mud. They wound up as muddy as a pair of hogs in a wallow, but it was only a matter of rolling back into the pond to wash their bodies clean again. For a time, they lay together in the shallows with her head cradled in the crook of his elbow as he washed wavelets over her gleaming brown flesh with his free hand. She looked up at him, her eyes filled with wonder in the sunlight, as she murmured, "Oh, this is terrible. I think I'm falling in love with you."

He didn't answer. He couldn't think of a thing to say that wouldn't get him in a whole lot of trouble. She studied his face dreamily for a small eternity, and then she said, "I know. It wouldn't work. I could never bring you home to my people, and your people would make me dress silly and go to church on Sunday."

He said, "I know. There's a mess of white gals it wouldn't work with, either. If I didn't have a job that made a permanent gal sort of complicated, I reckon you could pass for white enough in a Chicago-made Dolly Varden and maybe some shoes. Has anybody ever told you that you look sort of Irish?"

She smiled and said, "One of my grandfathers was an Irishman. He worked for the Hudson Bay Company in the Shining Times. The Sioux got him on the Saint Croix before I was born."

"Then you're a breed, like the Métis."

"No, I'm a Chippewa, just as the Métis are white, but don't know it. This business of grandfathers is a white man's idea. People are what they were raised to be. The Métis were raised to live as French Catholics, Just as I was raised to live and think as an Indian."

She snuggled closer as she added, "You would make a fine Indian. You know how to live."

He smiled wistfully down at her and said, "I've studied on that, honey. There's a lot to be said for the old free ways of the Shining Times."

"What's stopping you, then? There are still places where one can live as one wishes. Why do you have to go back to the world of laws and stuffy clothing?"

He looked across the rippling water to the ponies standing in the lost pond, and to the open rolling prairie beyond, and then he sighed and said, "I'm spoiled, I reckon. I like too many things that only money can buy."

She asked, "Can't you trade for them, or steal them? That's how *we* used to get tobacco and white flour."

He smiled crookedly and replied, "You just answered your own question. If we were laying here a thousand years ago, and nobody else lived within a thousand miles, we could make it without laws and maybe get by without tailor-made smokes and soap. It might be fun to rustle our own grub and dress up in hides. I'd like to have seen a lot of places before they messed them up with roads, fences, or taxes. It might even have been worth not having a dentist when you had a toothache, or a gun when you met a grizzly. But living off the country only works when the country's damned near empty. Even if the buffalo were still here, it'd take ten or twenty square miles of hunting ground to feed just the two of us. More, if we aimed to live fat cow, with side trips after special things like salt, fire flints, and such."

She said, "I know. You white people came to crowd the land and ruin it by draining the wild-rice beds and cutting down the forests."

He shook his head and said, "I plead not guilty, Your Honor. Columbus only speeded up what was fixing to happen anyway. Sure, you northern tribes were still spread thin, but you were getting bigger with each passing year, and you were fighting over hunting grounds before any of us got here. Further south, there were Indian cities as big as any the white man had at the time. If we hadn't come with our laws and cattle and wheat, the Aztec Empire would have built roads north to bring you *their* laws, along with beans and corn. Empty country draws settlers. And as it's settled, there have to be laws. I ain't sure I like it either, but folks can't live in any numbers if everybody tries to do just what he or she likes."

She moved his free hand down her wet belly and said, "Damn it, they told us all that at the mission school. Next you'll be telling me it's against some law to make love."

He glanced up at the sun and said, "I only hunt folks who break laws meant to protect innocent folks and their property. And speaking of which, we've wasted enough time with this bath. We'd best be on our way."

"Can't we do it one more time?" she pleaded, moving his hand between her wet thighs.

He started to say no. Then he laughed and said, "You're shameless, Dancing Eyes."

She smiled up at him and replied, "I know. Aren't you glad?"

He answered her question with a kiss, and as he remounted her, she said, "I'm getting used to that mustache, and I think I like it. Now that we're both so nice and clean, there's something else I'd like to try."

He said, "Tonight, maybe. Right now I'm in a hurry."

She wrapped her legs around him tightly and sighed, "Oh, yes, I noticed."

Chapter 11

Longarm would never forget the eleven days and nights that followed. He'd traveled with Indians before, though seldom with such pretty ones, so he already knew much that Dancing Eyes might have taught a greener hand about life on the open prairie. But Longarm was not a man to think he had all the answers before he'd heard all the questions, and so he watched and listened as they wended their way east across the old, deserted hunting grounds. Each evening, while there was still enough light, he got out his map and compared its often mistaken bench marks with the real world they'd just ridden over. Moose Jaw lay almost directly east of Medicine Hat as the crow might fly, but they weren't riding crows, and the Chippewa girl led them in some wide detours. Yet he saw that they were covering more mileage every day than he would have if he had followed the safe, proven trail along the winding river. Canada Jack's gang had a good lead on him, but Longarm had a hunch he was closing the gap, and there was a lot to be said for riding with such an acrobatic hunting companion.

The cloudless sky stayed blue, and the prairie firmed under the drying west wind. But the recent rainy spells had made a green garden of the open country they were crossing. They rode out of the stretch she called "the Land of Golden Grass," and through sod-covered sand hills that resembled a giant's golf course, with an occasional house-sized boulder left by the ancient glaciers to furnish golfballs for any passing Titans.

They rode stirrup-deep in wildflowers no one else would ever see, and camped by uncharted streams with musical, lovely old Indian names.

They circled lakes with necklaces of pine and paper-birch, and swam together in prairie ponds no white man knew. Dancing Eyes seemed to have a sixth sense for finding a swimming hole just at the hottest time each afternoon, and Longarm would never know whether she was suffering from the heat or just couldn't go more than twelve hours without making love. He had to admit, each time she suggested a swim, that he sure was feeling sort of sweaty all of a sudden, and the ponies enjoyed the rest in knee-deep water anyway. Since one was a gelding and the mare wasn't in heat, the ponies didn't get to have as much fun in the shallows, but the mare made up a game of her own. She liked to chase water birds for some reason. One time, a thundercloud of sandhill cranes rose loudly, just as Dancing Eyes was climaxing.

He laughed when she opened her eyes in wonder and asked, "My, did *I* do that?"

They made love, dry, in his bedroll every night. Later, sprawled naked on his back, with her head on his shoulder and a cheroot between his teeth, Longarm knew how the Mountain Men had felt about returning to civilization at the season's end. The stars hung lower out here at night, and he could feel the planet turning under him as he blew smoke rings up into the Milky Way. There were more shooting stars than a man could shake a stick at, and he'd given up asking Dancing Eyes to make a wish. The hot-blooded little Chippewa never wished for anything but more loving; sometimes he thought she could live on it alone. The second day out, he shot a pronghorn for them, but, while she cleaned and dressed it better than many a butcher could have, she only ate a sparrow's worth as she watched, naked, for him to finish his own haunch.

As they rode nearer to civilization, the girl's appetite for sex seemed to grow more demanding every night, and she spent more time crying, afterward. Longarm enjoyed the sex, but the crying was getting on his nerves.

He knew he'd done nothing to feel guilty about. Dancing Eyes was neither a virgin nor likely to get in trouble. When he'd gotten around to that cautious question, she'd assured him that Chippewa women seldom had papooses they hadn't planned on having, and he stopped her before she went into the details.

He knew she wasn't going to make foolish demands on his future, and they'd agreed, somewhat wistfully, that he'd drop her off at the reservation east of Moose Jaw before riding in alone. Yet he still felt sort of shitty. He decided it was because she was such a good sport about the whole thing. He was used to gals who wept and tore their hair when a man spoke the hard, cold truth, and he was used to harder-eyed gals who were just as tough about a romp in bed as any man. Dancing Eyes was neither. She was warm and loving and natural, with no false bravado to hide her feelings behind, and no sentimental notions that what folks felt while they were making love had to be engraved on stone for all eternity.

It was easy to say dumb things to a gal when you knew she didn't aim to hold you to them, and it made it nicer when she echoed them back at you with the campfire gleaming in her loving eyes. But they were playing with more than campfire, and he tried to ease off as they got closer to Moose Jaw.

Then, one morning, they topped a rise and Dancing Eyes reined in. He pulled up beside her as she pointed to a speck off to the southeast and said, "That's the windmill of the reservation I told you about. Turtle Claw will never look for me there."

He nodded and said, "I'll ride you over, then." But she looked at him with a puzzled frown and asked, "Why? Moose Jaw is straight ahead. You'll hit a wagon trace in a few miles, if you just ride into the sun."

He frowned back and asked, "Is this it? No long farewells?"

She smiled and said, "Oh, we can make love one last time, if you want. But I'm anxious to reach my relatives before they serve the noon meal."

He nodded soberly, and said, "I wouldn't want you to miss lunch."

She smiled, nodded, and heeled her pony away with a casual wave.

As she rode off, not looking back, Longarm sat his own mount and watched with a bemused smile as her trim figure faded out of his life. He didn't know what in hell he was feeling. It was the perfect ending to a perfect romance, and yet . . .

Women are such beasts, he told himself with a chuckle. Then he heeled his own mount and rode east, resisting the impulse to cast any further glances at the other rider as she diverged from him to his right.

He'd had the shoe on the other foot often enough to know it pinched. By the time he'd ridden a mile, he'd decided her abrupt goodbye was only rare common sense. In his time, he'd tried a dozen or more ways to ease himself out of some gal's life gently, and none of them had worked any better.

He suddenly spotted a stretch of bare sand ahead, and swerved his pony toward the wagon trace. A broken bottle in the roadside weeds told him he was back to civilization. He swung in the saddle and swept the horizon until he picked up a moving dot. Then, knowing she wouldn't see it, he blew her a kiss and said, "Don't forget to write."

Then, with romance out of the way for now, he heeled his pony into a lope to the east. The sun was in his eyes, but he saw smoke on the horizon, and knew the chimneytops of Moose Jaw would appear over the rim of the world in another hour's ride. Dancing Eyes had led him across the uncharted prairie as perfectly as she'd promised, and she hadn't asked one promise in return.

He shook his head and said to himself, *You've been too damned lucky lately, old son. The law of averages says it only stands to reason you just have to get in a real mess, any minute now.*

The town of Moose Jaw wasn't much. But as Longarm rode in, he could see that someone had shot the hell out of what there was of it.

Fresh bullet scars, dotting the weathered siding of the first building he came to, gave testimony with the shattered windows all around that he'd missed a lot of excitement by mere hours. He saw a knot of men jawing in the dusty street near a burned-out frame structure, so he rode over to them, dismounted, and nodded to the first townie who glanced his way.

The man asked, "You come to join the posse? You just missed 'em. They rode out towards Regina, after the Mounties."

Another man opined, "Goddamned fools should have fanned out for the border to the south. The Mounties don't need any backing, but if them rascals are headed for the States—"

Longarm cut in to ask, "What happened? I've been out on the prairie for a couple of days."

The informative townie looked surprised to discover that the whole world didn't know as he said, "Hell, we had us a real free-for-all *war* this morning, stranger! They was waiting outside the bank when the manager come to open up. But some of the boys spotted what was going on, and, whooo-eee! We had us a shootout as the sons of bitches come out of the bank with our money!"

Another man nodded and said, "We got three of the bastards, two right in front of the bank and the other down in front of the bakery. One of 'em's still alive, over to the jail. The other two never knew what hit 'em!"

Another man in the crowd chortled, "I got one. I'm sure I got one. I fired just as Clem and Rudy opened up and I still say it was my round that put him on the ground."

Longarm asked, "Who were they?"

But before anyone could answer, a morose-looking individual who hadn't spoken until then suddenly asked, "Before we get into who *they* were, mister, who might *you* be? I don't recall seeing you in these parts before."

Longarm had heard them say the Mounties had ridden after the bank robbers, so he smiled and took out his wallet, saying, "I'm on your side, Constable."

The Canadian lawman glanced at the wallet dubiously, so Longarm upped the ante by taking his badge from another pocket. The Canadian frowned and said, "Yankee federal man, eh? Ain't you sort of off your range?"

Longarm said, "I'm up here after some gents who've been killing on both sides of the border. If the ones who set fire to your bank over there are riding with a rascal named Chumley, they ain't as far ahead of me as I was worried about."

The Canadian lawman handed him back his wallet and said, "One of the outlaws we have over in the jail said his leader was Canada Jack Chumley, all right. But let's talk some more about you. Do the Mounties know you're up here?"

Longarm nodded and said, "I sent a wire to Crown Sergeant Foster at Fort MacLeod, saying I was in hot pursuit. There wasn't time to wait about for warrants and extraditions and such, but I suspicion Foster would have told me to stay put, if he didn't want my help."

A buzzing passed through the crowd, and the Canadian lawman said, "You just missed Foster by an hour or less. You say you know him personal?"

Longarm grinned and said, "Nobody knows Frosty Foster personal. I'd say he wears them stripes and crown to bed. But, yeah, we worked on a case down in the States together, a while back."

The constable smiled for the first time as he said, "That does sort of describe him, don't it?"

191

Then he shrugged and added, "Well, as long as you've cleared it with the Mounties, it's none of my business. I'm only the law here in town. You could likely catch up with the Mounties if you started now and rode sudden."

Longarm shook his head and said, "These other gents say half the town is already doing that, and they're right. Foster can handle any outlaws born of mortal womankind. I reckon I'll study some before I tear ass off to everywhere. You say you have one of the outlaws locked up?"

The constable's suspicious frown returned as he nodded, but said, "Yep, but you can't have him, if that's your game. I ain't even giving that son of a bitch to the Mounties. I caught him fair and square and, by jimmies, he's mine. The bastard is going to stand trial and hang right here in Moose Jaw."

"That sounds reasonable to me. I didn't know arson was a capital offense, though."

"It ain't. They left a gutshot clerk in the bank when they set fire to it on the way out."

Longarm stared at the burned-out bank and whistled softly through his teeth before he said, "That sounds like the bunch I know and love, all right. Jack Chumley's about three times meaner than he needs to be."

Then he said, "I have no intention of trying to extradite the one you caught, Constable. What the hell, it's all the same to Uncle Sam if he hangs up here. I would like to jaw a mite with him, though. You'll notice I'm asking, not demanding. As a fellow lawman, I know it's finders-keepers."

Mollified, the constable nodded and said, "Since you put it so neighborly, I'm willing to reply in kind. We've got the jasper on a pallet in the lockup. He was hit six ways from Sunday, and right now he looks a mite pale. But the doc says he thinks he can save him for the public hanging we're printing invitations to."

As they walked to the jail with Longarm's pony

192

trailing behind, the tall deputy marshal made small talk as he tried to fill himself in on certain details of Canadian jurisprudence. The constable explained that the Mounties acted like combined state and federal police might in the States. Local governments had their own courts and law officers, but the Mounties handled anything that happened between settlements in the unincorporated western territories. Longarm suspected that, as in any other country, including his own, there was some not-always-friendly rivalry between the big and little outfits. He was banking on it to aid him in his bluff.

They got to the jail and he tethered his pony to the hitching post out front before he followed the constable inside.

The prisoner lay, as promised, on a pile of blood-spattered blankets on the floor of the only cell. A deputy sat on a bentwood chair facing the bars, with a sawed-off ten-gauge across his knees. Longarm failed to see why. The shot-up outlaw on the pallet didn't look like he was about to escape; he looked like he was having enough trouble just breathing.

Longarm turned to the constable and asked, "Do you know its name?"

The Canadian nodded and said, "The bastard says he's from Iowa, and that we can call him Ben Taylor. You still can't have him, and our hangman's fixing to call him dead."

Longarm said, "I ain't asking you to take my word on sly extradition moves. You don't know me. But you look like a gent with common sense. Do you reckon we could agree on two things?"

"Don't know. Ain't heard about neither one, yet."

"Number one, that poor animal won't be alive when the sun goes down. I don't mean to be disrespectful of Canadian medicine, and I can see your doc wrapped a lot of bandages over the compresses. But I've been through one war and Dodge City before they tamed it, and I've seen men die with only half as many slugs in them. You can smell the acetone on his breath from out here."

The constable nodded and said, "I didn't know the chemistry, but I've sniffed that sickly-sweet smell before. Get to number two."

Longarm said, "We're both lawmen, and we could both use more than a name and a home state. I'll sweeten the pot by telling you, gratis, that there's no U.S. paper on any owlhoot named Ben Taylor. If we can wake him up for a dying statement, I misdoubt we can get him to confess anything for the good of his soul. From what I know of the gang, he ain't got one."

The constable nodded and said, "We're agreed on that, too. What's the play?"

Longarm said, "Let me talk to him, and you just go along with the dumb things I say. These critters play by ear, and he might grab at a chance to buy some time. Just remember that I'm lying a lot, and you'll follow my drift without a tedious rehearsal. I have you pegged as a man who's worn his badge awhile."

The constable smiled and unlocked the cell door. They went in and hunkered down together over the unconscious outlaw. Longarm took him by the shoulder on the side with the fewest bullet holes and shook him, saying, "Where are you from in Iowa, Ben? I know some folks in Omaha."

The dying man's eyelids fluttered and he murmured, "Sioux Falls. Do my folks know I've been hurt?"

"Sure. These Canadians sent us a wire, and I've come to take you home, Ben."

The Canadian frowned at Longarm, but didn't say anything. Taylor tried to blink himself awake as he asked, "No shit? Who are you, mister?"

"An American, like you. Canada Jack sure got you in a mess, didn't he?"

Taylor's brows knit as he gritted his teeth and muttered, "Crazy. The stupid limey is crazy as a bedbug! What in the hell did he want to rob that bank for? That wasn't the plan."

Longarm saw that he was going under again, so he shook him and insisted. "Wake up, Ben. Shamrock told me you were after the railroad to the east."

Taylor half-opened his eyes and said, "Right. Where is old Shamrock? Last time I saw him, he was riding beside Canada Jack between two houses, and the goddamn Canucks was throwing lead like they was watering the lawn with it! I reckon that's when I got knocked off my pony. Where in hell am I?"

"Hospital. Don't you pass out on me, boy! I can't take you home unless we can prove you're a U.S. citizen."

"Hell, of course I'm a Yankee. Everybody knows that."

"Maybe. Who can vouch for you? Would Jack and Shamrock tell us you were American? Where can I get in touch with them, Ben?"

The outlaw opened his eyes, closed them again, and sighed, "Beats the shit out of me. Jack keeps changing his goddamn mind. He says we're going one place, and then he decides at the last minute to go somewhere else. We were making for the railroad camps between Moose Jaw and Regina. Then, as we come down from La Coteau, he gets this crazy idea to rob some bank. Shamrock said it was risky, but Jack said he had a plan."

The dying man coughed before he added, weakly, "Some plan. I never heard so many guns going off at once in my whole damned life!"

Longarm shook him again and asked, "What about Regina? Does he have friends there?"

Ben Taylor didn't answer. Longarm shook him again and saw that he wasn't going to. He was still alive, but the way he was breathing said it was about over. The constable suddenly got to his feet and backed away in disgust, saying "For Christ's sake, he just pissed on my boots."

Longarm rose and followed him outside. He noticed that the Canadian locked the cell door after them.

195

Some men sure had suspicious natures. Ben Taylor was going to walk on water before he performed the greater miracle of going anywhere important.

The constable said, "Well, it was a nice professional try, but I can't say I learned much."

Longarm asked, "Do you have a telegraph line to Regina?"

The Canadian nodded and said, "Sure, and I'm way ahead of you. We wired down the line before the gun-smoke had cleared this morning. The gang has a Mountie patrol and a fifty-man posse chasing them into a trap. Regina is Saskatchewan headquarters for the Mounted Police. There must be a full troop of Mounties laying for the gang betwixt here and Regina."

Longarm nodded and said, "I know. Canada Jack has likely figured it out too. Let's talk about the money from the bank. Was it Canadian paper or specie?"

The constable ran a thumbnail along the stubble of his jaw as he thought and said, "One bag of Canadian, English, and Yankee notes was recovered off one of the bandits we shot. They got away with two sacks of mixed coinage—British sovereigns, mostly, with some Yankee twenty-dollar gold pieces. The bank workers who survived are still trying to figure out just how much it was, but it was more than a Saturday night's worth."

Longarm nodded and took out his Ingersoll watch, as if the time of day really mattered. He said, "Well, I'd best get cracking if I hope to catch up with old Bill Foster. The sarge is hard as hell on horses."

The constable followed him outside, saying, "I'll wire Regina that you're headed that way and that you'd like Crown Sergeant Foster to wait somewhere for you."

Longarm smiled pleasantly, all things considered, and said, "That would be neighborly of you, Constable. But I'm just an unofficial observer he sort of asked for a hand in identifying faces. Knowing him, he'll likely have the rascals by the time I catch up."

The constable said, "I know. Why don't I wire that

you'll meet him at the Mountie barracks in Regina? I know for a fact he's been ordered to report there, no matter how things turn out."

Longarm said that sounded like a fine notion, thanked the constable again, and went out to his pony to mount up. He waved goodbye and rode out of town at a comfortable lope before anyone else could get him in trouble.

He took the stage route to Regina, and waited until Moose Jaw sank below the horizon behind him before he cut south across the prairie.

He reined in well out of sight of the road, and took out his map. He scowled down at it in the sunlight, trying to decide which way he'd be heading if he were trying to jump the U.S. border with a sack of gold he could spend anywhere.

He had more choices than he wanted. The Moose Jaw River that gave the town its name had to be just over the next rise and, yeah, he was close to a ford. But if he rode due south, he'd run into the damned fool river again as it wound up to join Thunder Creek near town.

Jesus, he thought. *How many times does a man have to ford the same river in this fool country?*

He fished out a cheroot and lit it to steady his nerves as he let the pony graze. He deliberately ignored the map for a few minuees and then had another peek, trying to see it with fresh eyes. There were solid and dotted lines indicating watercourses all over the damned paper, but he squinted and tried to ignore them as he searched for a clear route trending toward the States.

Then, as he'd hoped, he suddenly saw it, the way a hunter suddenly makes out the form of a deer among the leaves that match its coat. If he forded the Moose Jaw once, rode south until he hit it once more, then kept to the east bank, almost to the prairie lake the river sprang from, he could ford it one more time and ride smack-dab south all the way to Montana without hitting anything much but grass!

It was not only the best way; it was damned near the *only* way. If Canada Jack had a lick of sense, he and the survivors of his whittled-down gang would take that route, and they were less than a day ahead of him now!

Longarm chuckled as he put the map away. He'd seen there were no more than a handful of trail towns and no telegraph lines between him and the border. Things were looking up. By the time Sergeant Foster knew he was in Canada, he figured to be safe in the States with his prisoners. It never occured to him to worry about getting the drop on a handful of mad-dog killers. Knowing he wouldn't have to tangle with the far tougher Mounties had made his day for him.

Chapter 12

The Indian pony he'd gotten from the Métis would have been laughed at in any horse show, but he was a tough little fellow who was used to living on buffalo grass and such water as the Lord and his rider saw fit to send his way. Longarm set a pace that would have killed a thoroughbred as he followed the high ground south-southeast.

He could see that others had agreed with him as to the route, but he didn't try to read signs seriously. A horse turd here and a hoofmark there only said other riders had passed this way. The ones he was interested in were likely to be pushing their mounts too, and the time to hunker down over signs was when the trail offered two choices.

It was late afternoon when he spied a windmill and headed for it. He soon rode down on a bearded man and a kid of about twelve who were branding stock. He pulled up by the brushwood fire, cast a quick look at their soddy a quarter-mile to the east, and saw that the roof and windows were intact. The gang had either mended their ways or been in a hurry, if and when they'd passed this way.

Longarm indentified himself and the man and boy stopped work to jaw with him. The small holder said he hadn't noticed a band of riders headed either way since sunup. Longarm thanked him, turned down an invitation to supper, and rode on with a frown. The gang could have avoided being seen from the spread by a simple detour in either direction, but Canada Jack hadn't shown much caution when it came to isolated families in the past.

He camped that night, without a fire, on a rise. He watched the skyline for winking orange stars a mite lower than the others, but the bandits were either over the horizon or foregoing bedtime coffee too.

The next day, as he kept pushing himself and the pony, Longarm was feeling less foxy about his map reading. Could the outlaws have headed for the border by another route? It made no sense. There wasn't another one that didn't call for an extra week in the saddle. On the other hand, even his own men agreed that Canada Jack wasn't long on brains. It was entirely possible he'd gone on with his farfetched plans to rob the C.P.R.R., in which case it was all over by now. There was just no way the gang was going to escape the pincers of two Mountie outfits riding to meet each other.

Longarm put the thought aside as unprofitable. If the Mounties had his prisoners, he was on a fool's errand. If he was estimating Canada Jack correctly, he was following the one sensible escape route. Everyone knew the killer liked to jump back and forth across the border to hit where he wasn't expected and be gone by the time the law on either side started taking the hunt seriously.

Longarm figured that if his notion was wrong, he was headed the right way, anyway. Billy Vail would be having a fit by now. There was a limit to how long the U.S. taxpaying public would put up with his vacation in Canada. He was going to get hell from Billy, even if he rode in with Canada Jack in tow. What the chewing-out would be like if he came home empty-handed was beyond human comprehension.

On the third day south, Longarm topped a rise and pulled up in awe. The wide, grass-paved draw ahead was a scene from the Shining Times. A herd of shaggy buffalo grazed down there ahead of him, as if they'd wandered through a hole in Time. If they noticed him at all, they didn't show it. This remnant of the great north herd apparently hadn't heard of Bill Cody or the other Mighty Hunters.

Longarm automatically tallied them as if they were steers, and came up with eighty-three head. It was pitiful next to the numbers he'd seen to the south just five years or so ago, but still an impressive mess of meat on the hoof. He knew he was far from civilization indeed.

He rode down the slope at a walk, not wanting to spook the herd or provoke an attack. It was well past the spring calving season, and no recent mother challenged his right to be there. He saw that the animals were in good condition as they drifted out of his way with an occasional wary glance. None were down or wounded. If Canada Jack and his boys had passed this way, they'd resisted the usual impluses the poor critters seemed to bring out in otherwise reasonable men.

He grimaced as he remembered the rotting carcasses piled up along the U.P. right-of-way, shot from the moving train by "sportsmen" who'd never ever been able to cut out a tongue to pay for the wasted shells and lives. Once the C.P.R.R was completed, this little herd would be boxed between railroads north and south. A Sioux had once told him the rails and fences had done more to wipe the buffalo out than all the hide-hunters together. The buffalo was a migratory animal. Unlike sheep or cows, it couldn't gaze the same range day after day. It had to keep moving, drifting across the unlimited plains with the seasons, as it followed its favorite plants or dropped by a certain dry wash for a dust bath at just the right time between rains. A few sentimental cattlemen had tried penning a herd for old times' sake. Longarm hadn't heard of its working, up to now. Holding them anywhere would call for a pocket of really varied topography, with timber, prairie, running water, and dry washes on the same spread.

He made it through the parted herd and up the far

slope without causing a stampede or provoking an attack. Then he put the buffalo out of his mind as he got back to more important hunting matters.

He could see the willow and cottonwood of the riverbank along the skyline to his right as he crossed high ground. Could the bandits be hugging the river? It didn't seem likely. A cluster of fresh horse turds ahead told him he was on the natural dry-shod trail. He reined in and dismounted to turn over a turd. The horse that had dropped it hadn't been grain-fed recently. That eliminated the man and boy he'd talked to back at their soddy. He'd noticed that their mounts were a mite sleek for cow ponies living on nothing but grass. He mounted up and rode on. The sign still left a mess of folks he could think of.

He rode until dark, then rode some more, trusting to the pony's night vision and the openness of the prairie to keep them from walking off any important edges. He rode until the sensible little Indian pony started balking and fighting the bit to tell him they were through for the day. Then he hobbled the pinto, spread his roll, and supped on a cheroot and some pemmican before he stole forty winks.

They were on the trail again before the lazy sun got up to join them. Longarm knew he was making better time than nine out of ten rangeriders considered reasonable. Where the hell was Canada Jack? His past record gave no indication that the spoiled young Englishman was ambitious. He and his pals were either scared skinny and riding themselves into the ground —or they'd taken another route.

"Dumb son of a bitch," Longarm muttered as he rode. He wasn't sure whether he meant the outlaw or himself. Longarm's rep for unusually clever captures rested on his ability to savvy what the men he hunted were up to by putting himself in their place. He mulled over all the moves *he'd* have made if he'd just tried for a bank and run into the same mess the James-

Younger gang had ridden into at Northfield. With your gang shot up and scattered, the sensible place to be was *far*. Chumley had enough gold to hole up in the whorehouse of his choice for a year. Nobody would be laying for him in Montana right now. Canada was hotter than a two-dollar pistol, so Canada Jack *had* to be making for the border.

Even if he wasn't, Longarm knew there was little sense in turning back. Crown Sergeant Foster would be thinking along the same lines by this time, and once the trap was sprung and empty, the Mounties would be heading down this way on the double. The only thing the outlaws had going for them was that there was no telegraph wire north and south. Even an anti-American government would wire the Montana law when the pursuit was this hot. Leaving the bank clerk they'd killed aside, the ugly murders on this side of the border were going to make it tougher than hell for the treacherous Englishman's fancy lawyers if the Mounties caught him now.

The afternoon after he'd ridden through the buffalo herd, Longarm consulted his map and decided it was time he thought about fording the Moose Jaw. As he swung to the west, he saw by the trampled grass that others had had the same intention. He rode to the gentle dropoff above the wooded prairie river, and once again he thought he'd wandered into a knothole through history.

There were a dozen tipis among the trees near the water's edge. A remuda of thirty-odd ponies was grazing all around. He noticed that an Indian kid had seen him and was running for the tents, so he shrugged and rode down the slope. If they were friendly, he'd soon know. If they weren't, he was in trouble, on a jaded horse with a long slope behind him.

As he approached the tipis, a grave-looking individual in a faded red blanket came out on foot to meet him with an upraised hand.

Longarm reined in and the camp chief said in Cree,

"Hear me, we are not bad people. I am Spotted Dog, of the Stonepipe Lodge. The Great White Mother has given us her permission to be here."

Longarm held his own free hand up as he replied in his best Algonquinoid, "My heart soars to hear my brother's words. I am not an enemy to the Plains Cree. They call me Longarm. I am hunting evil white men who might have passed this way."

Spotted Dog said, "Let us smoke and talk together about your hunt. My young men are out hunting. They are ranging far for a herd of buffalo we heard about. If you wait until they return this evening, one of them may have seen something."

Longarm decided the old man made a heap of sense. He dismounted and led his pony over to the chief's tipi as some women and children shyly peeked at him from a safe distance.

They sat down on a big blanket between the tipi and the water, and Spotted Dog unwrapped a calumet from a roll of buckskin. Longarm took out a cheroot and offered it. Spotted Dog gravely crumbled the little cigar into the stone bowl of his calumet, but broke with tradition by lighting it with a sulfur kitchen match.

He took a long, deep drag and handed the pipe to Longarm, saying, "That is very good tobacco. We have not been living well, lately, but the Hudson Bay people used to give us good tobacco. Lately, the stuff the white traders sell us tastes like it has dog shit in it."

Longarm took a drag and handed the calumet back as he said, "I saw the buffalo you heard about. They are in a draw to the north, less than two days' ride."

Spotted Dog smiled and said in English, "My heart told me you were a good person. I will tell my young men when they ride in, and we will live fat cow for at least one more winter. How many did you shoot?"

Longarm was pleased that he wouldn't be forced to stretch his meager knowledge of Cree dialect any further as he said, "I didn't shoot any."

"Is this true? I can see you have a rifle on your saddle. I never met a white man before who didn't like to shoot buffalo."

Longarm said, "Oh, I outgrew it a while back. When I first came West, the prairie was crawling with the critters, and I'd heard about the Great Hunters. So I shot me a couple before I figured out what I was going to *do* with them."

He grimaced and added, "There ain't much sport in shooting anything too big to miss when it just stands there, staring at you. I mean, I can see you folks hunting them for hides, tallow, and meat. But shooting them for the hell of it seems sort of wasteful."

Spotted Dog sighed and said, "I know. In the Shining Times, some of our people were as silly about it as whites, but there were few of us, and it didn't seem to matter if the young men ran some over a cliff now and then."

Before they could go deeper into game-management theory, one of the squaws let out a yell, and both men looked to see what she was pointing at. It was a Red River cart, coming their way down the slope. Longarm rose to his feet with a grin as he recognized the cart horse and the patches on the canopy. It was Claudette!

Longarm and the Indian walked to meet her as the Métis girl halted and dropped her ground anchor just outside the tent line. She recognized Longarm and jumped down to run to him with a friendly cry. Then she remembered her manners in front of the Indians, and they settled for a handshake.

Claudette said, "I was so worried about you! What happened back at Petit Arc? I left, as you ordered, when I heard about the gunplay. I thought you were following me to La Coteau."

He said, "It's a long story. Where are you headed now?"

"Back to the States," she replied. "I have to get word to Louis Riel about the terrible trouble near La Batoche. The Mounties have accused us of terrible things, and the Royal Artillery is marching from Fort Shilo to join them."

"Christ! Your revolution has started with your leaders out of the country?"

"*Mais non*! We have done nothing! Louis has said we must be calm and wait for a new government. Mac-Donald shows no sign of holding another election, but we have given him another few years before we intend to defy Ottawa openly."

"But you said the Mounties and the army are moving on you. Where's this La Batoche place, and what happened there?"

Spotted Dog cut in to say, "I know La Batoche is the center of the Métis settlements. I do not think I want to know what happened there. I think Louis Riel has a good heart, but my band wants no part of the flag that is red and white. The coming winter is enough for us to face with empty guns and bellies."

The old man walked away to resume his contemplations by the water's edge, and Claudette explained, "Two bodies were washed up on the banks of the Saskatchewan near La Batoche. They'd been shot to death. Both were known Orangemen and rabid anti-Catholics. None of our people know who shot them, but the Mounties insist we submit to a complete investigation."

He said, "Hmm, meaning a house-to-house search and a tally of such guns and ammunition as you might have. Naturally, some hot-headed Métis will resist, and, yeah, I see why they sent for field guns. Tell me more about the dead Orangemen."

Claudette shrugged and said, "We know only their names and reputations. They were the Duncan brothers, and they once beat up a Métis near Medicine Hat."

Longarm closed his eyes and said, "Oh, shit! I might have known!"

"Do you know who murdered the Duncan brothers?" she asked, surprised.

"Yeah, *me*. Only it wasn't murder. It was a fair

fight between a lawman and three rapists. They'll likely find the third body any minute, and I don't have any way to wire Regina from a safe distance. Do you reckon they'd believe you if you ran back with a message from me?"

Claudette smiled bitterly and asked, "A Métis girl, trying to prove her Métis friends are innocent without a witness? *Merde alors*, surely you jest!"

Longarm avoided her gaze as he said, "Yeah, I ain't on such friendly terms with the Mounties myself. I know what you want me to do, honey. It ain't my own hide I'm thinking about. Canada Jack and his boys are going to make the border long before I could ride back to Regina and set out after them again, even if the Mounties let me go—which I sort of don't figure on."

She grimaced and said, "You have no choice."

He sighed and said, "I know. I ought to make Regina in a few days of hard riding."

Claudette looked surprised and said, "That's not what I meant! If you tell the Mounties you shot those three Canadians, they will surely arrest you."

"True enough. But if I don't call them off before they get those cannon set up, there's no telling how many innocent folks will be killed on both sides. I don't expect they'll hang me, once I tell my tale to the judge. If push comes to shove, I've got a witness I can call. I'm going to catch hell from both governments, and I might lose my badge but what the hell? I haven't had much use for it lately, anyway. Maybe I'm getting too old for this job."

She put a hand on his sleeve and asked, "What about the men you are after?"

He grinned ironically and replied, "Yeah, what about them? I'm losing my grip, honey. A year or so ago, I was pretty good at tracking. Any lawman worth his salt would have had them rounded up by now. Canada Jack is a brainless, cowardly butcher, riding with a mess of young rascals any real lawman could bust over his knee for a spanking. When you see Louis Riel, tell him I'm sorry as hell for the mess I made of things up here. I'd give you a message to wire my boss, but I haven't thought up enough words to apologize the way I ought to."

She lowered her eyes and murmured, "If you rode with me to the border, and wired Ottawa . . ."

He said, "Honey, I'd like to be with you tonight more than I've got words to say. We both know it wouldn't work. That cart won't get you to a Yankee telegraph line in less than two weeks. If I don't ride for Regina right now, we'll never forgive ourselves for what has to happen at La Batoche."

He bent to kiss her cheek as he added, "Adios, kid. Take care of yourself."

"Will I ever see you again?" she asked, trying not to cry.

He said, "Hell, the way Ive been riding around in circles, I'm likely to meet up with you *twice* more!"

The town of Regina had mushroomed where the Canadian Pacific Railroad crossed the quicksands of Wascana Creek on a stretch of prairie stretched as flat as a drumhead under the big blue bowl of the Canadian sky. Between summer rains, the thermometer could top a hundred in the shade, and shade was hard to come by. Longarm studied on that as he rode in. He was used to the heat, but it was sort of unsettling to be out in the open, when open was carried to such ridiculous lengths. You could see the spires and roof-tops of Regina for hours before you got there. He knew that a man riding in would be visible from a second-story window for just as long. He realized, an hour or more before he reached the damned place, that he was committed. It would look funny as hell if a dot out on the prairie turned to go somewhere else; there was no-place else to go for miles.

He forded the creek and crossed some railroad tracks before he reined in and asked a couple of kids where the Mountie barracks were. They directed him around a corner and up the dusty street leading straight as a bowstring to whatever he was getting himself into.

The Mountie barracks at Regina were a mixture of primitive and polish. The Union Jack fluttered from a rough pole of tamarack, but the splintery wood was thickly whitewashed. As he skirted the parade ground, he saw a platoon of recruits doing monkey drill under the baleful eye of a sergeant who looked like a gorilla in a red tunic. He found a Mountie walking along the cinder path with some papers, and asked the way to the provost marshal's office. The Mounties said he was headed the right way. Longarm had been afraid he'd say a fool thing like that.

He rode up to the cluster of verandah-wrapped buildings and dismounted. He tethered his pony to the freshly painted hitching post and took a last drag on his cheroot before mounting the steps. It seemed doubtful that they allowed cigar butts within five miles, but he saw a quart can painted red and nailed to a post, so he dropped the butt in it and strode over to the door.

Inside, he found a red-coated sergeant major behind something too small to be a judge's bench and too grand to be a desk. The Mountie looked up with a noncommittal smile and Longarm said, "I've come to explain about some bodies you boys found up in the Métis country."

The sergeant frowned, nodded, and said, "Oh, right, the Duncan brothers. We've sent a team to investigate the murders, Mr., ah . . ."

"My name is Custis Long, and I'm a deputy U.S. marshal. There ain't no murders to investigate. I shot all three of the rascals fair and square."

The sergeant major was good. He never blinked an eye. He got up from his seat and said politely, "If you'll come with me, we'd best talk to Supervisor Collingwood about it, sir."

Longarm nodded and followed as the sergeant major

led him back to another office. He knocked politely, and only a lawman with Longarm's experience would have noticed the casual way the Mountie's hand hovered near the holstered revolver on his hip.

A voice inside replied in muffled tones, and the sergeant major opened the door. He waited for Longarm to enter first, and now his hand was *on* the grips of his service revolver.

Supervisor Collingwood was a vapidly handsome man of about forty, with a toothbrush mustache and a clipped English accent. He waited until the sergeant major explained that Longarm had just confessed to shooting the three Duncans before he indicated a chair near his desk and said, "It's very good of you to drop by like this, Deputy Long. Would you mind if Sergeant Gilmore hung your gunbelt somewhere while we chatted?"

Longarm asked, "Am I under arrest?"

Collingwood answered, "I really can't say. I haven't heard your story yet. We do have these rules about guns and all that, so, if you wouldn't mind . . ."

Longarm shrugged and unbuckled his gunbelt. He handed the rig to the sergeant major, who thanked him with a nod and stepped back by the door to cover him.

Longarm sat down and crossed his legs. Collingwood opened a cigar humidor with a questioning smile, and when Longarm nodded, he offered his visitor a smoke. They both lit up and leaned back. Then Longarm told him about the shootout at the Wilson spread, adding, "I heard the Métis were getting blamed for the killings, so I figured I'd best come forward."

Collingwood nodded and said, "Jolly decent of you. You say the rather boisterous Duncan brothers were about to rape the Wilson woman. Do you suppose she'd back your testimony?"

"I don't see why not. I shot the rascals before they got to do anything she'd have reason to hide."

Collingwood nodded and said, "It's a simple matter

of taking both of your statements, then. Do you have a place to stay in Regina, Deputy?"

Longarm frowned and said, "Not hardly. I figured, if you didn't arrest me, I'd just be heading home."

Collingwood sighed and said, "I'm not sure *what* the form is. It seems rather silly to arrest a guest of Her Majesty and a fellow lawman, what? I mean, you'd hardly have come forward if you had any intention of evading us. But you do understand, I'll have to ask you to stay in town until we can get a statement from Mrs. Wilson. How do you chaps handle things like this in the States?"

Longarm said, "I reckon a material witness can be released to his own self, if he gives his word he'll appear for the hearing."

Collingwood nodded and said, "Right. I'll have Sergeant Gilmore, here, take a statement from you before you leave. You can tell him where you'll be staying in town, once you make arrangements."

Longarm smiled and started to rise as the door behind him opened after one sharp knock and no invitation. As Longarm rose and turned, he saw Crown Sergeant Foster in the doorway. Foster saw him at the same time, of course, and a revolver appeared, as if by magic, in the big Mountie's rawboned fist!

Foster snapped, "You're under arrest, Long. Anything you say may be used against you."

"Oh, for God's sake, I'm standing here unarmed in the provost's office, you big fool!"

Supervisor Collingwood rose from his own seat with a totally confused look as he digested the exchange. He said, "I say, Deputy Long and I have just discussed the shooting at the Wilson spread in a most amicable way, Sergeant."

Foster smiled thinly and asked, "Did he tell you he's up here illegally, sir?"

Collingwood looked sadly at Longarm as Foster added, "We have copies of telegraph messages sent to him by his superiors in the U.S. Justice Department, sir.

211

He not only crossed the border in the company of a suspected rebel, but he did it against the direct orders of his own government."

Collingwood sighed and asked Longarm, "Do you have any answers to the sergeant's charges, Deputy?"

Longarm said, "I was in hot pursuit. Canada Jack Chumley was less than a day's ride ahead of me, and—"

"John Chumley?" Collingwood cut in, staring at his own sergeant major as he asked, "Isn't that the young chap we have in the guardhouse at the moment, Sergeant Gilmore?"

Gilmore nodded and said, "Yessir. Corporal Norris brought him in, the day before yesterday. We're waiting to hear from Ottawa about the disposition of the case."

Longarm swore softly under his breath and asked Gilmore, "Hold on, you say you boys captured Chumley *alone?* He crossed the border with a gang of at least a dozen, after killing some U.S. citizens!"

Before Gilmore could answer, Foster said, "I *owe* Deputy Long his explanation. He seems to think he's the only lawman in business, these days."

Foster waited until he saw there was to be no interjection from either of his fellow Mounties before he grinned at Longarm and said, "The reason we're holding Canada Jack alone is simple. My patrol caught up with them after they robbed that bank."

Longarm nodded and said, "You were always a fair shot, Foster. I remember you chiding me once, for shooting an outlaw you said I might have been able to take alive."

Foster shrugged and said, "I didn't approve of your rough-hewn methods then, and I don't now. The gang could have surrendered once we had them pinned down on a bend of the river. They chose to make a fight of it, and if the results saved Her Majesty the expense of a protracted trial, so be it."

Longarm asked, "How come you didn't finish off their leader, then?"

Foster grimaced and said, "Young Chumley was leading, indeed. He had the fastest horse and a full day's start on us by the time we finished off his gang. As you might have guessed, we'd wired ahead, so he rode right into another patrol, and the rest is a matter for the courts to decide."

Longarm grinned and said, "Well, fair is fair, and I have to take my hat off to you gents. Do you reckon he'll really hang, this time?"

Foster looked pained and didn't answer.

Collingwood said, "One would certainly hope so, but his brother is a belted earl and a friend of the Prince of Wales."

Longarm gasped, "Aw, hell, this time he killed Canadians, and some of them died ugly as hell!"

Collingwood said, "Quite. But we're police officers, not barristers. Now that we've rounded the blighter up, it's a matter for the courts to decide."

Crown Sergeant Foster asked, "May we get back to the matter of *this* arrest, sir?"

Supervisor Collingwood frowned and snapped, "I am quite aware of the charges you just made against this man, Sergeant. May I remind you that you are on my post as an uninvited guest from Fort MacLeod?"

Foster stood a bit straighter, which hardly seemed possible, as he said, "I am aware of that, sir. Like Deputy Long, I was in hot pursuit. It was my understanding Ottawa had wired clearance about our, uh, jurisdictional problem."

"They told me to give a free hand to a more experienced lawman. They did *not* say anything about turning over my command to a *junior*, Sergeant Foster!"

Foster's face went wooden-Indian as he replied, "No excuse, sir. I was out of line and I apologize."

Mollified, Collingwood said, "Oh, let's not get sickening about it. I quite agree that we have a sticky wicket here."

He turned to Longarm and said, "I'm afraid we're going to have to hold you after all, Deputy. I've no doubt you've told me the truth, in your own fashion, but there are rules, you know."

"In other words, I'm under arrest?"

"Well, at least until the American consulate can clear the matter up. I know it's a bother, but you did intend to stay in Regina until we took a statement from the Canadian woman you defended from those roughnecks. We'll wire Ottawa that we're holding you, and—"

"Don't you have an American consulate here in Regina?"

"Hardly. I'm sorry, but at the least, it's going to take a week or more to thrash things out. Meanwhile, we'll try to make you comfortable. As a fellow law officer, we may be able to work out an arrest-in-quarters, or—" Then Collingwood saw the look in Foster's eye and said, "All right, Sergeant. What am I doing wrong, this time?"

Foster stared hard at Longarm and said, "Your suggestion would be quite proper under ordinary circumstances, sir. But I happen to *know* this man."

"Oh? Are you suggesting Deputy Long might not be agreeable to arrest-in-quarters?"

"Sir, Longarm will *agree* to *anything*. But I've learned, to my cost, not to take his word too seriously."

Longarm frowned and said, "That ain't very neighborly, Foster. I disremember breaking any promises I may have made to you in the past."

Foster shook his head and said, "It won't work on me this time, you rascal. You're slippery as an eel, and your ideas of the truth are rather weird. But I know you of old, and with Supervisor Collingwood's permission, I'd say the best way he has of making sure you stay put long enough to make any difference would be to lock you up and bury the key a mile away."

Collingwood looked unhappy. Longarm shrugged and said, "Hell, let's get it over with, then. I've been in jail before, and Uncle Sam will get me out, if only to fire me."

Collingwood nodded and said, "Sergeant Gilmore will show you over to the guardhouse, then."

But Foster asked, "With your permission, sir. Could I have the pleasure?"

Again, the superior officer hesitated, so Longarm said, "Hell, let him do it. He's so eager he's about to wet his britches, and I hate to see a grown man cry."

Chapter 13

The Regina lockup, like the rest of the post, was no-nonsense and solidly put together. They had a drunk tank with a row of maximum-security cells farther back. Foster and the turnkey led Longarm past the drunk tank, and the sergeant patted Longarm down once again after the boys out front had taken his personal belongings and put them in a big manila envelope.

As the turnkey opened a cell door, Foster slid a palm up the inside of Longarms's thigh, and the tall federal man said, "I always figured you were hot for my body, Bill."

Foster said, "He's clean, but watch him. I wouldn't be surprised to see him slither through the drains like a reptile."

As the turnkey ushered Longarm into the cell, Foster turned on a bootheel and marched out grandly. Longarm saw that the cell was furnished with wooden bunks with no mattresses except a couple of thick Hudson Bay blankets on each. A young blonde man lounged on one bunk, so Longarm threw his hat on the other as the turnkey locked them in together.

Longarm expected the Mountie to walk away, but the turnkey stood there until Foster's footsteps faded away, then he said, "My name is MacLean. You *are* the Yank my brother told me about, aren't you?"

Longarm looked up with a frown and said, "I can't say. Who's your brother, and what did he tell you about me?"

The turnkey said, "Corporal Andrew MacLean. They have him over in surgery right now. Some Métis brought him in last night."

Longarm nodded and said, "I figured they would. Your brother was putting up one hell of a fight when I met him up north of here. How do the doctors say it looks?"

Turnkey MacLean said, "He'll be all right, thanks to you. Is there anything I can get you? Smokes and such?"

Longarm patted his vest and said, "They let me keep my matches and smokes, but I thank you for the thought."

MacLean said, "It was more than a thought. You saved my brother's life. How the hell did you get yourself into this mess?"

"It's a long, tedious tale, and I can see we'll have plenty of time to jaw about in the next few days."

MacLean nodded and said, "I'll see if I can get some apple pie to go with your supper. I hope you understand I've got a job to do."

"Hell, old son, if I aimed to escape, I never would have come here. You don't owe me, and if you did, I'd know better than to ask. Next time you see your brother, tell him I was asking about him."

The turnkey went away and the other man in the cell asked, "What was that all about?"

Longarm smiled across at him and said, "I've got some Mounties who're mad at me and some who ain't. They call me Longarm."

The blonde youth said, "John Chumley here. I'm being detained by a misunderstanding. I *told* the blighters I'm on Her Majesty's business, but they can't seem to understand the workings of British Intelligence."

Longarm didn't answer as he sized the other prisoner up. Considering his reputation, Canada Jack didn't have dripping fangs or even horns. Chumley was in his early twenties, clean-cut, and sort of pleasant-looking. Longarm could see he was a size bigger than most men, but he lounged on his bunk as if he were in some London drawing room, and his cool gray eyes were innocent as hell as he met Longarm's gaze.

Canada Jack said, "I doubt I'll be here long. They had to allow me to wire my solicitor in Ottawa, and he'll be on the train by now."

Longarm nodded and said, "That figures. What was that you said about being a British spy?"

Chumley laughed and answered, "Oh, nothing so dramatic, I assure you. My brother is in Lords, so, naturally, I volunteered my unofficial services while I was over in this perishing country."

"I see. You're sort of spying for Queen Victoria as a hobby."

"Quite. My brother's party is opposed to Gladstone's strange ideas on the Irish Question, and, as you may may know, Canada is a hotbed of Irish radicals. I came over here to dabble in cattle ranching, but when I heard of Shamrock O'Hanlon and his gang—"

Longarm grimaced and said, "Aw, shit! Are you trying to tell me you joined up with a gang of outlaws just to find out if they were Fenians?"

"Quite, and Shamrock *was*, you know. He confided in me, one time, that he has a police record in New York. I wasn't able to gather enough evidence on Murphy and O'Bannion before the Mounties brought them to justice, but—"

Longarm looked disgusted and said, "Save it for the judge, sonny. I know I don't look all that smart, but you're insulting such brains as I have."

Chumley smiled smugly and replied, "It's a good thing for me you won't be on my jury, then, isn't it? What are you in for, cowboy?"

"Damn foolishness," said Longarm, adding, "I might have known you'd come up with a whopper like that. Your family will likely get you off again, too. But to save you a mess of bullshit, I'm a deputy U.S. marshal, and I've been chasing you half the summer."

Chumley laughed boyishly, and said, "Things do get

confusing out here on the frontier, don't they? Would you like to make a little wager? I'll bet you even money I'm out of jail before you are."

Longarm shook his head and said, "No bet, now that I've heard the yarn your lawyers aim to spring in court."

"Do you really like it?"

"No, it's as full of holes as a screen door, but the trouble with trial by jury is that it only takes one idiot who'll believe one lie."

Chumley sat up with a frown and warned, "Careful, Yank. I never said it was a lie."

Longarm snorted, "You don't have to. Anyone with a lick of sense can see you're full of shit."

Canada Jack got to his feet and said, "See here, I'm not used to being spoken to that way, my good man!"

Longarm stared up at the other prisoner in dawning wonder as he saw that Canada Jack really meant it. The face stayed calm and detached, but there was something running around inside those eyes like a gibbering ghost. The young Englishman was really as crazy as everyone said he was. There was something busted loose inside his skull. Longarm remembered how others had said he tended to change his mind at the damnedest times, and it was starting to fit together now. Canada Jack wasn't simply ornery, he was insane.

Canada Jack said, "Well, I'm waiting."

Longarm asked, "Waiting for what?"

"An apology, of course. You called me a liar, and if you don't take it back, I'll have to thrash you."

Longarm laughed and said, "That'll be the day, sonny."

And then Canada Jack was all over him, kicking, biting, and screaming like a woman!

Longarm had been set for a sensible kick or punch, so it wasn't as bad as it might have been, just awe-inspiring. Canada Jack was almost as tall as Longarm, though not as muscular. But his madness gave him a strength beyond that of ordinary men, and his attack was totally reckless. His head banged into the wall as Longarm rolled under him, but the blow didn't seem to affect him. Longarm threw him off and rolled out of the bunk to stiff-arm him away as he rushed again, windmilling his fists.

Longarm said, "You're going to get hurt, sonny," as the madman kept trying to get inside his guard. Then Longarm saw that he was beyond reason, so he grabbed a fistful of blonde hair in his left fist, and threw his right.

It was like hitting a block of wood. Canada Jack's cheek was streaming blood, but the blow hadn't slowed him down at all.

Longarm saw that he'd cut the youth to ribbons if it went on this way, and the Mounties already had him down for gunning three men, so he dicided there had to be a better way.

He took a flurry of blows on his forearms and elbows to draw the maniac in closer. Then he opened his arms and stepped forward, taking a punch in the jaw and another in the gut as he bear-hugged and lifted.

Longarm had the weight advantage, if nothing else, so he was able to lift Chumley's feet from the floor and fall on top of him, pinning him to the floor on his back, with his arms pinned to his sides.

A voice called in, "What's going on?"

Longarm answered, "I wish I knew."

The Englishman he had pinned down suddenly went limp and sighed, "You win, darling. You've dominated me completely."

Longarm frowned down at the blood-streaked face, and a cold snake slithered around in his guts as he stared into the utter madness of the younger man's eyes. Chumley licked his bloody lips and pleaded, "Take me, Master. I am a slave to your lust."

"Lover's quarrel?" asked the turnkey, dryly.

220

Longarm said, "Not hardly. He's just loco. You wouldn't have another cell I could use, would you?"

The turnkey said, "I follow your drift, but we put you in with him because we figured you could handle him if you had to. The other cells are full or in reserve for Saturday night."

Longarm figured their fight was over, so he climbed off the madman and got to his feet. Canada Jack started to rise, then crawled over to put his lips to the tip of Longarm's boot, crooning, "Oh, you're so strong."

The turnkey nodded through the bars and said, "He seems to figure one or the other has to be in charge. It's probably the public school he went to, back in Blighty."

Longarm moved his foot away and said, "Go sit down and behave yourself, Jack."

The killer crawled to his own bunk to curl up coyly on it, smiling timidly.

The turnkey said, "Well, supper will be ready soon. If you want, I'll tell my replacement on the next shift that he's been at it again."

Longarm said, "Hell, I reckon we've got it straight now."

From his bunk, Canada Jack said, "Yes, he's the boy and I'm the girl."

It was about one A.M., and the cellblock was quiet. It was a weeknight, and the few drunks in the tank next door were sleeping it off. Longarm stood by the bars, staring out into the dimly lit corridor as he asked Chumley, "Don't they change guards at midnight? You were here last night."

Canada Jack said, "They're a bit late, I suppose. I think they hold a guard mount over at the headquarters building, and so forth. Why do you ask? I told you nobody comes back here at night unless we call out to them."

Longarm thought before he nodded and said, "Right.

221

That door-slam I heard a while back would have been the changing of the guard. There was a desk man and the turnkey when they brought me here."

"What are you talking about, darling? We've nothing to worry about."

Longarm turned around and said, "I sure wish you'd quit calling me darling. Put your boots back on."

Canada Jack simpered, "I told you the rules of the game. The man who can dominate the other gets to be the master. I haven't been beaten since I was at Eton, but the novelty might be rather piquant after all this time."

"Aw, shit, if I'm your master, put your damned boots on."

"Shall I take my pants off first?"

Longarm said, "Not hardly. We're busting out of here."

Then he went to his own bunk, sat down, and started hauling off one of his own too-tight army boots.

Canada Jack smiled and said, "Oh, yes, let's take off all our clothes and I'll lather my arse with soap."

Longarm grunted the boot off, took his derringer out of it, and held it in his lap as he hauled the boot back on, saying, "We'll talk about your ass later, after we get it out of here."

Canada Jack's eyes gleamed wolfishly as he gasped, "My God, I didn't know you'd smuggled in a gun!"

Longarm stood up, stamping the bootheel as he said, "The Mounties didn't, either. I was sure that god-damned Foster was going to feel it down past my ankle-bone, but he missed it. Hurry with your own boots, damn it."

The outlaw tugged his remaining boot on, but he hesitated and said, "I'm not sure this is such a good idea, Longarm. I've explained how my family solicitor is coming to get me out, and—"

"Look, sonny. Even if your fancy lawyer gets you off again—which is only an if—you figure to spend at least six or eight weeks in jail, right?"

"Yes, but you're a lawman. How do I know you're not just getting me out of here so that you can take me back to the States with you?"

"Shit, I've been arrested and likely fired, and we're a week's ride from the fool border."

He let that sink in before he added, "I'm counting on you to help me find a place to hide. Come morning, Sergeant Foster will be after me, frothing at the mouth."

Canada Jack got to his own feet, asking, "Oh, do you want to be an outlaw too?"

"Why not? So far, you jaspers have been having all the fun."

"Well, if we do tie in with other outlaws, this, uh, understanding we have will have to remain a secret."

"You have my word on that," Longarm said dryly.

"I can service you when we're alone, but most of these rough Canadian peasants don't understand the ways of the Grecian hoplites."

"We'll talk about your Greek whatever another time. Just stay put, and when I tell you to move, move the way I tell you, hear?"

He got Jack away from the bars and ran the muzzle of the derringer along them, making a loud clatter. He didn't want too many people coming, so he only did it once, and waited.

It only took a million years before a turnkey came back, muttering, "What's going on?"

Longarm said, "It's me. Look what I just found over here."

The Mountie stepped closer to the bars in the dim light. Then, as Longarm shoved the little gun through the bars at him, the turnkey froze and said very quietly, "You're not going to get away with this, Yank."

Longarm said, "Open this door and make it sudden."

The Mountie asked, "What if I tell you to go to hell?"

Longarm said, "You'll beat me there by a day or so. We can both see I'll be stuck in here and I'll likely hang if you decide to die out there with the keys. But I misdoubt you'll get much satisfaction. They don't invite dead men to hangings."

The Mountie said, "I don't know. I'm tempted to call your bluff."

Longarm said, "Well, sure you're tempted. I'd be tempted too. But I reckon, in the end, I'd open the fucking door."

The Mountie still hesitated, and Canada Jack said, "Oh, hell, shoot the bastard in the balls, darling!"

That did it. The twin brass muzzles trained on him might not have scared the turnkey, but the tinge of madness in the known killer's voice made his mind up for him in a hurry. He sighed and stepped over to the lock with his key ring, muttering, "All right, but keep that thing away from me!"

As soon as the door was unlocked, Longarm made the turnkey take his place in the cell, and led Canada Jack along the corridor. He opened the door at the far end and stepped boldly into the guardroom, training his derringer on the desk where he assumed, correctly, he'd find the other guard.

The Mountie behind the desk frowned thoughtfully at the little gun in Longarm's big fist and said, "You're being stupid. They told us the U.S. Consulate has a man on his way to bail you out."

Longarm smiled thinly and said, "Then there won't be such a fuss about our escaping, will there? Where's my badge, wallet, and such?"

"Behind you in that filing cabinet. I'll be damned if I intend to hand them to you!"

Longarm said, "I know just how you feel, old son. I'm going to lock you in with your partner. Then we'll help ourselves to horses, guns, and such, and be on our way. You'll be turned loose pretty soon, when the next guard is posted."

The Mountie got to his feet with a sigh and said, "Damn it, Longarm, they told us you were smart. You know you'll never in a million years get away with this fool trick."

"You may be right. That's why it makes sense for you to go along with my crazy play. Think of all the fun you'll miss if you ain't breathing when Superintendent Collingwood brings us back."

As the guard headed back grudgingly to join his comrade, he said, "You've got that a mite wrong, Longarm. Crown Sergeant Foster is the man who'll be trailing you."

Longarm frowned. "Foster? I thought he'd be on his way back to Fort MacLeod by this time."

The Mountie chuckled and said, "Nope. He and his patrol were invited to spend the night before riding back. In an hour or so, he'll hear the alarm and, by God, I intend to volunteer to ride after you with him!"

Longarm sighed and said, "We'd best get a move on, then. I'd sort of like to be off the premises before Foster and the rest of you count to ten."

Sunrise found Longarm and his prisoner alone but without cover on the dead, flat prairie. Canada Jack hadn't been told he was a prisoner just yet, and the Mounties probably thought they'd ridden south.

They hadn't. After getting his badge and gunbelt back, Longarm had found his saddle and possibles in the unguarded tack room of the nearby stable, and he'd selected a couple of stout-looking Mountie bays for the dash out. Canada Jack rode in a stolen military saddle with a Mountie's carbine in the boot, but he was still pouting about the Webley .38 he'd had to leave behind. Longarm had explained that the gun was probably in the superintendent's safe as evidence, and warned him not to draw the carbine unless he had a serious reason.

Having a gun again seemed to restore some of the lunatic's dubious manhood, and as they rode in the crisp morning air, he said, "I wouldn't want to leave you with the impression I was a homosexual, Longarm."

Longarm said, "You'd better not leave me at all.

I've heard all the talk about Greek soldiers and such. That ain't our problem right now. We have to rest these horses, but there's not a bump in the ground worth mention."

He swung in his saddle to gaze back the way they'd come before he added, "Shit, I can see a good five miles, and Regina ain't that far back. Let's just hope the Mounties have us figured for a beeline to Montana."

Canada Jack said, "I thought we'd be riding that way too. I thought about killing you a few times, in the dark, but as long as we're not heading for the States, I guess I can trust you."

Longarm said, "I heard you messing with the snaps on your carbine boot, Jack. You sure do change your mind a lot, don't you?"

Canada Jack frowned and said, "It upsets me to talk about my mind. I've agreed to let you be the dominant one, for now, but be careful. The first man I ever killed was a tutor who said I was . . . peculiar."

Longarm whistled silently as he considered how the renegade aristocrat was likely to sound to an American jury. Chumley's influential family wasn't going to do him much good in a Montana court, but insanity was a defense in any country.

He saw a break in the prairie ahead and said, "Looks like a dry wash running east and west. We'll get below the skyline, rest the critters a mite, and head west."

Canada Jack waited until they'd negotiated the steep bank down to the sandy bottom of the wash before he said, "I don't want to ride west. I want to go back east now. I'm about fed up with this perishing western nonsense."

Longarm swung himself out of the saddle and said, "Dismount and rest your horse."

But Canada Jack asked, "Suppose I refuse?"

Longarm said, "You can't. I'm dominating you, remember?"

"You said you weren't interested in me, and I'm

finding your company a bore. I think this is about where we'll be parting company."

Then he drew the carbine from its boot, pointed the muzzle at Longarm, and pulled the trigger.

He was levering the empty rifle with a puzzled frown when Longarm stepped over, grabbed him by one booted leg, and hauled him out of the saddle.

Canada Jack landed on his butt in the dust, rolled, and came up raging like a cross between a wildcat and an angry woman again. But Longarm was ready for it this time, and it seemed less important to keep his prisoner's face together now than it had been back at the jail.

So Longarm kicked the shit out of him.

Longarm wasn't a cruel man. He seldom allowed his feelings to get in the way of his duty, but he'd followed the trail of ugly death this maniac had left in his wake, and Canada Jack helped a lot by getting up again after anyone with a lick of sense would have stayed down.

Longarm fractured his nose and knocked out two front teeth before the killer suddenly covered his ruined face with both hands and fell to his knees, moaning.

Then, as Longarm watched in amazement, Canada Jack fell on his side in the dust, fumbled open his fly, and began to masturbate.

Longarm rubbed his bruised knuckles with a palm and muttered, "Jesus H. Christ! I never meant for you to *enjoy* it, you crazy bastard!"

Canada Jack had his pants down and was kneeling on his hands and knees, presenting his naked rump to Longarm.

Longarm muttered, "Shit!" and took the handcuffs from his coat pocket. He kicked the lunatic flat in the sand and hunkered over him to cuff both his hands behind him. Then he hauled Canada Jack to his feet and shook him, saying, "Cut it out. You don't have to convince me you're crazy. Save that shit for the judge and jury."

227

Canada Jack's eyes glared insanely as he spat, "Don't you dare say I'm crazy! I've killed men for saying that!"

"Aw, shut up. Hold still and I'll haul your britches up. You've spooked the horses up the wash, but I see they're grazing on some cheat grass now, so we'll give them a spell to settle down before we mount up."

"You're not taking me back to the States, my good man. I'll have you know my brother is a friend of His Royal Highness!"

Longarm buttoned the youth's pants and took a kerchief from his coat to wipe the dust and blood from his face before he said, "I can see getting hit don't bother you, but we've got to get this domination shit straight. I can't deliver you with half your face torn off. How did you get those other owlhoots to follow you, sonny?"

"By my natural ability to command, of course."

"Bullshit. One or two of them might have been raised as servants, but at least a couple were Americans, and I've met damned few Irishman who popped to attention just because someone yelled at them with a highfalutin English accent."

The renegade didn't answer as he explored the inside of his ruined mouth with the tip of his tongue.

Longarm continued, "When you ain't hurting other folks, you like to get hurt yourself. Was that the hold you had on Shamrock and the others?"

"Don't be an ass. I never muck about like that with social inferiors."

"I thank you for the compliment, but let's trail after the horses, you crazy bastard."

Canada Jack balked and said, "Don't talk to me like that. I told you it upsets me."

Longarm snorted in disgust and said, "You just get as upset as you've a mind to. I mean, I have run across some crazy sons of bitches in my time, but—"

And then he saw that Canada Jack had sunk to his knees, head down, and he'd started to bawl like a baby.

Longarm hauled him erect and said, "Oh, hell, this is ridiculous. I just tore your head half off and you acted like you enjoyed it. Now you're crying like a sissy just 'cause I said you were a mite touched, which we both know is the God's honest truth."

Canada Jack pulled away and fell to the sand, writhing in agony and screaming incoherent protests as Longarm studied him warily. Then, as Chumley whimpered, "I'm *not* insane! Those doctors didn't understand me," Longarm nodded and said to himself, *That's it. Everbody has* something *that hurts when you prod it.*

He walked up the wash, got the horses, and led them back to where Canada Jack was having his temper tantrum. He nudged the lunatic with his toe and said, "Come on, I won't say you're crazy no more if you behave yourself."

Canada Jack said, "Fuck you. I want to go home."

So Longarm said, "John Chumley, you are a raving lunatic. I'm going to tell everybody that you make faces at yourself in the mirror and talk to your own pecker in the dark."

Canada Jack howled like a trapped wolf and protested, "That's not true! I'm perfectly rational, as long as people do as I say."

Longarm sneered, "You spill your oatmeal down the front of your bib and piss in your pants when nobody's looking. You're a gibbering lunatic and you told me you were Queen of the Fairies and I'm going to make sure the whole House of Lords hears about it when I write to your brother."

"Stop it! I can't bear it!"

Longarm hauled him to his feet again and said, "All right. I'll stop calling you a maniac if you'll stop acting like one. Let's mount up and do some riding."

He got the outlaw aboard his stolen bay and mounted his own. Then, leading the handcuffed man's mount by the reins, Longarm headed west.

After a time, Canada Jack called out, "I have a toothache."

Longarm said, "Enjoy it while you can. The root will work its way out in a day or so."

After a few minutes of silence, Canada Jack said, "I think my right eye is closing. You *enjoyed* beating me, didn't you?"

Longarm grimaced and replied, "I sure did, but I disremember getting a hard-on while I was hitting you. I don't aim to hit you no more, now that I see you like it."

"Spoilsport," sighed the prisoner. Then he said brightly, "If we can get to a telegraph line, we'll be all right. I can get us some money when I contact my family solicitor."

Longarm said, "I don't need any money, and I don't reckon I'll let you wire your lawyer before we get across the border, either."

"Surely you jest. Don't you know the Mounties are trailing us?"

"Well, of course I do. Why do you think we're riding down here is this winding wash?"

Canada Jack nodded and said, "I can have them called off. Do we have a deal?"

Longarm's asked cautiously, "What sort of a deal, Jack?"

"Take me to Moose Jaw and let me send a few wires. I'll see that you are amply rewarded, and certain pressures will be brought to bear on those annoying Mounties—"

Longarm cut in to say, "Hold on, damn it. In the first place, you just robbed the bank in Moose Jaw, and they're a mite annoyed with you there. In the second, there's a limit to political pressures."

"Try me," the renegade suggested, adding, "You and I know I'm perfectly rational, but I do have ways of getting what I want from my brother's Tory friends in Lords, and—"

Longarm nodded. "I have it figured."

"Do we have a deal?"

Longarm didn't answer. He understood the whole mess now. Canada Jack had made himself the "leader" of his gang by simply wiring for money as the need arose. The others had been moronic thrill-seekers, content to follow a spoiled rich kid who could keep them supplied with pocket money and get them out of scrapes, they thought, through political influence.

The hold he had on his family was more complicated, Longarm now saw, than it had seemed. Chumley's brother and the conservatives in his party weren't simply idiots; they had a bear by the tail.

As they rode on, Longarm got some of the loose ends out of his prisoner through a few leading questions and a lot of listening.

It wasn't just that the younger brother of a belted earl was loco; more than one noble family had a dotty maiden aunt they kept in the attic.

It wasn't that Chumley was homosexual, although that was a jailworthy offense in England and most states of the Union. Longarm suspected there were a few queers in his own government too, if what Billy Vail had said about the gents' rooms in Washington was true.

No, a dotty younger brother who bullied the underclassmen at his high-toned school wasn't all that unusual, and friends in high places had covered up for him. Scandal was a political weapon that the enemies of a conservative lord would have used.

Canada Jack admitted to beating his private tutor to death in a fit of rage. His brother's influential friends had gotten him out of that by shipping him out of the country.

Before they'd figured out what it meant to cover up the killings of a mad-dog sadist, it had been a mite late. The trouble with blackmail was that it never stopped. Canada Jack was too crazy to stop raising hell, and sane enough to see that he was being protected. There wasn't ever going to be a trial in Ottawa, if the Mounties got him back. The conservatives in power couldn't afford to let him be tried; too many things would come out, things the man had done before he ever got to Canada.

As they rode along and Jack calmed down, he bragged of his exploits back in England the way some pool-hall loafers brag about the women they've known. But Canada Jack's conquests had included boys from families even Longarm had heard of, and he didn't vote in British elections.

To hear Canada Jack, one would think half the peerage of England was queer as a three-dollar bill, but Longarm took a lot of what he said with a grain of salt. It hardly seemed likely that the men who'd carved out the British Empire were a mess of sissies, and Longarm assumed that many of the young boys the English outlaw was bragging about had been more scared than queer. He knew what happened to younger prisoners in Yuma or Fort Leavenworth, and he knew the sort of bully Canada Jack was, too. Money was a fearsome weapon. If you had money, you could buy most of the gents you couldn't whip, and Canada Jack was a pretty fair free-for-all brawler.

Longarm was neither boastful nor modest about his own ability, so he was able to judge that the black-sheep aristocrat was able to lick maybe eight out of ten men his size, fair and square. The money and political clout could have made him dangerous as hell, even if he'd been sane.

The smart thing to do, Longarm knew, would be to shoot the son of a bitch and be done with it. It wasn't as if there were a reason in the world to keep Canada Jack alive. He'd be doing the owlhoot's embarrassed family, the Mounties, and the rest of the human race a favor if, right about now, Canada Jack got shot trying to escape.

As if to make it easier, the prisoner suddenly asked, "Haven't you ever had a boy, Longarm?"

Longarm shook his head and said, "Never had a sheep, either. I reckon I'm just lacking in curiosity."

Longarm kept his voice conversational as he asked, "How come you raped that old woman back near Petit Arc, when you had all them rosy-cheeked lads to play with?"

"Oh, that can be a change of pace too. You see, it's easy to get *most* women, when you're wealthy and good-looking. It's the ones who say no that I find most exciting. I remember this Irish scullery maid we had back home. Bit of a Holy Mary and all that, what?"

"I don't reckon I want to hear about it, unless it happened on U.S. soil, Chumley."

"Oh, I never hurt the slut, just raped her on the back stairs one day when we found ourselves alone. It was quite nice. One of the first real lays I'd had, and, of course, my first virgin."

Longarm decided it would be best for all concerned if he didn't answer. The wash was getting shallower as they rode west. After a time, their heads were above the skyline again, and he cast an anxious glance to the south. The horizon shimmered in the growing heat, and it was hard to make things out on the horizon. But if he couldn't spot anything bright red, he doubted that anyone wearing it would notice their darker clothes. Things were looking up.

He said, "By God, I do suspicion we've thrown Foster off."

Canada Jack asked, "Wasn't that the idea? He undoubtedly expected you to ride south."

Longarm nodded, but he didn't think they were in the clear yet. They were still close to Regina, and he knew that if Foster didn't cut some sign after riding south into virgin prairie, he'd tumble to what they'd done, and Foster was one hell of a tracker.

Longarm tried to place himself in Foster's saddle as he pondered his own next move. He nodded and muttered, "They'll circle, likely clockwise. Foster knows the best route to Montana, so he'll keep circling, trying to cut our trail, and if we go that way, he'll cut her sure as hell."

Longarm took out his tattered map and held it in his free hand as he studied it. The handcuffed outlaw at his side asked what he was looking for, and Longarm said, "The nastiest, most impossible way to reach Montana aboard two horses."

"That sounds rather silly, if you want my opinion."

"I don't. Hmm, here's one bitch of a tamarack swamp with some country to the south that's torn up all to hell. It looks impossible to cross, but if we cross it, we'll be in the Dakota territory just east of the Montana line."

"But what if we can't get through the swamps on horseback?"

"We'll be drowned, most likely. But what are you bitching about? You keep telling me you don't want to go back to the States."

Chapter 14

Longarm had ridden through some inhospitable country, and he'd transported some ugly sons of bitches,
but he couldn't think of a time when it had all ganged
up on him at once. Ten days alone with Canada Jack
was enough to make any man want to vomit, and more
than one would have shot him by the second day.

As his bruised face healed, the killer's spirits seemed
to improve. He was sure Longarm was lost, and that his
family solicitor would be in Regina by the time they
got back. When he wasn't bragging about some
godawful thing he'd done, he had a habit of looking
back as they topped a rise and asking, "I say, wasn't
that a flash of red back there?"

Longarm hadn't spied any red tunics on their trail.
He hadn't expected to. He figured Crown Sergeant
Foster for a good tracker, not a maniac, and some of
the territory scared hell out of Longarm.

They forded countless streams and bulled through
swamps his common sense told him no horse could get
through. They camped without fires and ate hardtack
and pemmican a few bites a day. When his prisoner
complained that his missing front teeth made it
difficult to chew, Longarm suggusted he chew with his
back teeth, or go hungry. They both caught something,
either from the chill nights or the bugs that pestered
them day and night, but Longarm tied Canada Jack to
his saddle and pushed on, ignoring his ringing ears and
puking every once in a while.

Then, one noon, as they stopped to water their

mounts in a sandy, braided prairie stream, Longarm consulted his tattered map and said, "The Lord must have had this day in mind when he created the world, sonny. This here creek is named after *me*!"

Canada Jack stared bleary-eyed at the running water and muttered, "Longarm Creek?"

"Nope. Long Creek. That's close enough. As you see, it runs southeast. It joins the Souris, which wanders over to Winnipeg, sooner or later."

"Winnipeg? That's in Canada. Not that I've any objection to going there."

Longarm smiled thinly and said, "We ain't following Long Creek as far as Winnipeg. Before it joins the Souris, it makes an oxbow into northwest Dakota. From there, it's open prairie all the way to Fort Peck, Montana, which is where I'm delivering you to a federal judge."

He saw that the horses had refreshed themselves, and led on as Canada Jack protested, "Damn it, I'd rather *die* than face trial in the States."

Longarm nodded. "I know. That's why I haven't killed you. I've been studying on what sort of jury you'll be likely to face in Montana. I don't reckon your crazy act will cut much ice, considering the way you and your sidekicks tore things up in Montana."

"I'm not crazy, damn it. You are. Even without a map, I can see you've ridden all over the place to get this far, and now you're talking about still another side trip! Why should we ride all the way west to Montana, when it's so much simpler to follow the Missouri down to—"

"The Union Pacific tracks? Forget it. I didn't go to this much trouble just to see you beat the charges. The judge will likely let you send a wire. Judges are funny that way. Your lawyers in Regina might be able to get to Fort Peck, by transferring around a mite. But there's no direct rail connection, and I mean to suggest a court-appointed lawyer."

"You son of a bitch! Why don't you just shoot me and be damned?"

Longarm said, "I told you I'd studied on it. When you ain't hurting other folks, you admire feeling sorry for yourself. I've met few Indians who minded physical pain less. But I mean to see you pay for at least a mite of the hurt you've dished out. You're going to get a fair trial, sonny. You're not going to have any fancy lawyers pleading with the judge and jury to feel sorry for you because they picked on you in school. No Montana judge or jury gives a shit about embarrassing the conservative party, up here or back in England. Not that you deserve the hint, but I warn you not to bring it up unless you aim to swing a few days sooner."

As they crossed the stream and followed the western bank south, Canada Jack whimpered, "I was keeping an eye on the Fenians, I tell you. It was Shamrock who actually pulled the trigger those times!"

Longarm chuckled and said, "Make sure you mention that in court. I'd say the odds of having a couple of Irish-Americans on your jury would be even money."

Jack sighed, "Well, as much as the idea galls me, I suppose I can always plead insanity."

"You can plead insanity if you've a mind to." Longarm replied. "I always thought Jack McCall shot Hickock for a crazy reason, but they hung him anyway. You've been telling me how sensible you are, ever since we met, so I'll have to back you on that in the witness box."

Privately, Longarm was worried about this. He knew that if they sent Canada Jack to a lunatic asylum, someday his friends would get him out.

Longarm decided to shut up. His prisoner was right on the razor's edge between criminal insanity and just being loco. As long as he knew he'd done wrong, it was fair to hang him. The minute he wised up enough to decide he was Napoleon, or maybe the Empress Josephine, all bets were off.

They were coming to a willow thicket, and Longarm swung wide to avoid it. Then he gasped, "Son of a bitch!" and heeled his own mount right into the willows, with the prisoner trailing.

He backhanded Canada Jack off his mount and snapped, "Lay flat and keep your head down!" as he swung himself out of the saddle, drawing his Winchester on the way down.

As he tied the two horses to willow branches, a familiar voice called out, "Give it up, Longarm! We have you spotted!"

"Is that Sergeant Foster?" Canada Jack asked, grinning broadly.

Longarm said, "It ain't that funny, sonny. I'll gut-shoot you before I turn you over to them. So lay still and don't get any silly notions."

He spied a blur of scarlet through the willow branches to his left, and called out, "That's close enough, Foster!"

Foster's voice called from another direction as the sergeant explained, "There's a squad of us, and we have you surrounded. What in hell do you think you're doing in that brush?"

"You come in here after us and you'll find out, Foster. I'm forted up good and the border can't be more than an hour's run, mounted or on foot."

Foster laughed and called back, "Don't be an ass. We've been laying for you here, all morning. I scouted that thicket earlier. You can't dig in; the ground water's only a few inches down. If I were to order a volley through those thin branches, it would be all over."

"Maybe, but you'd likely kill my prisoner, so fire and be damned."

There was a long silence as Longarm relived the frantic last few moments since he'd rounded the willows and spotted the Mounties camped on the far side. He hadn't taken time to count them.

He thought for a moment, and then he called out, "Hey, Foster?"

"We're still here, Yank. What's your pleasure?"

"How the hell did you get out in front of us? I knew you were a fair tracker, but this is ridiculous."

Foster laughed and called back, "I didn't track you, Longarm. I just read my own map, picked out the wildest, most impossible route from Regina to the border, and took some shortcuts. Did you swing all the way west to the Old Wives' Drainage?"

"Sure. We cut across a couple of divides, cross-grained. I have to hand it to you, you wise-ass bastard. I figured we'd lost you sure in them swamps to the west."

"We rode around them. As I said, once I figured where you meant to jump the border, there was no sense in killing our mounts. Frankly, I expected you to get this far on foot!"

"Well, we stole some good horses from you."

Someone laughed, off to his right. Longarm didn't think it was Foster, though he suspected that the Mountie was hugging himself right now for being so damned smart.

Longarm looked at the sun, hoped he was wrong, and checked his watch. It wouldn't be dark for at least five hours.

Foster called out, "Do you want to deal, Longarm? Or do you want to move this thing from push to shove?"

"I'm listening, Foster. What are your terms?"

"Honorable surrender. We'll drop all charges against you and, what the hell, you can even keep the horse."

Longarm glanced at the grinning prisoner, prone in the sand at his side and, though even a lunatic knew the answer, he called back, "I ride out scot-free and you get to take this murdering son of a bitch back to Regina, right?"

Foster's voice was insufferably smug as he replied, "That's about the size of it, Longarm." Then he added, "How does it feel to be on the receiving end of it?"

Longarm answered, "Can't say I like it all that

much, Foster. But if you'll think back, I let you take your prisoner back to Canada that time, remember?"

Foster's voice was grim as he said, "I remember. The prisoner you let me take away from you was dead, overripe, and the wrong man."

Longarm chuckled and said, "Tell you what. Why don't you boys shoot this bastard and saddle me with a corpse in high summer?"

Foster called back, "I've a better idea. Why don't you surrender?"

Longarm didn't answer. Foster waited for a time before he called out again, "Longarm?"

"We're still here, as you might have guessed."

Foster's voice was a bit gentler as he insisted, "I know you're trying to come up with something, Yank. It's no use, this time. We've got you, and you know it."

"Then what the hell are we jawing about? I ain't ready to come out, and I don't reckon you gents are fixing to come in, just yet."

Foster laughed. Longarm was starting to hate that laugh. The sergeant said, "We could take you the hard way, if we had to, but we don't have to. You're in the only cover for a dozen miles. We're spread out nicely along the edges of it, thank you very much. If you make a break with the prisoner, my men have orders to shoot."

Foster let that sink in before he added, "On the other hand, if you break cover alone, we'll hold our fire and you can simply ride off. We don't want you. We know your damned government will only bail you out after we've had all the trouble of guarding and feeding you for a week or so."

Longarm yelled, "Uncle Sam's likely to be sore as hell if you gun a U.S. deputy, too."

Foster answered, "You're right. That's the only reason we're holding our fire. But don't bank too hard on it, Longarm. My orders are to bring back John Chumley, and my orders are from Ottawa."

240

"Goddamnit, Foster! You know this pissant's lawyers will get him off in any Canadian court!"

"That's not our problem, Longarm. Are you going to hand him over, or do we have to come in and take you both?"

"Folks are likely to get hurt, Foster."

"I know. That's why I'm willing to meet you halfway. But we're starting to talk in circles, Yank. I'm giving you five minutes to make up your mind. You do what you feel you have to."

Longarm checked his watch as the prisoner beside him chortled, "You have no choice, you know."

Longarm drew his sixgun, pulled the hammer back, and aimed it thoughtfully at the suddenly less certain-looking killer. Then he nodded, lowered the hammer, and sighed, "Fair is fair. When you're right, you're right."

He hauled the prisoner to his feet and called to Foster, saying, "I get me, and you get this animal, and we part friendly, right?"

Foster called back, "One more condition. I want your word that you'll ride right for the border. No turning back, no more funny tricks. I want your word that you'll not try to recapture my prisoner."

Longarm swore and muttered, "The bastard is a mind-reader!"

Then he called, "You have it. We're coming out. If you shoot me, I'll never speak to you again."

"Giving up, eh?" Canada Jack said with a sneer, as Longarm took him by one elbow and guided him through the willows. He let a willow branch slap Canada Jack across the bruised lips, and answered sweetly, "Yep. I ain't as crazy as you and your gang. I doubt if any of this will sink in, but after they let you out again, you'd sure better steer clear of the U.S. of A!"

Leading the ponies as well as his prisoner, Longarm came out of the willows, feeling pretty sheepish.

Crown Sergeant Foster was standing near his own mount, looking like he'd just broken the bank at Monte

241

Carlo. As they headed for him, Longarm saw other Mounties breaking cover all around, leading their horses. A couple had put their carbines away, and one of them was toting a damned fool Mountie flag.

Longarm stopped a few paces from Foster and said, "All right, you won fair and square, but this bastard sure deserved a better fate."

Foster smiled thinly and said, "I quite agree. I was expecting you to shoot him, Longarm."

"It crossed my mind, but I reckon I'm a sissy. I never have been able to gun a man with his hands cuffed behind him."

Foster nodded and said, "I know the feeling."

Then he barked an order, and his patrol began to mount up. Foster remained standing, however, as he said, "I'd say this makes us even, wouldn't you, Longarm?"

Longarm smiled wistfully and said, "Yep. I outfoxed you last time, and this time you outfoxed me. It's getting sort of tedious."

"You admit I licked you, fair and square?"

Longarm nodded and said, "Go ahead and rub it in, if it makes you feel good. I'll put this pissant on his horse and hand you the reins after you mount up."

Foster grinned and followed Longarm's suggestion. By the time all three were in the saddle, the patrol was lined up as if they expected Queen Victoria to pop out of the willows and inspect them.

Longarm reined in near Foster and held out the reins of his prisoner's horse. The crown sergeant ignored them and said, "I have you on one more point. Do you have any idea where you are?"

Longarm looked around and said, "Sure. That bend in the creek puts us six or eight miles north of the border."

"Are you sure, Longarm? How do you know we're not six or eight miles *south* of the border?"

Longarm shook his head morosely and said, "I wish

like hell we were, but I just checked my map. What are you up to now, Foster, a border incident?"

Foster stared at the prisoner next to Longarm and said, "I don't think I'd like to risk one. I'm sure you're mistaken. If we're not on U.S. soil, we're perilously close to it. When this young man's solicitors ask you, as I'm sure they will, would you be good enough to inform them we did our best?"

Longarm understood, but he didn't believe it. Canada Jack came unstuck sooner and wailed, "I demand to be taken back to Regina! I'm a British subject, my good man!"

Foster smiled and said, "A credit to the Empire, I'm sure, sir. But, as you see, this Yankee rascal has you on his side of the border, despite our best efforts."

Then Foster started to swing his mount away.

Longarm called out, "Hey, Foster?"

"Yes?"

"What in the hell were we just doing?"

Foster stared with distaste at the prisoner as he explained, "I thought you knew. We were proving we were lawmen."

"Bullshit. You tracked me down and got me to surrender my prisoner just to show me how good you were."

Foster's smile, this time, was much less coldly correct than his stiff code might have called for as he nodded and said, "You're damned right, I proved it. But, frankly, I was hoping you'd shoot this maniac when you thought we had you boxed."

"You should have known me better than that, Bill."

"I guess I do now, Longarm. Take care of yourself, and, for Christ's sake, *try* to stay out of my territory."

Again, Foster turned to ride away, and again, Longarm called out.

Reining in and turning in the saddle, Foster asked what he wanted.

Longarm said, "I was wondering how much they pay you Mounties."

Foster frowned and said, "It comes to about fifty cents a day in your currency. Why?"

Longarm said, "You're worth more."

Then he threw the little Mountie flag a U.S. Cavalry salute, and wheeled his horse about to lead his prisoner south.

SPECIAL PREVIEW

Here are the opening scenes
from

LONGARM AND THE BANDIT QUEEN

seventeenth novel in the bold new
LONGARM series from Jove

Chapter 1

The icy bite of the twilight wind cut through Long-arm's clothes and crept down inside the leather tops of his stovepipe cavalry boots, curling his toes and numbing them. He wondered if they might not be turning blue. His hands, on which he wore thin leather gloves—the only pair he'd found when rummaging in his saddlebags—felt like they were blue, too. Longarm wasn't about to pull the gloves off to find out. His fingers were so chilled that he was afraid one or two might come off with the gloves.

A stray gust sent an icy thread trickling down his collar to rustle the hair on his chest.

Damn me for a double-dyed jackass! he thought as he pulled the lapels of his long, black Prince Albert coat closer together. *If I'd thought it'd be this cold so far south along the Arkansas in September, I'd have brought my sheepskin instead of leaving it hang in Denver where it ain't doing nobody any good.*

Letting go the reins of his Texas-bitted cavalry mount, Longarm slapped his palms together to bring back some feeling. They flexed enough, with a little beating, to let him slide one hand inside his tight-pulled coat lapels and fish a cheroot out of his vest pocket. He chomped his strong teeth over the tip of the cheroot, clamping the thin cigar in his mouth while he fumbled a match from his coat pocket.

He made two tries at flicking the match into flame with a thumbnail before remembering that he had on gloves. *For all they're keeping your hands warm, old son*, he told himself, *you might as well not be wearing them.*

Lifting a foot out of the stirrup, he hoisted his leg upward high enough to bend it, and struck the match on his bootheel. The puff of blue smoke that he loosed to mingle with the chill air, almost as visibly blue as the smoke itself in the fading light, made him feel a little bit better.

But not enough to mention, his thought ran on. *Billy Vail's just too damn tight with voucher money lately, telling me to get a remount at Fort Gibson instead of letting me stay on the train all the way to Fort Smith and renting a livery horse there.*

By now, the fragrant smoke from the cigar was beginning to soothe Longarm's spirits somewhat.

But I guess it ain't all Billy's fault. It's them damn pencil-pushers back in Washington. They set on their padded swivel chairs all day and figure how to cut off a penny here and whittle away a nickel there, and I wind up freezing my butt for fifty or sixty miles on a cavalry nag traipsing across the ass-end of the Cherokee Nation, when I still ought to be at least halfway warm in a coach seat on the damn train.

Which don't mean it ain't Billy's fault that I'm here in the first place. I got about as much business being down here between the Creek and Cherokee Nations, trying to pick up a smell of Jesse James's trail, as a butchering-sized hog has trying to fly. Seems like every day that goes by and the James boys stays hid out, the hotter everybody gets about finding them. Hell, I'll stand by what I told Billy when he put me on this case. I'll put up a mint-new double eagle against his plugged two-bit piece that Jesse's right close to where he calls home, over east in Missouri. And he ain't going to be found until those neighbors of his start flapping their jaws. Trouble is, nobody's listening when I try to tell them what only seems like good sense to me.

Ahead of him, Longarm caught the glint of a campfire's light flickering among the trunks of the big sweet gum and blackjack oak trees that grew thickly on both sides of the river trail. The trail meandered more or less parallel to the banks of the Arkansas River as it flowed sluggishly southeast toward the line between the Indian Nation and the state of Arkansas.

He picked up the reins and twitched them to send his mount in the direction of the promised warmth. There was still a good distance between him and the fire. He nudged his horse with a spurless bootheel to speed it up a bit, anxious, now that he'd seen the blaze, to stop and settle down beside it, and share its warmth with whoever had built it.

He'd covered most of the distance to the flickering spot of light, zigzagging between the trees and skirting the heavy brush, when a scream split the darkening night. For a moment, Longarm couldn't be sure there was a connection between the scream and the fire. He was still too far away to see anything but a suggestion of dark shapes silhouetted against the glow that spread around the fire. There were three or four figures moving around, but he couldn't tell whether they were those of men or women. Just to be on the safe side, though, he slipped his Winchester out of its saddle scabbard and flicked off the safety. Then he dug both heels hard into his horse's flanks, and the animal spurted forward.

Twenty seconds and two or three screams later, Longarm was close enough to get an idea what was going on around the campfire, as the diminishing distance sharpened the blurred edges of the shapes of four men and a woman. As the distance continued to lessen, he saw that the men had been chasing their companion, and as he watched them, the men wrestled the woman to the ground. Three of them held her—one holding each of her legs, the third stretching her arms above her head. The fourth ripped away her skirt and underclothes, and fumbled at his belt.

By now, Longarm was close enough to see more than silhouettes. The men became defined as bearded,

248

butternut-jean-clad individuals, but the woman was only a stretch of bare flesh, tinted deep pink by the lurid firelight. Dark pubic hair broke the sweep of her skin between waist and legs. The man who'd begun fumbling with his belt had let his jeans drop now, and Longarm could see his protruding erection as he dropped to his knees between the writhing woman's widespread legs.

Her screams increased when she felt him probing to enter her. She twisted as best she could, trying to avoid his eager efforts, and her body arched against the strain her captors were putting on her arms and legs. The kneeling man struck her with his fist, and the woman's screams stopped abruptly, as did her struggling. One of the men said something. Longarm was too far to make out the words, but he heard the raucous laughter that followed the remark.

That was enough for him. Rape was rape under any circumstances, and rape wasn't something that Longarm's personal code would countenance. It was also against the law, and he was the law. He pulled up the horse with a sliding of hooves. Shooting against firelight was tricky, as he'd learned through long experience. He caught the kneeling man in his sights, and squeezed the Winchester's trigger.

For a split second, the kneeling man froze, then the impact of the high-velocity .44-40 slug toppled him over. He fell across one of the woman's pinioned legs. His companions let go of the now-sagging limbs they'd been struggling to hold still, and clawed for their guns.

Longarm reduced the odds with a snapshot at the man at the group's head. His shot was quick, and the flickering firelight made sighting chancy. His target crumpled, then floundered on the ground. Longarm swung the Winchester, but the other two were on the move even before he'd started shifting his aim. Before he could trigger a third shot, the two remaining rapists were running into the deep shadows among the trees around the vest-pocket clearing where the fire blazed.

While Longarm was searching the dappled shadows for a shot at the running desperadoes, the man who'd been his second target struggled to his feet and hobbled, bent double, into the sheltering woods. Longarm was in easy pistol range now. He sheathed the Winchester and dropped the horse's reins over its nose. The cavalry-trained animal stood placidly.

Longarm dismounted, drawing his Colt, and struck off to one side of the fire. He had no way of knowing where the three men were, but instinct and experience told him they'd probably not gone far. The odds were that they'd taken shelter among the big boles of the gumwood trees and thick foliage of the scrub oak that surrounded the little clearing.

Longarm could almost see them, shielded behind a protecting tree trunk while they waited for him to enter the revealing circle of firelight to bend over the body of the woman, who still lay unmoving on the ground beside the blaze. The twilight had slid into darkness during the moments it had taken for him to reach the fire, and the ensuing minutes that had been consumed in his brief surprise attack. Neither moon nor starlight penetrated through the thin gray overcast that had veiled the sky when it had last been visible. Longarm stopped to let his eyes grow accustomed to the gloom, and to listen for sounds of movement.

There was a constant rustling in the wooded area. The wind was still brisk, and it whined softly as an undertone to the shushing it caused among the autumn-hardened leaves, still green and thick but dry now after the sun of summertime. Bit by bit, his ears grew used to the forest murmur, his eyes to the freshly dark night. Directly in front of him, a twig cracked under the pressure of a booted foot. Slowly, Longarm edged ahead.

He felt his way, lowering each foot slowly as he stepped forward, putting his weight on the foot gradually, ready to pull back if the springiness of the loose leaves that blanketed the ground was interrupted by the hard line of a dry tree limb or twig. His caution saved him a bad fall, for he was still balanced on one foot when the foot he was advancing touched the ground briefly before the earth crumbled away under its pressure. Still, he had to shuffle to keep from pitching forward, and the movement set up a soft rustling in the vegetation underfoot.

A line of fire cut the darkness in front of him, and the sound of the shot and the ugly, high-pitched whistle of lead zipping past, mere inches from his chest, sounded at almost the same instant.

Longarm hit the ground, squeezing off a shot toward the spot where he'd seen the muzzle blast as he fell. Two gunshots cut the night now, a few feet apart, but they were high. When he'd gone to the ground, Longarm had fallen into a shallow ditch. He rolled, measuring it by feel, finding that it was no ditch, but judging from its size and shape, a grave.

For that woman they were about to rape, he thought. *Figured to get rid of her after they'd had all they wanted from her.*

He lifted himself to his knees, and reaching out one hand in front of him, encountered the earth that had been lifted from the grave. It was as good a breastwork as anybody could ask for. Longarm put a shot into the darkness from behind the shelter of the dirt pile.

Two shots replied, and he answered them instantly, shooting to the side of the muzzle blast. One of his slugs found flesh. A cry of mixed anger and pain sounded from the darkness.

"Son of a bitch winged me!" a man's voice grated. "Shit on this! Whoever that is, he's better than I am at sharpshooting in the dark! I'm getting the hell out of here!"

"Not without me, you ain't!" a second voice replied. "Come on! Lucky we didn't unsaddle before we went for the woman!"

There was a loud pounding of feet on dry leaves and the slapping of scrub-oak branches against bodies.

251

The noises faded, then there was an angry exchange of words in tones too low for Longarm to make out what was being said. Finally, the drumbeat of hooves thudded noisily beyond the waning fire, then faded into the distance, telling Longarm that his antagonists had ridden off with more haste than caution.

Longarm waited until the hoofbeats died, to make sure, before he stepped out of the shallow grave, that the three riders weren't going to regain their courage and circle back.

Unreplenished, the fire had waned to little more than a bed of red coals from which an occasional flicker of bright flame burst when the heat ate into a sap-pocket. The woman was still unconscious. Longarm studied her with a frown.

She was young, younger than she'd sounded to him, but the noises she'd made had been dragged out of her in fear and rage. He put her age at somewhere in the middle twenties. Her face, in repose, was unlined—a square-shaped face, with a firm jaw under slightly over-full lips. Her nose was upturned and small, with wide nostrils, under full, heavy brows. Her cheekbones were high, her brow inlined. She had thick black hair that grew in a half-circle around a narrow forehead, and streamed out loose on the ground under her shoulders.

Her clothing was still disarranged. Her white shirt-waist was rumpled, its collar ripped half off, and the corduroy riding skirt that had been pulled away by her attacker had fallen or been pulled high; it covered her breasts in a rumpled mass that hid their contour. Her body was bare from the waist down. A gently rounded stomach glowed in the firelight. Below a thick black vee of pubic hair, her thighs tapered plumply to calves still covered by high-laced boots, with thick stockings folded over their tops. Her knee-length under-pants lay in a tattered wad at one side.

Across one of the woman's legs, the man Longarm's rifle slug had killed lay sprawled, his arms thrust up-ward. Blood stained the side and front of his butternut shirt, where the bullet had taken him. His narrow hips and buttocks were bare.

Longarm pulled one of the dead man's arms aside to get a clear look at his bearded face. It was not one that he recognized, either from a past arrest or from any of the wanted flyers at which he'd looked recently. In death, the face might have belonged to anybody, a storekeeper or a farmer. It had lost whatever villainy it might have possessed while the man was still alive.

Longarm grabbed the corpse by its limp wrists, and dragged it away from the woman. Then he eased her skirt down to cover her thighs before he took stock of his surroundings.

At the edge of the clearing, two horses were tethered to a bush. Both were still saddled. Behind them, a mule was also tied up; it bore a lightly loaded packsaddle. There was nothing in the clearing, except the dying fire and a small stack of chopped tree limbs at one side of it, to give any sign that the group had intended to make camp there for the night. There were no bedrolls, no cooking utensils, not even a water bucket.

Longarm brought his own horse up and tethered it where the others stood, then he threw a few of the pieces of cut wood on the coals, hunkered down, and stripped off his gloves. He'd forgotten about the cold wind in the flurry of action he'd set off. In the clearing, the trees cut the force of the breeze, though its presence was still indicated by the waving of the treetops. Thoughtfully, Longarm took out a fresh cheroot and lighted it while he continued to study the little glade.

From the evidence, it was impossible to tell whether the woman had been traveling with the four men, or had encountered them on the trail and been forced to accompany them to the secluded spot. Longarm gave up on the puzzle. When the woman woke up, he'd get the answers to his questions.

He did not have long to wait. The young woman sighed, and her arms moved fitfully. Then her eyes snapped open. A scream started from her lips when she saw Longarm squatting beside the fire, but she choked it off before it had gained enough volume to emerge from her mouth as anything louder than a surprised gasp.

"You startled me," she said, struggling into a sitting position.

Longarm let a small frown gather on his brow, though it was hidden by the wide brim of his flat-topped Stetson, as he tried to put a location to the odd intonation in her voice. It was not from the South, nor was it one that carried the casual overtones of the West or the flatness of New York. Rather, it was a nasal voice, produced in her head rather than flowing easily from her throat. Longarm had heard words inflected that way before, but not very often; the predominant regional accent of the West reflected the elongated vowel sounds of Southern speech.

She went on, "Something happened that I don't remember. I don't remember you at all."

"No reason why you should, ma'am. Far as I know, you never did lay eyes on me before, any more than I've seen you before now."

Her brows knitted together thoughtfully as she struggled to remember. "Then, what happened to me?"

"You got hit. Real hard, judging from the length of time you've been out. You don't need to worry about anything, though. Nobody laid a hand on you while you were unconscious. You're all right."

Longarm studied her while she was looking around the clearing. She was a bit older than he'd first judged h to be—in her early thirties, perhaps. Her eyes, which he was seeing for the first time, were dark brown. Her gaze, darting around the little glade, fell on the dead man who lay on the ground at one edge of the clearing.

"My God!" she gasped. "He was—he was the one—"

"He was the one that hit you," Longarm filled in when her voice trailed off.

"More than that." She began to tremble as memory

254

came rushing back. "He was one of the guides I hired at Fort Smith. He—they—there were four of them. And they were going to rape me."

Longarm nodded. "That's about the size of it. I watched it all, from the time they commenced chasing you around until I got busy and changed their ideas."

"Is that a polite way of telling me that you killed him?"

"Well, now, I wasn't trying to be polite, ma'am. No more than I usually am, to a lady. But now that you remember what was going on, it won't bring back more bad memories than you've already got. The reason you don't know how all of it come about is that you'd been knocked cold just before I dropped that fellow there."

"My God! What kind of place am I in? You're saying you shot that man in cold blood?"

"No, I wouldn't exactly say it was cold-blooded. I was mad as hell, if you don't object to me swearing a mite. I don't like to see four men ganging up on anybody, let alone a woman, trying to hurt her."

"Hurting's one thing. Killing's another. I've never been raped, and I don't suppose it would be a very nice experience, but at least I'd still have been alive when they finished. That man lying there is dead!"

"Yep. Just about as dead as anybody'll ever be."

"You killed him deliberately, with a gun, instead of just stopping him from—from what he wanted to do."

Longarm was losing his patience. He looked into the woman's angry eyes for a moment before he replied, "If you'll recall, ma'am, there were four of them. And they weren't the kind I'd want to walk up to and try to reason with, seeing as how all of them were wearing guns."

"He should have been tried in court, not summarily executed! Even the most disgusting criminal deserves a trail before a judge and jury. You deprived him of his life without giving him a chance to defend himself!" Her eyes were fixed scornfully on Longarm's apparently emotionless face.

"Oh, he defended himself. Him and his three friends all had a few shots at me before I winged two of them and they lit out."

"But they didn't—"

Longarm's temper finally let go. "Now, you just be good enough to keep quiet a minute, ma'am."

She looked at him questioningly, and started to say something, but Longarm was already standing up, his back to her. He went to the fire and selected a branch, choosing one that had a good flame at one end and was long enough to serve as a torch.

"You follow along with me, if you feel able to," he told the woman.

"Follow?" She shook her head. "I don't understand."

"You will," he assured her.

Longarm waited for her to stand up. She got to her feet by kneeling first. The loose, unfastened skirt dropped away. She stood up quickly and grabbed for the skirt, which lay on the ground. Draping it around her waist, she fumbled for a button or snap, but whatever had secured the garment had been torn off by the dead man. She settled for holding the skirt with one hand as she took a step toward Longarm. He led her toward the edge of the glade.

"Where are we going?" she asked suspiciously.

"Not far, just a few steps over here. There's something I want you to see."

Wordlessly, still puzzled, she followed him as he led the way to the shallow grave. By the light of the burning branch they could see a short-handled spade sticking in the ground beside the pile of dirt that had been taken from the long, narrow excavation.

"Good God!" she gasped, as the significance of the hole's shape dawned on her. "You've already dug a grave for the man you killed! I suppose you're getting ready to bury him out here in this wild place, without a prayer?"